Mensa's MATCH

A Riot MC Biloxi Novel

KAREN RENEE

I0715567

Copyright © 2025 by Karen Renee

All rights reserved.

No part of this publication may be reproduced, distributed, or transmitted in any form or by any means, including photocopying, recording, or other electronic or mechanical methods, without the prior written permission of the publisher, except as permitted by U.S. copyright law. For permission requests, contact [include publisher/author contact info].

The story, all names, characters, and incidents portrayed in this production are fictitious. No identification with actual persons (living or deceased), places, buildings, and products is intended or should be inferred.

No artificial intelligence (A.I.) or predictive language software was used in any part of the creation of this book.

Without in any way limiting the author's and publisher's exclusive rights under copyright, any use of this publication to "train" generative artificial intelligence (AI) technologies to generate text is expressly prohibited. The author reserves all rights to license uses of this work for generative AI training and development of machine learning language models.

ISBN: 978-1-957194-32-5

Paperback ISBN: 978-1-957194-38-7

Cover Model: Zach Fox

Photographer: Golden Czermak/Furious Fotog

Designer: Karen Renee

To Heather Ann –
You're gone far too soon.
I'm honored that we spent time together in the book world.

AUTHOR'S NOTE

This book is enjoyed best after reading *Finn's Fury*. However, if you like to break the rules and live a little dangerously by reading a series out of order, this has been written so that you will still be able to appreciate Mensa and Whitney's story.

This book is intended for readers 18+. There are scenes of gun violence and abduction, which may trigger or upset some readers. Please do not read if you are uncomfortable with those types of scenes. Thank you.

PLAYLIST

Don't Come Around Here No More by TOM PETTY AND THE HEARTBREAKERS
I Want You to Want Me by CHEAP TRICK
EX's and OH's by ELLE KING
Hand in My Pocket by ALANIS MORISSETTE
You Ain't Seen Nothing Yet by BACHMAN-TURNER OVERDRIVE
Headstrong by TRAPT
Here Without You by 3 DOORS DOWN
Risky Business by ZHU
I Am Here by P!NK
Easy Come Easy Go by IMAGINE DRAGONS
Nobody Knows by SLIGHTLY STOOPID

Chapter 1

Fate

Whitney

"I CAN FIND SOMEBODY else, Whitney. I don't want to be the reason you give up on your dream," Aunt Nadia said.

My eyes met hers and I offered a wan smile. "That's sweet of you, Aunt Nadia, but life happens."

My aunt narrowed her green eyes and scoffed. If she didn't visit her hairstylist routinely, I suspected her grays would be more white these days, but nobody knew for sure because her hair was always a vibrant auburn. For a woman who wanted to retire, she still had plenty of spunk and style. A big part of me hoped I could live up to her example when I was her age.

She put a fist on her jeans-clad hip. "That boy, Ben, did you wrong."

I dipped my chin. "He did, but that doesn't change the fact that it's time. I've been burned out for a while, and I've realized I want other things from life."

"That isn't what you said—"

This wasn't the first time we broached this subject, and no matter how angry it might make her, I interrupted.

"That was a while ago. Between this wake-up call and your need to retire... it's a sign."

Aunt Nadia frowned, then she spied my purse on the counter. "You goin' somewhere?"

I grinned. "I thought I'd grab a slice of pizza. You want to come with me? Or I can bring you something?"

She dropped her hand and blew out a breath. "No, ma'am. You go ahead. I have to sign for those jerseys if they ever get delivered."

With a quick nod, I ducked out of her embroidery and screen-printing shop, Hard Pressed.

In the nick of time, I snagged the last two-person table at Bayou Moon Pizzeria.

My conversation with Aunt Nadia wouldn't stop repeating in my mind. It took restraint not to tell her just *how* wrong Ben had done me. My cell rang, and I answered without paying close attention to the display.

"Whitney, it's Ben."

I clenched my teeth and exhaled quietly through my nose. "What do you need?"

"I just saw your texts. Are you sure, Whitney?" Ben asked.

Ben and I had been agents on an FBI public-corruption squad. During our last case, he'd been forced to fire his weapon, which required a separate investigation to prove deadly force had been necessary. He'd shared with the review panel a number of things, such as our involvement together and his suspicion that I'd become too engrossed in the case.

He should have received three texts; the first, telling him I needed to speak to him, went unanswered for over two days. Even though I was loathe to do it, I sent a second text saying our relationship was done. The last one, sent ten minutes later, informed him I had resigned from the Bureau and that I'd boxed up the few things he'd left at my place, and I provided the tracking number for the shipment.

I resisted the urge to pull my cell phone from my ear and chuck it across the room. No amount of deep breathing could calm me down, but I tried again anyway. It gave me time to control my tone of voice. "Yes, Ben. I'm sure. There was more than just one text and all of them were rather clear."

"It's just a misunderstanding, baby."

My jaw shifted and I considered getting up from my seat inside Bayou Moon Pizza. The lunch rush was in full swing, though, and seeing as how my order hadn't been called, if I stepped outside I'd never get my table back.

I firmed up my tone, but kept it from being bitchy.

Who was I kidding? When Ben didn't hear what he wanted to hear, he always called my firm tone bitchy.

"Agent Heston, we're done. You voiced your opinion that my judgment as an agent was questionable, added to that the fact we had been involved, and rather than both of us getting benched, only I did. I'm being as civil as I can, but hear this. I'm *very* sure that we are finished."

Ben went on a tear that I only half-listened to, since I'd heard it before. He claimed it was all to keep us safe, and reminded me that my mental health evaluation played a bigger role. That was true to an extent, but he was a master at painting himself in a good light.

The door opened, the bells tinkled, and I found myself thoroughly distracted. Three Riot MC members sauntered inside wearing their colors.

Thank God, I sat in full view of the front door.

I ducked my head down in hopes they wouldn't notice me. Many would assume that my FBI training developed my habit of sitting with my back to the wall, but Quantico didn't teach me that, Aunt Nadia did.

Aunt Nadia taught me a lot of things. Like not taking shit from anyone. Like living life to the fullest. And most recently, embracing life's curveballs and seeing the silver lining – though that lesson was still a struggle.

"Are you listening to me, Whitney?" Ben demanded.

"Can't say that I am. We're done. Stop calling me, Ben."

I ended the call, and my order was announced. My stomach growled as I sat down with my two slices of mushroom and pepperoni.

I heard the bells tinkle again, looked up, and sighed. This couldn't be happening. I specifically came to Bayou Moon because it was a pizzeria. He wasn't supposed to be here, seeing as how he carried an EpiPen for his dairy allergy. Nevertheless, Kenneth "Mensa" Ragstone sauntered inside, and my heart rate accelerated.

Nothing about this was right. I gravitated to the good guys. I didn't go for the bad boys. I only wanted to see Mensa one way: him walking in front of me with his hands behind his back, wearing handcuffs *I* had put on him.

Yet, that wasn't to be. I hadn't been sent here to investigate him. I'd been ordered to befriend a judge's daughter. The judge was suspected of defrauding the Social Security Administration, and other things.

Over the course of the investigation, I'd come across Mensa's file. My superiors thought he might be in on the fraud, but we found no evidence to support that. In fact, aside from a drunk-and-disorderly when he turned twenty-one, it appeared that Mensa hadn't so much as jaywalked in the past fifteen years. Rumor had it he came by his road name due to his brilliance at not getting caught doing anything. He wasn't a book-smart genius. He was a genius thanks to his street-smarts.

Thus, the idea of bringing him in appealed to me. He may not have been caught, but my gut said he'd committed plenty of crimes. That made my attraction to him all the more irritating and baffling.

My damned hormones were getting the best of me – had to be.

Nothing else explained my eyes seeking his whenever we were in the same room, or the fact I went out of my way to do the opposite of whatever he wanted, like when he wanted me out of the Riot MC clubhouse back in November, but I'd stuck around until after midnight.

Now that I'd resigned, I had no reason to give a damn about Mensa. Hell, other than Aunt Nadia and her shop, and that my assignment turned into a genuine friendship with Riley – a definite silver lining – I had no reason to stay in town... but I couldn't decide where I wanted to go. Or what I wanted to do.

You want to do Mensa, a little voice inside my head suggested.

I clenched my teeth.

I despised that I lusted over him. He wasn't my type, and not just because he was an outlaw biker. My prior lovers had been over six feet tall, clean-cut men. Sometimes they were built, other times they had the beginnings of the classic 'Dad bod.' I didn't care as long as a man was funny and friendly. The ability to take instruction or at least listen to what I wanted in the bedroom didn't hurt, either.

Mensa didn't qualify on most of those counts.

According to the dossier I had compiled on him, he stood only two inches taller than my five-foot-eight-inches.

His brown eyes weren't soulful, no, they were so cold he could stare down the devil himself. When we argued, some foolish part of me craved the moment that I earned that stare-down.

The way his wavy hair curled along his neck, I wanted to run my fingers through it and give it a good tug. He probably wouldn't go for that, which made me want it even more.

He was built, but he didn't flaunt it.

He wasn't the least bit friendly to me, which meant I had no idea if he was funny – though he made his MC brothers laugh plenty.

And obviously, I had no idea about his behavior in the bedroom.

Hard to say what I hated more – the fact that I was attracted to him or the fact that he could be so freaking attractive with his messy hair and scruffy beard.

While I ate my pizza, I noted where each Riot MC brother sat at their table. Mensa had his back to me. I had an excellent profile view of Gamble and Brute. Har faced me, but his focus was on the other men.

I sipped my Dr. Pepper to wash down my last bite while I read an article on my phone. Someone pulled the chair across from me out from under the table. I glanced up to see Mensa sitting down. That was unexpected, but I kept myself from showing a reaction.

"I've been looking into you," he said.

I lifted my chin an inch.

His nostrils flared. "But I can't find anything."

I resisted the urge to smile that almost overwhelmed me.

He narrowed one eye at me. "That tells me my gut is right."

I turned my head, and noticed Gamble and Har were watching us. My lips tipped up when I looked back to Mensa. "And what is your gut right about?"

He shifted the chair back. "That you're trouble. Do us all a favor, stay away from Riley."

That rankled.

"She's my friend. Or isn't she allowed to make those decisions for herself?"

"That's low," Mensa hissed.

I shrugged a shoulder. "You're part of the same family tree as her; for all I know you've got the same controlling ideas that her Daddy did."

His lip curled. "I don't operate that way, Blume."

I nodded once. "That's a relief – and I mean that."

"The fact I can't find out anything about you tells me you're not from here."

"Your point?" I asked when he lapsed into silence.

He shook his head. "When are you leaving town?"

I assumed an innocent expression. "What makes you think I'm leaving town?"

"Your brother left. Figured you won't be too far behind him."

If I hadn't resigned, he'd be right – not because I was following Wyatt, but because I'd have been assigned to a new case by now.

The idea that Mensa wanted me gone bothered me.

It shouldn't, but it did. He wasn't the first person who didn't take a shine to me, and seeing as that feeling was mutual it spurred more confusion. Why did I care what he thought of me? He wasn't the sort of man who interested me. Why did I want him to want me to stick around?

I couldn't contemplate that with his eyes boring into mine.

I concentrated on putting my phone in my Boho bag before I looked up at him. "This might disappoint you, but I don't know that I will leave town. Biloxi isn't such a bad place. The weather's nice, there's a beach, and Aunt Nadia's cool as hell. I could see myself sticking around a while."

He twisted his head to the side and exhaled hard. He turned back, those eyes blazing. "You're full of shit, and you're hiding something. I mean it, stay away from me, my brothers, and damn sure my cousin, Riley."

"Or what?" I asked, unable to stop myself.

He stood and looked down his nose at me. "Or there's gonna be hell to pay."

***

The security system gave a whiny, high-pitched double beep when I opened the door to Hard Pressed. The business was Aunt Nadia's pride and joy. But seventy was on the horizon and six months ago she'd asked me if I wanted to take over.

At the time, it had been an easy answer: not a chance. I was working interesting and challenging cases with the FBI.

Now, I was ashamed that I'd resigned.

And yet... if I were honest with myself, I'd lost my drive somewhere along the way. My five-year anniversary with the Bureau would have been in two months. Part of me felt the loss of not hitting that milestone, and another part of me recognized it had been past time for me to move on. An agent had to be able to move if there was a greater need on another mission. In the past, I'd been down for all of that, but since hitting thirty-four, it had lost its appeal.

Was it a total waste to turn my back on law enforcement after the last four years? (That year spent in the academy didn't factor into my tenure with the Bureau.) I didn't really think so. I had done more good than most people would ever know during that time.

Despite Aunt Nadia's encouragement to keep after my dream, her offer was still on the table. Dealing with ordinary citizens appealed to me... no, being my own boss appealed to me. Just because something appealed to me, didn't mean it was the right decision though. Part of me wanted to get that drive back and prove that I still belonged in law enforcement.

"It's about time you got back," Aunt Nadia called from the register.

I stepped behind the counter and tucked my purse into a drawer. "Yeah, I'm sorry that took so long."

"They must have been busy at Mick's place."

"No more than usual," I muttered.

"Really? Then what was the hold up?"

I wobbled my head. "To start, Ben called."

Aunt Nadia pulled off her glasses. "That boy…"

"Yeah," I murmured.

"Something else happened."

"It doesn't matter."

"Don't lie to me, Whitney Janelle."

I forced a smile. "The next time I'm craving Bayou Moon's pizza, I'll have to get it to go, that's all."

"Why? Did you get on Mick's bad side somehow?"

I scoffed. "I know better than that."

"Then why would you have to settle for take out?"

"I ran into Kenneth."

Her brows drew together and her lips curled in distaste. "Who's Kenneth?"

I sighed. "Mensa, okay. I'm surprised you only know these people by their road names."

"Sandy only refers to them using those names. What does Mensa have to do with you not going out for pizza?"

I glanced out the front window. "Nothing. Like I said, it doesn't matter."

"You're supposed to be smart, but you've lost half your IQ if you think I'm gonna fall for that. Hell, that's a sign it absolutely matters."

I leveled a dry look at her. "I'm attracted to him, but that's irrelevant. He's not my type. He can't stand me. And I'm not getting involved with a man again for quite a while."

She cackled.

I widened my eyes. "Don't laugh at me like that. I know what that means. You think I'm full of it."

She sobered. "No, I think those are famous last words, my dear. You're so determined to have no man in your life right now that fate introduces you to Mensa."

I shook my head. "Don't bring *fate* into this. There's no way I'm entertaining that idea."

Her knowing grin unsettled me. She shrugged a shoulder. "Have it your way. It still doesn't explain why you have to steer clear of Bayou Moon."

I returned her a knowing grin. "He warned me to stay away from him, Riley, and his Riot MC brothers. And because I'm a glutton for punishment, when I asked what he'd do if I didn't heed his warning, he threatened me. I'm pretty sure fate has nothing to do with this one, Aunt Nadia."

"I'm surprised he'd do such a thing to you. That's disappointing." She shuffled to the other end of the counter, and nudged a box with her foot. "While you were gone, the jerseys for the softball team came in. You can get to screen printing them while I finish up another patch for a VFW member."

CHAPTER 2

THAT LOOK

MENSA

MENSA PARKED HIS BIKE behind the Riot MC clubhouse, swung off, and climbed the steps to the back door. He wanted to kick his own ass. A tall gin and tonic might help him take the edge off his shame. He didn't threaten women, so it surprised him when he'd threatened Whitney. Her insinuating he was anything like his Uncle Jack sure as hell hadn't helped matters.

She ticked all his boxes for what he *didn't* want in a woman.

He'd convinced himself that she was hiding something. His conviction was so strong some of his brothers threatened to make him a tin-foil hat.

Inside the clubhouse, he went behind the bar in the common room.

"You got that look again," Finn said, putting away a cue stick, moving to the bar, and settling on a stool.

"I don't have a look," Mensa muttered.

"When you're stewing about Whitney, you do."

Mensa kept his reaction in check by pouring gin over the ice cubes in his glass. "Not stewing. Just wondering how she fooled you and most of the other brothers."

"She's still pretty new to Biloxi. I got no reason to distrust her."

"Her twin brother is an FBI agent, and that only came to light because of the investigation into my uncle."

Finn shrugged a shoulder. "Since your uncle was abusing his power – he had that coming."

Mensa added a splash of tonic and shook his head. "Not what I mean. She's hiding something, and I'll bet she's part of the FBI, too. She lied to Riley—"

"Lied about what? They only discussed Riley's dad once – assuming Whitney was in on the investigation."

Mensa swallowed a sip of his drink. "How do you know they only talked about Uncle Jack once?"

Finn went behind the bar and grabbed a bottle of beer. "I asked Riley, because of how dead-set you are against Whitney."

"Yeah. Bet Whitney's a master at steering the conversation."

Finn returned to his stool and took a swig of his beer. "You're losing it, Mensa. She's not from here and she's helping her Aunt Nadia."

"My gut says she could have been investigating the club."

"So what if she was?" Block asked, sauntering to the bar and sitting next to Finn.

Har was a pace behind Block and nodded. "We got nothing to hide."

Finn set his beer down. "Except Riley says Whitney's between jobs... so she isn't investigating shit."

There it was, the thing that should have had them all on alert. Anyone who was 'between jobs' wouldn't hang in Biloxi. They'd be fighting tooth and nail to get back on the job or finding another opportunity to make money.

He didn't buy the excuse of taking care of her aunt either. Nadia was as fit as a fiddle, as far as Mensa knew. Taking care of her sounded like a cover – and a bad one at that.

Sandy bustled into the common room from the kitchen. "You better hope she sticks around, otherwise you boys are gonna be in a lurch when you need new patches stitched. Or when one of you decides to take an ol' lady... you'll have to special order a cut from out of town."

"She's officially hanging it up?" Block asked.

Sandy grabbed a lemon from a small fridge behind the bar and turned to Block. "Her arthritis is gettin' worse, and she wants to travel."

Finn caught Mensa's gaze. "You got nothing to say to that?"

Mensa swallowed some of his cocktail. "No, because that's the first true statement I've heard." He arched his brows. "And none of that pertains to Whitney."

Sandy strode back to the kitchen.

Finn lifted his beer bottle toward Mensa. "I stand by what I said months ago. One night, make an approach and hate-fuck her out of your system."

Mensa glowered at Finn.

Block laughed. "No way. That shit don't work. I'm proof."

Finn smirked. "Yeah, and you're happier for it."

Block gave a small nod.

Mensa downed the rest of his drink and made another. "Block, you never hated Heidi." He shifted his gaze to Finn. "It isn't the same sitch here, Finn. Back off."

Har leaned forward. "I want to know what you said to her at lunch. Her reaction made it clear she wanted to kick your ass."

Mensa picked up his glass, ready to hit his room. "I told her to stay away from all of us or there'd be hell to pay."

"You threatened her?" Block asked, his tone outraged.

"I'd never make good on it."

"I don't think she'll give a damn about that, Mensa," Block said.

Finn tossed his empty beer bottle into the trash. "Thought you were the smart one."

"A woman can make any man crazy, Finn," Har said.

A wide, knowing grin spread across Finn's face. "You're right, Prez, but Mensa says this isn't like that."

Mensa glowered at Finn. "Whatever. You assholes had your fun. I don't plan to see her ever again. I'm headed to my room."

<hr>

Mensa closed his door just as his phone vibrated with a text. He opened the thread and saw a message from Cynic.

Tomorrow, you're on for Open-Mic night

A half-hearted smile crossed his face. Part of him looked forward to the Open-Mic-slash-karaoke because he loved music so much. Another part of him hated it because it immediately brought Whitney to mind.

Last November, Sandy had roped Nadia and Whitney into helping her arrange an impromptu karaoke night at the clubhouse. The way Whitney had belted out "Devil Won't Go" by Elle King made a lasting impression. She wasn't as good as Riley, but she likely hadn't had any training. He couldn't deny that Whitney had a great fuckin' voice.

Once he sent Cynic a text to tell him he'd be there, Mensa lay back on his bed with a book. Any other time, he'd watch a movie, but for the past three months he'd start a flick and compare the actress to Whitney. With her crystal blue eyes and shiny blonde hair, she was a stunner. Those fucking eyes, though – hers gleamed in a way he didn't see from most women. She didn't look like a California girl, she looked like the California girl's cousin who could kick your ass if you said the wrong thing.

Fuck him, but he was curious about that. He had been since Finn and Riley tied the knot in the back yard of the clubhouse a month ago. Especially since Whitney had wasted no time cornering him to bitch about the tents. Someone – his money was on Victoria – had shared that he'd suggested the tents.

He'd more than suggested. He'd insisted on them in order to keep the women out of the clubhouse. Being insistent was risky, but Har had relented. It was good that he did, too, or Mensa might have lost his battle to his inexplicable attraction to Whitney.

All of Riley's bridesmaids wore navy blue dresses, but they weren't all the same type of dress. Whitney came down the aisle first in a halter-style gown, and Mensa's fingers itched to tear the gauzy-looking fabric off her.

Recalling that vision of her, his mind wandered to what she was like in bed and he got angry with himself. The woman compared him to his crooked uncle, and the heat in her eyes made it clear she held a grudge against Mensa. There was no way he'd bring that woman to his bed. He snatched up his book with a disgruntled sigh, opened to the bookmark, and shoved thoughts of Whitney out of his mind.

Chapter 3

Silence

Whitney

R**ILEY HURRIED INSIDE** H**ARD** Pressed, her wavy, golden-brown hair in a ponytail swaying with her stride. She pointed at me. "You're a liar."

I bit down ever so subtly to hide my surprise. *Did she find out about my assignment?*

I hated being discovered. It was nerve-wracking during the best scenario, but in this case I could lose a friendship. One I had quickly come to value. Not that I didn't value all friends, but Riley and I got on like we were sisters separated at birth. A friendship like that was rare, and I'd put off coming clean with her.

She stared at me with her chestnut-colored eyes, waiting for a response. Silence had saved my ass plenty over the years.

"Riley, girl," Aunt Nadia said, and I'd forgotten she was in the room.

Riley came to the counter. "You're not busy tonight. Why are you really skipping Open-Mic night?"

"I just need a quiet night," I semi-fibbed.

Riley narrowed her eyes. "Nope. I don't believe that, either."

I threw my hands up in slight surrender. "It's the truth."

"Gamble said he saw you at lunch yesterday."

Funny how criminals and law enforcement had certain things in common. Nothing got by those Riot MC brothers... and I did my damnedest to make sure nothing got by me, either.

"He did, but that doesn't change the fact I'm staying in tonight. Let's plan to hit the Beau Rivage on Tuesday—"

She curled her lip. "It's too crowded there. Besides, Mensa will be running things tonight." A calculating look crossed her face. "Which reminds me, Gamble said Mensa talked to you yesterday. Is that the real problem?"

My face froze. Seemed those Riot boys gossiped like women.

"She's following his orders," Aunt Nadia said.

I aimed some side-eye at my aunt. "Not orders."

Aunt Nadia's chastising look should have left me quaking in my sandals. She smiled. "You're right. Not orders, you're keeping his threat at bay."

"Threat? He did not threaten you," Riley said.

I shrugged a shoulder. "Not like Aunt Nadia makes it sound, but he wants me to stay away."

Her eyes widened. "Well, he doesn't get to decide that."

Aunt Nadia tossed her hands out. "That's what I'm saying, and I don't understand why my niece is heeding that boy's warning."

I glanced between the two of them. "I'm not in the mood to poke the bear." With a head tilt at Riley, I added, "You go and crush it tonight."

Her brows arched. "I could crush it better if you were there."

I smirked. "Now who's a liar?"

"Whatever. Good vibes create *more* good vibes. Think about it."

Aunt Nadia wandered toward the other end of the counter. "There's nothing for her to think about. She had no problem ignoring what Mensa wanted when you and Finn tied the knot." She gave me a sideways glance. "Go give that boy a hard time. It's a free country."

I stared at Aunt Nadia. "It's where he works. That's not cool."

Riley chuckled. "And he lives at the clubhouse. What's the difference?"

I just stopped myself from saying Mensa had a studio apartment near I-10 in Ocean Springs. That would have blown it.

I needed to come clean to Riley.

Which would mean Finn, Mensa, and all the Riot MC brothers would know.

No doubt they'd assume I'd been looking into the whole club, but all I really wanted was to investigate Mensa and lock him away. Nobody was that squeaky-clean. Nobody.

My eyes locked with Riley's. "The difference is that I *know* he works at Twisted Talons. I didn't know he lived at the clubhouse when I complained about your wedding reception being inside a tent."

"That's fair, but he really needs to get over himself. I don't understand why he has a problem with you. Who cares if your brother works for the FBI?"

"Whitney," Aunt Nadia said.

I jerked my head toward the back. "Come on back to the office. You want some sweet tea?"

Riley's eyes skated between me and Aunt Nadia. "Is it that blackberry stuff I had a few days ago? Because that is pure nectar."

"As long as it's blackberry season, Riley, I'm gonna make blackberry tea," Aunt Nadia declared.

I led Riley to the back and poured her a glass of tea from an over-sized travel thermos Aunt Nadia kept in her office mini-fridge.

Time to face the music.

She sipped from her glass and her eyes rolled back in her head for a moment. "I don't know how she does this without tons of pulp."

I grinned. "Wish I could tell you, but she never makes it when I'm in the room, and she guards her recipe like a hawk."

Riley waved her free hand at the office. "Why did you want me to come back here?"

"You mentioned my brother working for the FBI, but I did, too."

Riley gave two quick nods. "Yeah, I suspected that when you visited me in the hospital." Her expression turned wary. "But you mentioned you were between jobs to take care of your aunt."

"Yeah, my status changed not long before shit hit the fan with the case against your dad."

"What do you mean? I thought there was a man involved in this."

I nodded. "Yes, but that isn't what I wanted to talk about." I blew out a breath. "My superiors assigned me to you in order to figure out how much, if anything, you knew about your dad's activities."

She put her tea down on the desk, and frowned at me.

A sour feeling grew in my stomach. "I didn't want to keep it from you any longer. I'm sorry that—"

She shook her head. "But you asked me about Dad *once*."

I tilted my head. "Right. The way you shut that down, my gut said you had nothing to do with it." I paused. "When I wasn't with you, I'd follow you. It became clear your story about avoiding and staying away from Tyndale was true. I'm sorry I didn't do anything about your car being sabotaged. From where I watched the house, it looked like he was trying to take care of the car."

As much as silence saved my ass, it unnerved me when others went too quiet.

After enduring her long stare, she said, "I interrupted you a moment ago. What were you going to say, you're sorry that... what?"

"I'm sorry that I deceived you."

Her head tilted. "I don't think you're sorry about that. I mean, you were doing your job. So was your brother."

I shook my head. "Wyatt wasn't on that case. I was just as surprised as you to see him at the hospital. You're right, though, I was doing my job. I hope you don't think we're friends because I was assigned to you."

Her lips twisted with skepticism. "Were you *assigned* to loving karaoke? Hmm? And don't tell me you don't love it because nobody gets as good at it as you are without loving it."

My lips tipped up. "No, I've always had a thing for karaoke."

"And those wrong, but incredibly strong, opinions about Ben Stiller? Were those a front?"

"No... and you're the one who's wrong. *The Secret Life of Walter Mitty* is his best movie by far."

"*Zoolander*, but there's my point. We'd have been friends no matter what spurred our meeting."

I stared at her in admiration. "I love how open-minded you are, Riley. Most other people find out I had to cozy up to them because of a case and I'm cut out like a cancer."

"Like I said, we'd have been friends regardless."

I nodded once. "I appreciate that. Nobody's ever been as understanding as you, so thank you."

She swallowed a sip of tea. "You're welcome. Now that we have that out of the way, you're coming to karaoke tonight."

"No, I'm not. The farther away I am from Mensa, the better off everyone will be. We can't stand each other, and for good reason."

"You don't mean that. I've seen how you look at him."

I smiled. "Sure, with suspicion and scrutiny."

Riley laughed. "Yeah, if that's what you want to call checking someone out."

I rolled my eyes. "I don't check him out. He's not my type physically, and we're definitely wrong for each other morally."

"Morally?" she asked, her tone bordering on disbelief.

"No offense, I know he's your cousin, but I doubt he has any morals. Or, no, that isn't fair. His sense of right and wrong are the very opposite of mine."

Riley stared at me for a beat. "Nothing's ever black and white with him, that's for sure."

"I see shades of gray too, Riles."

She tipped her head, a questioning expression on her face. "If that's true, then the two of you are more alike than you think."

I shook my head. "It doesn't matter. Once you tell Finn, the brothers are going to agree with Mensa. Keeping me out will be their priority."

"But you aren't working any more."

I twisted my hands up. "Yeah, but the brothers won't care. And something's got to give soon. I need to figure out what the hell I'm doing. I definitely don't have time for dancing around a man like Mensa."

The breeze from the Gulf tickled the back of my neck before I set off on my jog. Part of me couldn't believe that I routinely came to the public beach access to torture myself this way. Even though I'd been on my high school track team, I didn't like running; I'd done the shot-put. But training at Quantico had been no joke – mentally and physically – I didn't like running, but I quickly learned that a long run was the one time I could zone out the noise of the outside world.

I needed to zone out in the worst way because I had a ton of big decisions in front of me. After a few stretches, I wandered to the sidewalk that lined Beach Boulevard, and jogged.

It didn't take long for my mind to clear so I could focus on the decisions I needed to make.

If I took over Aunt Nadia's shop, I'd have to pack up my place in Jackson and move down here. I wondered if running Hard Pressed would be fulfilling enough.

If I still wanted a job within law enforcement, I needed to figure out what that looked like. Did I want to work with the Biloxi PD? Did I want to put out feelers for a job in the private sector?

I couldn't ignore one of the biggest reasons I had resigned.

It sounded cliché, but my clock was ticking and I felt like I'd been married to my job, which wouldn't have been fair to my future family. It wasn't that field agents couldn't have families. Most of them did. It was that I didn't want that for my day-to-day life. By the flip side, I didn't want my life to revolve around being a mom. There wasn't anything wrong with that; I just needed to have an identity along with being a mom.

Being this aimless was new to me.

Another voice in my head asked if it was a waste of my education to settle for running Aunt Nadia's shop? Considering that I'd majored in business (in case I didn't get into the FBI academy), my education would actually help me. Not to mention keeping her shop in the family would be its own kind of achievement.

My breathing had become more labored as I hit my stride. Running along the Gulf of Mexico was so much better than running almost anywhere else.

It struck me that what I'd spouted off to Mensa at lunch had been true. I really loved it here. It was one-part tourist town, mixed with one-part Southern small town, and a dash of suburbia creeping in, depending on where you were in Biloxi.

The only downsides were that it wasn't that close to Mom and Dad in Baltimore, and Wyatt would likely put in for an office transfer at some point. Then where did that leave me?

If I decided to go into the private sector or local law enforcement, my biggest fear was in the backlash of this situation. Dating a co-worker was very unusual for me, but I had thought that Ben and I had clicked. We weren't the first two agents to connect – and it didn't violate Bureau policies, either.

But I'd never expected Ben to throw me under the bus like he did.

In a conversation with our case manager, Ben said I had an obsession with nailing the Riot MC. He felt I had too much of a chip on my shoulder where Mensa was concerned. He'd repeated that during the questioning with the deadly force review panel. Add in my deepening friendship with Riley, and multiple people questioned whether I was capable of maintaining my cover.

They might have been right.

Being undercover wasn't for the faint of heart. It was lonesome, grueling, and often felt like the case would never break. Those factors made it easy to get burned out. Plenty of people got burned out at their jobs, but losing any edge in an undercover case made a world of difference.

When I returned to Quantico for the routine stress test and mental health evaluation, I had expected to pass like I had six months prior. Yet the psychologist zeroed in on my issues immediately. While the recommendation was for me to take time off to get myself sorted, to my bones I knew it was time to hang it up. The competitive side of me despised this idea, but I couldn't deny such stark clarity.

I resented that this realization came at the hands of Ben, a man who claimed to care about me. We'd gotten to that relationship stage where we talked about moving in together. I hadn't fallen in love, but I had deep feelings for him.

My instinct said he'd been using me. Were the signs there all along? How did my judgment get so impaired where he was concerned?

I approached a major intersection along Beach Boulevard and turned around. Another bolt of clarity hit me: I wasn't getting involved with another man any time soon. No matter what Aunt Nadia said to the contrary.

CHAPTER 4

DIDN'T NEED TO KNOW

MENSA

"TWO GLASSES OF RED wine," Riley ordered with a huge grin on her face.

Mensa arched a brow. "Both of those for you... or did you bring your newest, former-FBI friend?"

"She brought her oldest friend, not that it should matter to you," Aurora said, her straight dark hair draped over her shoulder.

Mensa dipped his chin, turned, and poured two glasses of Merlot.

Once he set the glasses on cocktail napkins, Aurora put a twenty on the bar. "You can keep the change because if I have anything to do with it, I'm getting her newest friend to sing tonight."

"Aurora! I told you Whitney isn't coming out," Riley said.

Aurora tipped her head toward Mensa. "Yeah, because he doesn't want to see her."

Riley shook her head and grabbed her glass. "She has a lot going on right now."

Aurora stared at him, but nodded a couple times. "Yeah, all the more reason to come out for karaoke."

Mensa lifted both hands in surrender. "You want her here, have at it. I've done what Cynic asked of me since I got the sound system set up, and I've trained Finn on how to handle any snafus. It's slow tonight. I'm out of here in forty-five minutes, if not sooner."

"You're no fun," Riley complained.

He shook his head. "I'm just glad to know my instincts were right about her being in law enforcement. I'm done with the drama. Have fun, and get your name on the list now."

<hr>

He jinxed himself. His plan to cut out early imploded when their three latest prospects arrived. Cynic had neglected to tell Mensa that he and Finn would be training these men during Open-Mic night.

The unexpected training meant he had a full view of Whitney strutting her fine ass inside Twisted Talons. Between her tight, dark-wash jeans and the fire-engine red sleeveless blouse, she commanded attention.

Four men tracked Whitney's progress to where Aurora and Riley sat, and Mensa ground his molars together. One of those men watching her wore a cut. Mensa hadn't caught which club the man was with, but he'd noticed the name patch said 'Rod' and right below his name was a Vice President patch.

Whitney showed up exactly forty-five minutes after Aurora and Riley had been at the bar giving him shit. He never should have said a damned thing to them.

He'd jinxed himself all right.

Finn sidled up to him. "I got the prospects in the back. This might be the only lull we get for a while, go get your dinner. I ate about an hour ago."

The smartest thing he'd done that evening was order a gyro from DeeLight's to be delivered. The food at Twisted Talons was great...or so Mensa had heard. Too much of the menu contained cheese for him to know for sure. And even the items without cheese were off limits because the batter contained whey, which was a milk by-product.

This didn't bother Mensa most of the time. He'd long become accustomed to limited options at restaurants. If anything it made him more grateful for the local restaurants that made food he could eat without wondering if he'd need to grab his EpiPen.

Gyros were one of his favorite foods, but unless he made it himself, he had to be careful. Not every place left off the tzatziki sauce, and some places had dairy in the pita bread. Two years ago, he'd found DeeLight's, a locally-owned restaurant that made great fucking gyros. When he explained his predicament, they bent over backward to accommodate him.

Dontrell, the owner of the restaurant, came inside with his order.

"Surprised you brought this yourself, man," Mensa said.

Dontrell put the bag on the bar. "Sometimes it's good to get away. See how the staff does when the cat's away and all that. For Open Mic night, this place seems slow."

"It's only eight-thirty. Give it time. You want a drink?"

Dontrell declined, but didn't move to leave. Instead, he shared with Mensa his opinion on the NBA playoffs. Mid-conversation, Dontrell grinned as his focus shifted down the bar. "Houston! Been a long time since I saw you."

Thinking of a man he went to high school with named Houston, Mensa turned his head, but his expression dimmed when he saw Whitney striding toward them. He'd done his best to ignore her being in the bar. Whitney's eyes were locked on Dontrell, and she appeared to be oblivious to Mensa's presence. The way she smiled at Dontrell, she had a girl-next-door quality about her. Her smile was so friendly, it filled her eyes with a brightness he didn't get to see from her.

"My last name isn't Houston, Donny, but thanks for the crazy compliment."

He turned his head back to Dontrell with a questioning eyebrow arch. "Donny?"

Dontrell shrugged. "Only the pretty ladies can call me that."

"What are you doing here?" Whitney asked, her eyes pinned on Mensa, the friendly light snuffed out.

"I work here, Blume. What happened to your quiet night?"

She stepped up to the bar. "I changed my mind when I heard you wouldn't be here."

For some bizarre reason, that stung. He shifted his eyes toward Dontrell and back to her. "How do you know Dontrell?"

A coy grin twisted her ruby-red lips. "Finding the best gyro is one of the top ten things I do when I move to a new city. DeeLight's is my favorite place in town."

He didn't want to know that about her.

"You gonna swing by for lunch soon, Houston? Been too long since I saw you," Dontrell said.

"Absolutely. Might bring Aunt Nadia by to see you."

Dontrell laughed. "You do that, but I won't hold my breath. Until she retires, that woman's gonna work through lunch."

No matter the night or the customers on the other side of the bar, Mensa scanned the room routinely. He watched Aurora hurry to the doors with her keys dangling from her fingers. His eyes slid to the right, and he saw Rod sat at a low-top table, nursing his beer, and staring intently at Whitney. For the first time, Mensa wished the brothers had insisted on no club colors being worn inside Twisted Talons. He didn't like this guy, but he didn't have any rational basis for it.

The occasional whiff of Whitney's gardenia scent hit Mensa and it drove him crazy. Any other patron, he'd let her carry on this conversation with Dontrell. Instead, he leaned forward an inch. "You need another drink, Blume?"

She turned to him with an annoyed expression she tried to hide from Dontrell. "No. Finn brought us another round. I'm actually on my way to my car. I need to give something to Riley."

Dontrell swung his arm toward the doors. "Don't let us hold you up, Houston. Get back to your girls."

She grinned. "Thanks, Donny, and you should stick around. I'm supposed to sing in ten minutes."

Mensa wiped down the bar intending to hit the break room during her song. He'd forced himself to deal with watching her in the bar, and catching her enticing scent, but listening to her sing again would push him over the edge.

"I'm gonna hit the john. Tell Whitney that I'm sticking around to hear her sing," Dontrell said.

Less than a minute later, Mensa jerked his head up to see Whitney storming to the bar, her cell phone in hand.

"Can you pull your security feeds, Mensa? Somebody stole my car that was parked right out front. It looks like there's a camera trained on that parking space, so—"

Her volume had risen and Mensa held up a hand. "If it's the camera along the fence line, it was struck by lightning during a thunderstorm on Saturday."

Her head tilted at a perfect angle and he struggled against the urge to kiss her.

Shit. This was not the time and she wasn't the woman for him.

Rod, the biker sitting alone, sauntered to the bar. He appeared to be stockier now that he was standing. As he came closer Mensa noted the Corrupt Chrome MC patch. Rod's eyes were on Whitney. That wasn't surprising. A gorgeous woman like her... any red-blooded man would fixate on her presence. Something about Rod moving to the bar struck Mensa strange.

"And you haven't fixed it?" Whitney asked, drawing Mensa's gaze.

"Repairs are scheduled for tomorrow," Mensa said in a low voice, then turned to Rod. "You need another Coor's?"

Rod ignored Mensa and caught Whitney's gaze. "You remember me? We met at that gyro joint."

Whitney quickly hid her trepidation. "Um...sorry, I can't say that I remember you."

She turned back to Mensa, but Rod stepped closer. "How about I jog your memory. You drive that tricked-out Hyundai... or was it a Toyota? I remember talking to you about it while we waited on our gyros."

Whitney shook her head. "Sorry, I'm in the middle of something."

Undeterred, Rod kept talking. "Did I hear you say your car was stolen? I can help you."

He practically leered at Whitney.

Whitney paused, nodded, then spoke in a neutral tone. "Thanks. We're going to let the police handle it."

Rod glanced at Mensa and back to Whitney. "He ain't gonna be able to help you. He's working behind the bar."

Whitney gave a circular nod. "I'm still going to call the police."

Rod's eyes narrowed. "The cops are always stretched thin. And the Riot MC brothers aren't going to be able to help you, sweet thing. Let's go outside. We'll call some friends of mine."

Finn lifted the bar flap and moved behind the bar. Before Finn lowered the heavy piece of wood back into place, Mensa moved out onto the floor.

He didn't get toe-to-toe with Rod since that would have garnered unwanted attention. He positioned himself close to the line of barstools, and within arm's reach of Whitney. "You heard her. She wants the authorities involved. If you aren't ordering another round, you should leave before you really insult my club."

Dontrell rounded the corner and sidled up to Whitney. "You singing soon—"

Rod's eyes zeroed in on Dontrell. "Barlow? What the fuck are you doing here?"

Dontrell squinted one eye at Rod. "It's none of your damned business what I'm doing here."

Rod leaned toward Dontrell. "Your time's up, Barlow."

Mensa and Whitney looked back at Rod.

"I ain't paying a bunch of thugs to protect my business," Dontrell said, standing straighter.

Rod glanced at Mensa and back to Dontrell. "You pay up now, or you're gonna pay an even higher price."

"I pay you, and what then? You aren't protecting me from shit. You'll just raise the damn price, and for what?" Dontrell demanded.

In a smooth motion, Rod pulled a gun from behind his back and aimed at Dontrell.

"Oh shit," Finn muttered from behind the bar.

Whitney stood between the two men. Rod pulled back the safety. Instinct kicked in and Mensa tackled Whitney to the floor, his animosity toward her forgotten. The sound of gun shots filled the small space before they hit the ground.

The karaoke song ended abruptly and screams filled the bar.

Whitney squirmed beneath him and he tightened his grip. He moved them both toward the exit. Two more shots rent the air, but at least one of them came from a different direction. Either Finn had his gun on him, or another brother had stepped into the fray.

"Don't move," Rod yelled.

Mensa looked over his shoulder realizing the asshole was yelling at them. A second later, Rod shot at them.

Mensa wasn't sure what kind of gun Rod had, but by his math, there were at least three more bullets, which were three too many.

"Put your fuckin' gun down," Two-Times yelled.

Mensa glanced back and saw Two-Times behind the bar, holding a Glock.

"Fuckin' hell," Whitney whispered.

Mensa fought a perverse grin since he had the very same thought. He rolled off Whitney and pulled her to her feet. Another shot rang out. He looked over his shoulder and saw Two-Times aiming at Rod, who had dropped to his belly.

"Run!" Mensa shouted, then felt a rush of humid air hit him. He whirled and followed Whitney out.

She was three feet ahead of him, and half a dozen other patrons were running out of bar.

Mensa sprinted, caught up, grabbed Whitney's hand, and yanked her toward his bike.

"What are you doing?" she demanded.

"You're coming with me and we're on my bike. Hurry."

"We need to call 911 and wait for the police."

His eyes widened. "There isn't anywhere to take cover, Blume. Rod's shooting at us *now*. His club isn't far from here, so twenty other bikers could be here any second. We're leaving."

She opened her mouth then closed it, and kept pace with Mensa to his Harley. The faint sound of sirens filled the air, but they weren't very close.

He swung on his bike, put the key in the ignition, and Whitney hauled herself up behind him like she'd done it fifty times before.

Something else he didn't need to know about her.

Rod barged out of Twisted Talons. He hollered something, and in the side mirror, Mensa saw two other bikers in the parking lot. Even over the pipes of his Harley, he heard one of the bikes roar to life.

"Hang on," Mensa yelled, and they shot forward.

He tore through the parking lot and hung a left onto the main thoroughfare.

Whitney tapped his shoulder. "Head toward the interstate, you can drop me at my apartment."

He shook his head. "No. There's another Corrupt Chrome member behind us."

From the side mirror, he saw her whip her head around and turn back, scowling.

A car ahead turned right, and Mensa accelerated to get away from the biker behind them. It was the one time he didn't like his loud pipes because it gave away the fact he'd twisted the throttle.

"Are we going to the clubhouse?" Whitney yelled.

The entire situation was fucked up. He'd prefer to lead this asshole to Har's body shop and have it out with him. The clubhouse would be his second choice, but he couldn't do either with a law enforcement officer on his bike. (Even if Riley had shared that Whitney had resigned from the FBI, Mensa didn't care. Once a cop, always a cop, as far as he was concerned.)

His options were limited.

He considered a casino, but the rider was too close for Mensa to lose him.

Roman had a mother-in-law suite, but he actually had his mother living there.

"You got an extra gun?" Whitney asked, pressing forward.

He heaved out an exhale. He'd just sold his spare gun to Tiny, who wanted Sierra to have a small gun in her purse.

"No," he yelled, and forced himself not to think about her tits against his back.

"You sure? I won't report it."

"It was registered, and I sold it."

Mensa steered the bike onto I-10 westbound. The Corrupt Chrome rider was forced to stop for oncoming traffic. That was the first break they'd had.

Through this stretch, the interstate was two lanes. It wasn't a problem typically, but they were approaching a bottleneck with a minivan ever-so-slowly passing two semis.

If it were just him being chased, he'd split the lanes.

"Take the shoulder," Whitney called.

"No."

"He's going to catch up!"

The minivan finally moved to the right lane and the Honda Civic in front of them gunned it. Mensa followed, passed the minivan, took one of the last exits for Gulfport, and headed south. He intended to catch US-90 and go back to Biloxi, but something told him the Corrupt Chrome MC member expected that.

Mensa's bike needed gas soon. He spotted a busy truck stop, hung a right, and parked as far from the entrance as possible.

"Are we hiding?" Whitney asked.

"Let's just give it a moment," he said, shutting down the engine.

"He might expect you to try something like this," she muttered, swinging off the bike.

He dismounted. "Where are you going?"

Her expression held a hint of cockiness. "To the front doors to watch for the Corrupt Chrome MC. I'd invite you, but you're a little conspicuous in your cut."

He wanted to argue, but she was right.

"And what are you gonna do if he shows up?"

Her lips tipped up. "Tell Mary, because while I'm waiting, I'll be talking to an agent I used to work with about this. Hopefully Donny is all right."

She turned away, and Mensa grabbed her bicep. "Donny's weathered far worse than Corrupt Chrome MC. You don't need to worry about him. Calling your FBI contact won't help here."

Her eyes glinted in the harsh outdoor lights. "I have to, Mensa."

He sighed. "Do you really? I heard you resigned. I don't care if you call in the situation at Twisted Talons, but don't mention the asshole following us."

"It doesn't work that way. You haven't broken any laws, Kenneth."

He clenched his jaw at her using his given name. From the road, he heard a motorcycle engine. He crept closer to the corner of the building. An older man in a pastel blue crew neck shirt put down the kickstand of his Triumph.

Mensa turned and Whitney was in his space. It took all of his self-control to ignore her closeness, her scent, and her sheer sexiness. Once he had a lock on it, he glanced down at her. "Not him."

"Cool, but unless you want the bastard to see you...I'm thinking you shouldn't stand in the light at the front here."

He stared at her for a beat. "Don't call anyone."

Her lips pursed and she glared at him. "Or what? You're gonna leave me here?"

His lips tipped up. "It crossed my mind."

She lifted a shoulder. "I'll Uber it back to the bar... and send you the bill."

His brows drew together a fraction. "Why the bar? If your car's been stolen, you won't be able to get home."

She blinked and her eyes skated to the side as she contemplated it. "I hate how much sense you're making right now."

He chuckled. "Didn't get much of that in your government job?"

Her eyes burned with the glare she aimed at him. "No, I'm surprised you're capable of making sense, Mensa."

Roaring pipes filled the air and Mensa's body tensed. He paid close attention to the sound and realized it was coming from the Interstate... and had quickly trailed off as the motorcycle kept speeding away. That might have been the person following them, or it might have been coincidence.

"So, what's your plan biker-genius? We aren't hanging out here at a truck stop all night."

He considered something for a moment – a question had come to mind earlier, but Whitney giving him guff threw him off track. He focused on her when it came back to him. "You keep your registration in your car?"

"Yes," she drawled.

"Does it list where you live in town? Or some other address? Now that I know your background, I'm assuming you have a place back in Jackson where the FBI field office is located."

The light in her eyes dimmed. "It has my apartment here listed." She turned her head and hissed, "Shit."

CHAPTER 5

THE H-WORD

WHITNEY

I PULLED MY CELL phone from my back pocket, but Mensa waved a hand at me. "Just give me a minute. I'll have Block swing by your place and see if everything's good."

My gut told me it wouldn't be good, not in the slightest.

A few minutes later, Mensa tucked his phone away. "Block's gonna call me back when he's checked out the parking lot at your complex and the area surrounding it."

I did a slow nod. "That's great, but what's the plan right now? I haven't had dinner, and the adrenaline is wearing off, which means I really need to pee."

Mensa twisted his head to the side for a moment, then focused on me. "Let's not talk about adrenaline. For now, we wait. If we get the all-clear, I'll take you back to your place. If they got the drop on where you live...I'm not—"

I should have kept my trap shut, but I couldn't stop myself. "You could take me to your studio apartment."

He opened his mouth and closed it. I had never seen him speechless before. It gave me a delicious, even if perverse, thrill.

Finally he muttered, "Lease ran out on that place two months ago."

My head cocked to the side. "That's the second time you let me down tonight. Asked if you had another gun, you sold it. Asked about your studio apartment, you dropped the lease."

He narrowed an eye at me. "You assume I'd let you stay with me."

My eyes widened. "You *are* the reason I'm in this mess."

"How the fuck do you figure that?"

I scoffed. "If you hadn't kept me from running to Aurora's car, I'd be just fine."

"Yeah. Aurora left while you first chit-chatted with Dontrell, so you'd have run out into an ambush. Maybe you'd be 'just fine' being held at the Corrupt Chrome compound in Ocean Springs."

My mouth clamped shut at that because to my knowledge the Bureau wasn't aware of another MC in the Biloxi area, let alone that they had a compound so close by.

Before I could ask anything else, Mensa's phone rang and he took the call.

"Block," he answered.

Mensa's eyes cut to me. "What's your unit number?"

I gave him my apartment number.

There was a pause while Mensa listened.

"Hang on a minute, Block." He looked at me. "You got a neighbor who can check on your place?"

My lower lip stretched out and down with my grimace. "No."

Mensa nodded. "She doesn't. Did you see anyone suspicious? If Corrupt Chrome took her car, they'll be listening for a Harley, expecting me to drop her off."

After a pause, his chin dipped. "Yeah, walk around the complex and call me back."

He ended the call and tucked his phone into a holster on his hip.

"Thanks for having him do that," I said.

He lifted his chin and turned to watch the traffic outside the truck stop.

After a few minutes, he paced back and forth on the sidewalk and ran a hand through his hair. "How the hell did this shit happen?"

"Well, gee, if you hadn't put me on the back of your bike back at Twisted Talons, we wouldn't be in this mess, handsome."

He glared at me.

My words replayed in my mind.

Shit.

"Did I use the h-word?"

With a scoff he nodded. "But don't worry, I'm not and even if I were handsome, I know you didn't mean it."

Oh my God. A man who didn't realize how good looking he was – that was rare indeed.

My heart melted a little bit, but I had to keep focused. No doubt about it, I was cramping his style. My every instinct said if I hadn't been in the vicinity when Rod threatened Dontrell, Mensa would have taken matters into his own hands.

His phone rang. "Yeah, Block."

Mensa stared at me while Block spoke. After a beat, he squinted one eye. "You know everything *looking* okay from the outside doesn't mean shit, Block."

"It probably *is* okay," I muttered.

Mensa gave a short head shake. "Block has a feeling the building is being watched."

Mensa's eyes shifted to the side, and he said to Block, "She *isn't* going to the clubhouse."

"I've been there before," I muttered.

"Don't remind me," Mensa muttered back.

Anger suddenly washed over his face at whatever Block said.

"That is the *last* damn time anyone says that to me."

I didn't know what that was all about, so I ignored it.

Mensa ended his call.

I crossed my arms. "Here's an idea, drop me at Aunt Nadia's, and I'll get a girlfriend to take me to my place in the morning."

"It's late. You'll be lucky if she doesn't shoot you."

"That's ridiculous. I'll chance it, Mensa."

"Maybe I can't."

My head tilted. "Like you care about me."

He cocked a brow. "No, but I'll feel guilty about Nadia blaming herself for shooting you. Besides, I'm gonna have to walk you up, make sure it's safe."

I tossed an arm out to my side. "For crying out loud, they wouldn't know anything about Aunt Nadia."

"You don't know that. Rod came off like a trigger-happy idiot, but—"

"But you're paranoid."

"I'm surprised you aren't."

I sighed. "Let me call Aunt Nadia, then we don't have to worry about freaking her out."

"There's no need to worry her right now."

My gaze wandered to the property across the street and I spied a fast food restaurant. A Holiday Inn Express was nestled behind it.

Mensa blew out a sigh and tucked his phone away.

I met his gaze. "This truck stop makes me feel like we're sitting ducks. Since taking me back to my place isn't an option, we could see if that Holiday Inn Express has rooms. Then in the morning, I'll get a ride home from someone."

Mensa turned his head in the direction of the hotel, then I watched his lips bulge as he ran his tongue over his teeth. "Might be the best idea you've had all day, Blume."

I let that go. "Seriously, though, before we head over there, I'm raiding this convenience store. I'm hungry enough, roller food won't bother me tonight."

"There's only *one* room available? You're kidding, right? The parking lot isn't even that full," Mensa groused.

"Sir, there are three tour buses in the back lot," Rose, the front desk clerk, said.

My earlier raid of the convenience store had been thorough, and I shifted the two cellophane bags to my other hand and leaned on the counter. "He's doesn't mean to be rude, but is this last room a double? Or better yet a suite for some privacy?"

Rose looked at me, her expression dry. "The suites were all taken by the guests on the tour bus, miss."

I tugged Mensa toward the double doors. "I appreciate you getting me to safety, but how about you leave me here and someone else can get me in the morning?"

He raked a hand through his wavy hair. "I should say yes to that, but I got a bad feeling you're gonna be cornered at your place tomorrow. So if the person picking you up isn't an FBI agent or someone with some street smarts, I'm sticking around."

That was quite admirable of him.

"My gender doesn't factor into your protectiveness, does it?"

He gave me a pointed look. "Your lack of a weapon is the only factor. I'd like nothing more than to ride back to the clubhouse without you, but I won't leave you here like a sitting duck."

I bit my lower lip. "This is overkill."

"Overkill trumps being killed."

I couldn't argue with that.

"Do you want the room?" Rose asked.

"It's just sleeping," Mensa said.

Oh sure.

I wandered to the counter and pulled my card from my back pocket. "We'll take it."

"You aren't paying," Mensa bit out, sidling up next to me at the counter.

"Then I should pay for your gas."

While I stared up at him, our eyes locked, he snatched my card off the counter and put his down in its place.

Rose made a humming noise, then said, "I could split the charge—"

"No," Mensa said, his tone final.

Rose ran his card, clacked her nails on the keyboard, and looked up at us. Her face paled.

"What? Is the room no longer available?" I asked.

She offered a wan smile. "It's yours, but it's a king."

I turned wide eyes to Mensa. "It's just sleeping."

If I thought Mensa had a problem with me before, I was wrong. His disdain amplified the moment the hotel room door closed. He prowled the entire space looking for non-existent threats, and avoiding eye contact.

While he made a show of being disgruntled, I emptied one of the shopping bags.

"Did you buy the whole store?" he asked.

I tossed two packages of Skittles onto the credenza. "No, just the important stuff like toothpaste, toothbrushes, and wine."

He laughed at my mention of wine. "Those Skittles are the opposite of toothpaste."

I shot him a grin over my shoulder. "Wine and Skittles are a winning combination. You should try it."

"Not tonight, I won't. One of us should stay sober."

With a thunk, I set the bottle of pinot grigio on the credenza. "That Corrupt Chrome asshole isn't going to come hunting for us at a roadside hotel set back from the main drag behind a fast-food joint. Your bike could be any weekend warrior on a road trip, Mensa. I highly doubt he committed your license plate to memory."

After a lengthy stare-down, he crossed to the small closet, opened the door, and pulled out an extra pillow along with a thick flannel blanket. "I'll take the floor."

A little voice told me to let him make his own choices, but my inner smart-ass couldn't be contained. "What happened to 'it's only sleeping'? It's not like I have cooties. But hey, if you want the floor, have at it, buddy."

That earned me his cold stare and strange excitement shot through me.

"I'm finally coming down off that adrenaline high, and if I'm in the same bed as you, I'm gonna have an entirely different struggle on my hands. One I'm not sure I can best, so I'm doing you a favor here by taking the floor."

The curious side of me wanted to help him with that struggle, but my more rational side held me back. Getting physical with Mensa – even one time – wouldn't help my reputation. Even if I was done with the FBI, my reputation meant something to me. Deep down, I still wanted to figure out a way to arrest him... though, from everything I'd seen tonight, he wasn't as bad as I'd thought.

"You have nothing to say?" he asked.

I shrugged and turned to him. "You can suit yourself, but there's a shower in that bathroom that might help with your struggle. After that, won't we just be... sleeping?"

He turned his head so sharply to the side, I worried he'd strained his neck. What more could he have to argue about?

CHAPTER 6

'THAT WOMAN'

MENSA

IF SHE THOUGHT A shower would help with his struggle, she needed a reality check. Even if he could jack off in the shower with her mere feet away, it wouldn't be enough.

Worst of all, he couldn't tell her that without giving himself away.

Hell, he'd lied about the adrenaline. Block's words on the phone had stuck in his head like a bad pop song. He'd repeated Finn's suggestion that Mensa 'work' Whitney out of his system.

As though one quick fuck would do that for him.

As though her every curve didn't hold a promise of pleasure he couldn't find with any other woman.

As though riding for the last forty-five minutes with her at his back hadn't felt perfect.

As though she were as expendable as a sweet-butt.

No.

Block and Finn didn't have a clue.

Mensa couldn't fuck Whitney out of his system. Hell, one taste and he'd probably lock them both in that room for the next five days.

Shit. That thought made his blood rush south and his jeans felt tight.

After that won't we just be sleeping? Her question was so forthright, that he wished he hadn't been so convincing downstairs.

It would never be just sleeping next to her. He'd already cataloged the many ways he could take her. His favorite so far was from behind in a spoon position, but watching her come while dominating her in missionary held a very close second place.

He blew out a sigh and swung his arm toward the bathroom. "You hit the shower first, Blume. You're right, it's just sleeping, and I'll get my shit tight by the time you're finished."

Her expression shifted... and fuck him, was that disappointment?

He did *not* need to know that.

She shook her head. "I'll shower, right after I report my car stolen. I'm serious, though, don't sleep on the floor. That's ridiculous."

Half-an-hour later, Whitney had reported her car stolen and gone into the bathroom. With her out of the room, he threw the extra pillow on the bed and put the flannel blanket back in the closet.

He shrugged off his cut and put it on a hanger. The remote control caught his eye and he grabbed it. Rather than turn on the television, though, he sent a group text to Har, Brute, and Cynic.

> Rod, the VP of Corrupt Chrome MC opened fire at the bar tonight. He shot at me and Whitney. Two-Times returned fire and I got Whitney out. I'd have stuck around, but some other Corrupt Chrome member chased me on my bike.

Moments later Cynic texted back.

> Yeah, I'm at the bar dealing with BPD. What about Whitney? Did she report her stolen car?

His phone rang and Har's name came up on the screen.

"Hey, Prez."

"Tell me exactly what the hell happened."

He ran it down for Har.

Humor laced Har's tone. "And you took her to a roadside hotel instead of your room at the clubhouse?"

"Prez—," he drawled.

"You really can't stand her."

He ignored the sarcasm in Har's tone. "We'll be out of here in less than ten hours. It's not a big deal."

Har chuckled. "That's one way of looking at it. Drop by my shop with her in the morning. Gamble will be there and Finn's been bringing Riley in every morning. We'll figure shit out then."

A strange sense of possessiveness came over him. He didn't want to hand Whitney off to Har, Finn, or Gamble. For some bizarre reason, he wanted to see that Whitney got into her apartment safe.

"You still there?" Har asked.

"Yeah. I don't want to rope any other brothers into this shit. Bad enough I had Block check her apartment complex."

"You know better than that, Mensa. We're a brotherhood. Hell, you can take her home, but as often as you've mentioned not trusting her and disliking her...I figured this would make shit easier."

"I appreciate that, Prez."

"Something about that doesn't sound right...almost sounds like you care about her."

He gave a humorless chuckle. "No, Har. Just a case of being in the wrong place at the wrong time."

"For both of you, I'd say."

"I wouldn't. I don't know why Rod threatened Dontrell, but that man doesn't deserve whatever Corrupt Chrome is doin' to him."

"You want to wade in on that, too," Har surmised.

The sound of the shower distracted him for a moment. "If Dontrell doesn't lose his mind, yeah."

"We'll need to have church."

"Make it in the evening so I can get more info from him."

The shower cut off a moment before Har hummed in agreement. "You got it. Also gives you time to get some sleep. My guess, you won't get much sleep tonight in the same room as 'that woman.' That's what you call her, right?"

He rolled his eyes at himself. He never should have made his feelings about Whitney so widely known. "Yeah, and she'll be back in the room soon, so I'll text you in the morning."

He tucked his cell away. The toothbrush laying next to his favorite candy on the credenza caught his eye. He wandered closer to the bathroom. "Did you forget your toothbrush?"

"No, that's for you," Whitney called back.

She was thoughtful.

"Thanks," he called.

"You're welcome."

She was making it hard to dislike her.

She opened the door, and padded out with a her hair twisted up in a towel. To his surprise, she wore an over-sized shirt that hung to her mid-thigh. The design on the shirt made it look like she was a cartoon character in a red, polka-dot bikini.

The fuck? He did a double take. "Did you get that at the—"

"Truck stop? Yes. You'd be surprised what you can find at a high-traffic truck stop – if you're willing to pay their prices."

Her bra hung from her fingers and he blinked – willing himself to forget that she was braless.

He focused on her baby-blues. "Did you get *me* any pajamas?"

She tilted her head. "No. I wasn't sure of your size."

He arched a brow. "It wasn't in your FBI file on me?"

Her grin held an edge to it. "No, we focus on more useful intel. And we were investigating your uncle, not you."

She talked a good game, but the quaver in her tone when she said the last two words gave her away.

"All yours," she said, sweeping her arm toward the bathroom. "You're welcome to use the shampoo... and the conditioner, if that's how you roll."

"The bar of soap works for me."

Her eyes widened so drastically, he battled against his laughter. "You use bar soap and get waves like those? Are you shitting me?"

His brows drew together. "No. At home, I use shampoo. For tonight, I'm sure I'll be fine—"

She put her hand to his chest, and he tipped his chin down giving it a scathing look. "Please, don't be so proud. Use the damned shampoo."

His eyes traveled from her hand in his chest to her earnest gaze. "Move your hand, and stop being so dramatic, and I'll use your damned shampoo."

She dropped her hand and in a bizarre twist, he immediately missed having it there. "Sorry. I know better. I'm having some wine, and I can pour you a glass if you want."

He needed his head examined because for some reason, he nodded. "Sure, but just one. I need to be on my toes."

"Because a Corrupt Chrome member can come hunt you down?"

His lips tipped up ever so slightly. "No. Because a former FBI agent insists I share a bed with her tonight. Never in my life did I think I'd be a literal example of strange bedfellows."

She grinned, coy as hell. "I'm not a fellow, Mensa. Enjoy your shower."

Half an hour later, Mensa threw his empty plastic cup at the trash can across the room. It hit the target, but the rustling sound of the trash bag wasn't half as satisfying as hearing the cup thunk would have been.

If Whitney decided to give up law enforcement, she had to consider going into sales. She was just that convincing. His one glass of wine had turned into two-and-a-half. Mainly because she tempted him with Skittles and an asinine assertion that they 'paired' well with the dry white wine.

He doubted his love of Skittles was in the file.

There was zero doubt he'd ever pair Skittles with pinot grigio again.

"That's impressive. Getting an empty plastic cup into the trashcan isn't easy. They aren't dense enough, and most people over throw because of that," Whitney said, her plastic cup held near her mouth. She had her ass planted in the bed, her back against the headboard, and her long legs tucked under the covers.

He shoved himself out of the uncomfortable chair at the desk. "I'm talented, what can I say? I'm gonna brush my teeth now before they rot from sugar overload. You need the bathroom?"

She shook her head and kept the cup in front of her mouth. "Nope. You do your thing."

He felt her eyes on him as he crossed to the bathroom, tagging the toothbrush along his way. Midnight was fast approaching. Four hours ago, if someone would have told him he'd be holed up in a hotel room with this woman, who rubbed him the wrong way for months... he'd have busted a gut, just before busting that someone's nose.

After he finished getting ready for bed, he came out to find Whitney with her phone in her hand and if he wasn't mistaken, she was scrolling through various sounds on her phone.

"What in the hell are you doing, woman?"

She looked up at him with a serious expression. "I am hell on wheels when I don't get my sleep. I'm pretty low maintenance most of the time, but when it comes to sleep... no. The idea of sleeping in my clothes turns my stomach. Hence, buying a sleep shirt. Sad to say, those people who make memes have it all wrong. Southerners *aren't* the only people who can sleep through gunfire, thunder, and tornadoes, but sit up wide awake without their box fan. I'm not Southern, and I cannot go without my fan."

He made a rolling motion with his hand. "Okay, but what's that got to do with your phone?"

She lowered her chin a touch. "I'm looking for the right white noise. They have a box fan option, but it sounds so fake it's laughable."

Her finger touched the screen, the room filled with a noise that sounded like a fan in a huge warehouse.

"That's the box fan?"

"Yeah."

He wandered to the opposite side of the bed. "Put it on the beach or ocean waves and be done with it."

"Typical," she muttered and bent to her phone.

With her attention turned, he quickly shed his jeans, and pulled back the covers.

Her sharp inhale got his attention. "Seriously? You're sleeping in your underwear?"

He slid under the covers. "You didn't buy me any pajamas, Blume. What do you expect me to do? Sleep in my Levi's? Fat fuckin' chance."

"Do you normally sleep in your underwear?"

He couldn't resist fucking with her. "When there's a woman in the bed, I sleep naked, Blume. Efficiency is the name of my game. Believe me, I'm doing you a favor this way."

She stared at him. "You are a liar."

He grinned. "So are you, babe. Don't you need your beauty rest, Miss Hell-on-Wheels?"

The bed jostled violently as she exited the bed, but it was her annoyed huff that made him choke on laughter.

Chapter 7

Not Going to Plan

Whitney

THIS WAS NOT GOING to plan.

Who was I kidding? What plan?

I'd bought a large bottle of wine in an effort to build a rapport with Mensa. Instead the man made it clear he knew what was up by sharing he had to stay on his toes. The fact he knew I was lying threw me like nothing else.

Thinking back on it, my voice had held just a hint of a quiver when I said I hadn't been investigating him.

Him mentioning a file... there wasn't an official one on him, unless you counted my personal collection of notes. I watched him like a hawk, and his love of Skittles was clear, but Sierra confirmed it when she'd shared a story of Mensa spending an afternoon at her house in order to keep her safe.

Now, I had to sleep next to that man while he wore nothing but his t-shirt and underwear.

Gah!

I finished in the bathroom and padded to the bed. Mensa had turned out all the lights. He'd turned on the TV, which gave me enough light to see.

And boy, did I see. Mensa had taken his shirt off and his muscular tattooed chest stole my attention. My mouth went dry. I lifted the covers and climbed into bed.

Mensa pointed the remote at the TV. I grabbed my phone and set the noise app to a continuous setting.

After I set the phone on the nightstand, I rolled to my side, away from Mensa. "Sleep well."

He sighed. "You too."

It took more time than usual for me to find sleep. It was cold in the room, but I felt like I was producing ten times my normal body heat. I forced myself to stop thinking about my body heat, and eventually, I fell asleep.

———

A door down the hall slammed and I woke with a jolt.

"Fuckin' pricks," Mensa mumbled.

I heard and *felt* his mumble. Then I realized I'd somehow rolled to my left and tangled a leg with his. My arm rested along the curve of his hip.

His hand clamped down on my wrist when I made to pull free. "Don't. Move."

"Mensa... you hate my guts, and I never meant to—"

"Don't hate your guts. You were wriggling around non-stop until I put an arm around you. Once you started breathing Darth Vader-style, I rolled away."

"But—"

"Then you rolled into me," he murmured.

Embarrassment flooded my system. "Still, I can let you—"

His tone sounded defeated. "Just stay where you are. It's three-thirty. We only gotta make it three more hours. Go to sleep."

Another three hours? Shoot me now.

I took a deep breath. My breasts tingled at the thought of how solid his body felt against mine. He really was different from any other man I'd shared a bed with. Dark hair, even more tattoos than I'd ever imagined, and I'd spent some time imagining.

53

I told myself to stop thinking this way. It felt good that he didn't hate me, but we were still wrong for each other.

"You aren't sleeping," he muttered.

"Neither are you," I whispered.

"Keeping a lock on my control is what matters right now. You go to sleep, I might be able to do the same."

Control? I moved my arm a little and his hold tightened.

"Blume, I mean it. Stay still."

"Did it occur to you that I'm in the same boat?"

His voice became husky. "You're not. You're just in the same bed."

He let go of my wrist, and I skated my hand along his abs. They weren't quite as ripped and muscular as his chest. His abdomen clenched.

"Sorry," I whispered.

"Are you?" he asked in a velvet murmur.

That gave me pause. "Yes."

He slid his hand down and over mine. "I don't hate your guts. I just don't like... what you stand for."

"What I stand for? You hardly know me."

"Law and righteousness." He made a low hum as he paused. "And pop music."

"Pop music? You are not to be believed!"

"Raise your voice a little more, Whit, and the whole floor will hear you."

I yanked against his hold.

He moved my hand lower. "You don't like me either. Admit it."

I sighed. "I *do* like you... I don't want to like you so much."

"Same," he grunted.

"You don't *want* to like me? Why?"

"Could ask you the same thing. We aren't compatible."

"Donny's fabulous food notwithstanding," I muttered.

"Great food is great food. Hell, it'd only give me one more reason to dislike you if you didn't dig his grub."

He held my hand to his lower belly, and with every breath he took, I swore he inched my hand even lower.

Anticipation had me tingling somewhere *other* than my breasts. "What is your point, Mensa?"

"Not sure I have one."

I scoffed. "Then let me roll over—"

"Seems you *do* have control."

"You were testing me?"

"I was testing myself, but I can see why you'd say that."

Again, I tugged, but he rolled toward me. "Hate me, yet?"

Moonlight filtered in through a gap in the curtains, giving me an excellent view of his features. I stared into his eyes. "No."

"Are you fighting it?"

I pushed my head back into the pillow. "Fighting what? Hating you?"

He leaned forward an inch, and when he spoke his voice was deeper and huskier. "Control."

Then I noticed he'd let go of my hand. His tone, his weight... hell, just the wait for a moment like this with him, it stoked a fire inside me.

My body buzzed with need and my control felt like a melting ice cube. There, but quickly dissolving to a slippery shard.

"Yeah," I breathed.

He backed away, and to my surprise, I let out a low whimper.

"I want a straight answer to this. Someone suggested I... bang you and get it out of my system."

My timing sucked because I inhaled sharply through my nose right when the A/C cycled off.

Of course, he heard it.

"If you don't want that, I'll lay on the floor."

I wanted him, but I also wanted *more* than just a quick bang to work me out of his system. Nobody else had to know about this... especially if it was just for tonight.

"I didn't hear a question. Or was that the question?"

He brought a hand to the side of my head and his thumb stroked my cheekbone. "Thing is... I don't think you can be honest because I'm not sure once will be enough."

I didn't either, but I kept quiet.

In the ensuing silence, my need grew to an ache.

After a long moment, he said, "It can't mean anything, and you strike me as the meaningful type."

That crazy voice in my head pointed out that 'can't mean anything' was worlds apart from 'won't mean anything.'

Fool that I was, I let that notion take root even if I didn't openly acknowledge it.

With a deep breath, I reminded him, "I still haven't heard a question, Mensa."

"Do you want to sleep? Or do you want me to fuck you hard enough that you *have* to go to sleep?"

"Does the latter involve kissing and you fucking me more than once?" I asked.

"As long as we're on the same page, definitely."

I ran my free hand into the hair at the side of his head. "I'm not going to sleep... and neither are you." Then I leaned up and pressed my lips to his.

The moment we kissed felt like pure magic. Surprise, joy, wonder, and the certainty that I didn't want it to end.

He drew in a sharp breath and leaned into me. I went along with his lean, but kept my hand in his hair, which helped to keep his lips locked with mine.

Once my head hit the pillow it was like he realized what I'd done. He swung his hips to the right, forcing my legs to spread, and he fell through. The bulge of his erection tested my self-restraint because I wanted to buck my hips something fierce.

I touched my tongue to his lips. He groaned and opened his mouth. Rather than let me in, he pushed his way inside my mouth.

My free arm rounded his bare torso and glided along his back. He had defined muscles there, and I couldn't wait to see those dips and valleys in the light.

That felt like a record scratch.

It can't mean anything.

Would I get to see him in the daylight? Hell, would I get to see him *at all?*

If this was it, I would damn sure make the most of it.

I pulled free from the kiss. "Lights."

"What?" he hissed.

"Lights. I want to see you because you're determined to get me out of your so-called system."

He chuckled. "'So-called'? What's that mean?"

I shoved a hand into his boxer-briefs. "Don't worry about that. Hit the freaking light."

"Goddamn, you're bossy," he complained.

"Genius, you ain't seen nothing yet, then again, it's still dark in here."

He leaned away, but stopped. "Did you just fuck with my road name?"

"Does it matter? Or are we going to bump uglies?"

"I'm thinking you need to shut up."

"Why?" I chuckled.

His forearms hit the pillow on either side of my head and he lowered his face to mine. "Because I don't 'bump uglies,' with anybody, Blume."

"Really?" I drawled.

"Yes, really, because nothing about a sweet, wet pussy is ugly. And when I take this pussy of yours, it will be *far* from bumping."

I laughed. "Is that so?"

"Are you laughing?"

"That's obvious. Turn on the light before I do it."

He leaned down and buried his face in my neck. Then I felt him playfully bite me there... and suck on my neck.

"Mensa!"

He sucked harder.

I gasped.

"Oh my God, you have to stop. I can't have—"

He increased the pressure and I moaned while my traitorous hips bucked.

Suddenly he let me go and exhaled against me. "You can't have a hickey? Too fuckin' bad. You mouth off to me, I'm sucking on your sweet skin. Any-damned-where I please. Now, I'm turning on the light, and you're gonna stay still."

"Who made you the boss?"

"Not who, but what, baby. I got at least seventy pounds on you, and I'm damned sure gonna use them for the rest of the night."

He leaned to the side and yellow-ish light flooded the room from the nightstand lamp.

I'd been trained to adjust to bright light, and in seconds, I saw the outline of his erection against his brick-red boxer-briefs. Instantly, I wanted his cock in my mouth.

He was quite right. I was bossy. I knew it, and I didn't give damn. Even when others expressed their disdain (or disapproval) of my assertiveness, I didn't back off. The bedroom wasn't any different for me.

I shoved his boxer briefs down and his cock sprang free. Hair lined his crotch, but it was well-maintained. That wasn't something I encountered most of the time, and I definitely liked it.

Dammit. I couldn't think about the many things I appreciated about him.

No, I had to enjoy this night and that was it.

It had to be.

"Fuck," Mensa groaned. "Woman, I told you—"

His words trailed off as though his train of thought broke. Likely because I shimmied my way down the bed under his frame until I was in position. If I wouldn't feel bad about tearing them, I'd totally have ripped his underwear down the center... but that shit was harder than it looked with cotton boxer-briefs. Still, his hard cock was in my face, and I wasted no time licking up the shaft and guiding him into my mouth.

"Oh... goddammit," he hissed.

My eyes crinkled with what would have been a grin, but my mouth was otherwise engaged. And did I ever engage. Mensa was thick, he had length, and he tasted damned good. After four bobs on his dick, he let out a frustrated growl and hauled himself away from me.

"Goddammit, Whitney. You're not sucking me off right now."

It might have been playing with fire, but I couldn't keep myself from asking in a playful tone, "Not right now? So definitely later. You're sure?"

He pushed forward and I fell to my back. His hands had gone up and under my sleep shirt; he found my panties, and he yanked them down. "Damn sure. Time to get my first taste of you."

Using my legs, I helped him get my underwear off.

His eyes blazed at me. "Sleepshirt. Now. Or else, I tear it off."

A huge part of me wanted to see him tear my clothes from me, but this wasn't the time. With a short, excited exhale, I arched my back, pulled up the over-sized shirt until it bunched around my armpits, then leaned up, tore it over my head, and tossed it aside.

His eyes lit with fire now that I was naked. He brought his hands up my inner thighs, along my hipbones, to the outside of my torso and up, until both hands cupped my breasts.

"Oh... shit," he breathed.

I chuckled. "That doesn't sound good."

His eyes met mine. "Because it isn't."

My brows arched. "Oh?"

He stared into my eyes for an eternity. "Three hours isn't going to be enough, so I hope you don't have to be anywhere before ten."

I hated myself for it, but I giggled. "Ten? Really?"

His intensely serious tone caught my attention. "Yeah, really. It's after three-thirty, and I plan to eat you out... no. I'm gonna suck on both your gorgeous tits, then eat you out. Luckily that doesn't require protection."

"Mm-hmm," I murmured.

He grunted a chuckle. "I'll see your mm-hmm in t-minus twenty minutes. You're going to be screaming after I put my mouth on your clit. Besides, after I got you good and primed, I'm gonna fuck you missionary and watch you come because I've thought of nothing else for fifteen months."

"Fifteen?"

"Yeah. Now, *you* stay focused. The second time I take you will be in a spoon position on our sides, and not to jinx it, but that one's been my favorite for months now, even if I haven't implemented it with you."

My legs squirmed beneath him with my excitement. To say I wanted all of that was like saying preschoolers wanted Christmas gifts.

Listening to him, I wondered if the rumors were true. I'd heard from 'sources' that Mensa believed firmly in being a giver. He wanted women to get theirs before he ever took his orgasm.

I couldn't wait to be the recipient of his giving nature, even if I wanted to give back to him at the same time.

He had hold of my hands and hovered over me. Then he lowered himself so we were chest-to-chest and crotch-to-crotch. "Last time, Whitney. Do you want this?"

I stared up at him. "Yes. I want this, Mensa. If you don't, now's the time to say so."

CHAPTER 8

HEADSTRONG

MENSA

HE TURNED HIS HEAD to the side. She had a helluva knack for turning shit around on him.

His cock was weeping with the need to be buried inside her, and here she was, throwing his shit back at him.

Again.

Still.

His mind replayed the last two minutes, and her words resounded crystal clear.

"Yes." And, *"I want this, Mensa."*

She wanted him, and God knew he'd wanted her for a long time.

Those lips wrapped around his cock were sheer heaven.

He wanted to get back to that, but first, he had to take care of her.

"Is something wrong?" she asked.

Her body under him made him crazy. He felt like he was even more on the verge of losing control. That didn't happen to him.

This didn't mean anything. It couldn't.

He stared down into her gorgeous blue eyes. "Nothing's wrong."

Her lips quirked into a half-smirk and he kissed her. That wasn't the best move, but he couldn't help himself. He'd wanted to kiss her smirk off her face for months. Now that he could, he took her mouth hard.

Best of all, Whitney gave it right back to him. Her fingers drove into his hair and she hooked a leg around his hip. He felt her wetness against his cock.

She hummed into the kiss before tearing away. "I need—"

"Know what you need," he said, grinding his hips.

Her hand grabbed his cock. He gripped her wrist. "What the hell are you doing?"

Those blue eyes glinted with her resolve. "I'm clean and on the pill."

He dipped his chin. "But you don't know shit about me."

Her cocky grin set his teeth on edge because he felt it in his dick. "I heard you tell Cynic your blood work came back a-okay in February. I'm so on-edge it isn't funny, Mensa. So fuck me."

Every so often, she reminded him of how he underestimated her. "February, woman. It's late May. That's plenty of time for me to fuck that blood work up."

Her smile fell away and her eyes narrowed. "Last week, Finn said you were so crabby because you haven't been laid since February."

He wanted to punch Finn, but he kept focused. "You're gonna trust that?"

"I know I've never been this wet for another man. Even though you're holding out on me right now, I also know once will *not* be enough. Let's go, Kenneth, so I can fuck you in the positions *I've* imagined over the last fifteen months."

He crushed his lips to hers again, but only gave her a hint of tongue before he cut it short. "I'm tasting you first or it'll eat at me. Now keep your voice down, Blume."

He trailed his lips down her neck to the slope of her breasts. His hands shoved them together and gave one a playful nip.

She gasped, bucked her hips, and threaded her fingers into his hair to hold him there.

He smiled against her soft skin, then lifted his head. "You like rough?"

"I like sex, and for some fucked-up reason, the more you infuriate me the more I want you."

He grinned. "Misery definitely loves company."

He drew her nipple into his mouth and sucked – getting a better idea of what she liked. Her hips shifted, but he made a mental note that she didn't buck like when he bit her.

He snaked down her body, kissing here and there. She smelled like hotel soap. It disappointed him that he didn't get a nose full of her usual gardenia fragrance.

She widened her legs once he made his way to her center. She kept herself well-trimmed. He skimmed his finger through her wetness.

She spoke the truth: her pussy was soaked for him. He lifted her legs, tossed them over his shoulders, and set to devouring her.

He'd heard her half-whimper ten minutes ago. Now she whimpered in earnest and he looked up her body. She had an arm flung over her head, a hand in the headboard, eyes full of lust.

He felt her push toward him.

On a chuckle, he squeezed her thighs. "Serious, Whit. Keep it down."

Her eyes widened and the annoyance shining at him pleased him.

They were so fucked up.

Glutton for punishment that he was, he dug that even more.

That thought reminded him that he had to keep this physical.

Redoubling his efforts, he licked around her clit. She cupped the crown of his head to hold him there. He drove a finger inside her, then added another.

"Yes! Don't stop, honey. I'm so close."

He sucked her clit for a moment, pulled away, but left his fingers inside her. "How close?"

"Very," she growled. "If you hadn't stopped."

He grinned. "Good."

With a curl of his finger, he found her g-spot, began stroking, and went back to eating.

His girl did not lie. He set her off moments later, and lapped up her orgasm with gusto. She tasted better than any woman he'd ever had.

His balls ached and he shoved his boxer-briefs off. In a fluid motion, he rose to his knees, lifted her hips, lined himself up, and pushed in to the base.

No whimper this time, she cried out, "Oh God."

"Quiet, baby."

He leaned forward, and savored the experience of being fully-seated inside the woman who drove him crazy. Centimeters separated their noses.

She stared up at him. "I haven't even come down yet."

"Even better because I want to feel you come again on my dick."

Her chuckle forced her pussy to clutch his cock tighter. He hissed at the sensation.

"Sorry, bad boy, but I'm not sure that's in the cards seeing as how I just came. I've never had a double."

He laid a hot and heavy kiss on her, stroking in and out gently. On an inward thrust, he pulled his lips from hers. "Tonight, that changes."

He withdrew, pushed up on one arm, used his other arm to hike her leg up. The new angle felt so good he almost blew. Once he had that under control, he checked off one fantasy by fucking her hard, dominating her sweet body and watching a second orgasm come over her. Feeling that sweet pussy milk his cock was pure icing on the cake.

She raised her hips to meet his thrusts and her hands dug into his ass, her nails stinging his skin.

"Shit," he hissed, feeling the tell-tale sensation in his balls.

Moments later, he came inside her with a long groan. His arms gave out. She took his weight without any complaint, wrapping her arms and legs around him.

"Fuck," he breathed.

"Yeah... we definitely did that," she muttered.

He laughed.

She brought a hand up to his cheek, guiding his face to hers. He shouldn't have let her do it, but once he was close enough, she kissed him.

Still inside her, she took her time while taking exactly what she wanted from the kiss. It hit him that letting her take control would be just as satisfying as dominating her.

He'd just come hard, but hell, if he didn't feel like he could recover faster than usual.

Dammit. What was she doing to him?

She ended the kiss by softly brushing her lips against his. He rested his forehead on hers, his eyes closed.

"That was... that was something else," she whispered.

He opened his eyes. "Yeah. You want to clean up? Or do you want me to bring you a—"

Her eyes went wide. "I can handle it. If you let me up, big guy."

He pulled back, but that felt so good and he glided back inside.

She inhaled sharply. "Mensa."

He grabbed her hands and rested more of his weight on her. "Right here, woman. I'm letting you up, but you better be quick. I'm not done with you. Gonna roll to my back, so I can watch you ride me... and maybe I'll play with your tits."

She leaned up and kissed him again. "So many promises. You better deliver, Ragstone."

Her using his surname hit him hard and his control snapped. He leaned down to nip at her neck just below her ear. He caught a hint of her gardenia scent, and he sucked her skin into his mouth.

"Oh, fuck, Mensa. That shouldn't feel so delicious."

Her voice had gone husky.

He pulled away and gently pulled out of her. "Clean up, and be quick. I got plans for you, Blume."

Mensa woke up to three conflicting sensations. First, the bright sunshine in the room indicated it was well into the morning, which alarmed him because he'd never expected to sleep past dawn and he hated not doing what Har expected of him – getting Whitney to the body shop first thing in the morning. The second sensation was almost primal. He didn't want to leave the room. His initial thought yesterday, that he'd hole himself up with Whitney in the room for five days, had been completely accurate.

The third sensation was physical pleasure. The moment he opened his eyes, he knew why.

After two more rounds with Whitney, he'd fallen asleep naked. From what he could see lifting the covers, she had slithered under the sheets and down the bed. She'd wrapped her fingers around his cock and taken him fully into her mouth.

Goddamn. Her mouth needed a permit. Yet, he was eager to discover how she would suck him off.

He tossed the covers off and her eyes met his. The way she looked up at him, hit him deep. He wanted to see her like that a year from now and beyond.

Her free hand moved from his balls and she touched herself.

She enjoyed what she was doing and that turned him on even more. His hips began to thrust and he called on some restraint so he wouldn't fuck her mouth outright.

He groaned. "Get up here, woman. You can't handle me fucking your face yet."

She stopped and semi-glared at him. "Shouldn't I be the judge of that? I mean, how do you know what I can handle?"

He curled up, slid his hands under her arms, and hauled her on top of him. "I don't know, but I want your cunt right now."

"Could fool me. You didn't see your face when you finally woke up."

He gave a short head shake. "Your mouth is a fucking dream, Blume, but I don't want to get too rough with you right now."

"Thought we were pretty rough last night," she murmured.

He slid a hand down to massage her breast. Keeping his hands off her was harder than he'd ever thought it would be. "Yeah, but we slept in and we don't have much time. That means, you're gonna kiss me, and then I'm gonna fuck you from behind so we both start the day right."

"Be better if I just ride you. I'm already in position—"

He craned his neck and kissed her silent. She also enjoyed his kisses, that was clear early, but he liked how with just a kiss he could convince her to do things his way. Just like four hours ago, her body relaxed and practically melted into him. Then he noticed she hadn't run her fingers through his hair.

Her hand wrapped around his cock and guided him toward her.

He opened his eyes and broke the kiss. "Whitney."

She grinned. "You can't blame a girl for trying. Besides, you *really* liked watching me ride you."

He couldn't deny that. If they'd been at the clubhouse, she'd have gotten her way on both the blow job and riding him.

Two could play her game, and he reached down to glide a finger through her wetness. "I did, but this ends once we leave this room, and I'll be damned if I don't get everything I want from you."

Her eyes filled with a strange combination of expressions. A blend of defiance, resolve, and it might have been disappointment or sadness. She quickly hid it, and squared her shoulders. "Then you better make it damn good, Genius. Because I guarantee, I'd have made it damn good for you."

Forty-five minutes later, they stepped off the elevator into the small lobby. Mensa clocked the two cops at the counter immediately. They were in plain clothes. Both stood with their sides to the counter, facing each other, which meant they clocked him and Whitney, too. One was younger and had brown hair cut in a crew cut, his brown eyes narrowed on Mensa. The other officer had short, gray hair and light blue eyes.

"Agent Blume," the younger officer said with a fake grin.

Mensa's defenses went up immediately, but he forced himself to stay calm.

If the officer's behavior bothered Whitney, she disguised it well. She stepped forward and stretched out her hand to the older officer. "Whitney Blume, Officer..." she let that trail with a questioning tone.

The gray-haired man shook her hand, his lips quirking every so slightly. "Detective Robinson. This is Detective Fortner. You reported your car stolen last night."

"Yes, sir. Do you have any leads?"

Detective Fortner aimed a pointed look at Mensa and back to Whitney. "Is this your boyfriend? Or can we talk with you alone?"

Mensa stepped closer to Whitney. "I'm her ride to her car, if you've found it."

"That's what's strange about this. Why didn't you take her home last night?" Fortner asked.

Mensa answered before Whitney could. "She told me her registration was in the glove box. That lists her address, and I sent a buddy to her place. He didn't see anyone, but he felt like the place was being watched."

"He 'felt' that?" Detective Fortner asked.

Mensa slowly dipped his chin. "Yes, sir. In your line of work, I suspect you trust your instincts even when they defy logic."

Detective Fortner stepped away from the counter. "You don't know a thing about my line of work."

Whitney put her hands out in a calming gesture. "He didn't say that he did. Do you have news? Otherwise, why come here and not...," she trailed off.

The detectives being there signaled that something else had happened.

"Why were you at Twisted Talons last night? And why was Dontrell Barlow there with you?" Detective Fortner asked.

"Is this official questioning?" Mensa asked.

Fortner ignored him.

Mensa looked at Whitney. "Wait for a lawyer."

Her brows lowered over her blue eyes. She wasn't going to listen to him – as usual. That had to be the number one thing that bugged him. She was so damned headstrong.

"The answer to his first question is in my report from last night, Mensa." She looked at the detectives. "I went to Twisted Talons for karaoke. Dontrell was there to deliver food to him." She tipped her head toward Mensa. "I saw Dontrell, not knowing he was making a food delivery, and decided to say hello. I ran out to grab something from my car, saw it was gone, and I came back in to see if Twisted Talons had access to their security feeds. That's when a man wearing a Corrupt

Chrome Motorcycle Club cut joined me and Mensa. His cut indicated his road name was Rod. He offered to help me find my car. Dontrell came back from the restroom, and Rod threatened Dontrell."

Fortner's lips twisted with skepticism and he glanced at his partner.

"We haven't found a member of Corrupt Chrome MC with that name or a member who fits the description you provided when you made your report last night," Detective Robinson said.

"He's probably laying low," Mensa muttered.

"Why did you leave the scene when shots were fired?" Fortner asked.

Mensa glanced around the small lobby. "Why are we doing this here? Out in the open?"

Detective Robinson crossed his arms. "Can we trust you to come down to the station?"

Mensa nodded. "Sure. I have to gas up my bike, and we'll be there."

"Mind if we follow?" Fortner asked.

Mensa locked eyes with the detective. "Are we under arrest?"

"No."

"Then we'll be at the station in thirty minutes. We haven't had breakfast."

The detectives exchanged a look. Fortner frowned at them while Robinson led the way out.

After Fortner cleared the doorway, Whitney edged closer to him and spoke through clenched teeth from the sound of it. "Why did you play it that way?"

He shifted so his back was to the doors and his body shielded her from view. "Call it a protective instinct. Nothing about that is right and I don't like it." She opened her mouth to speak and he held up a finger. "Fortner kicking this off by calling you Agent Blume didn't sit right, and something tells me he did that to make a fucked-up power-play. Not sure why you're no longer with the FBI, but my gut says you got screwed over. I'm not gonna stand here and watch those two twist your words."

"Okay," she drawled.

He shrugged a shoulder. "You're all about right and wrong. When you answer their questions, have a lawyer there."

She nodded. "I could ride with them, save you the hassle."

"No way. Have you ever heard of them before?"

"No, but Mensa, I can't know every detective in town. They're hardly going to—"

"Whitney, I'm sticking to the plan which is that I get you to your apartment, or your car – if it's been recovered."

"Fine. After you," she said, tossing an arm toward the door.

A ghost of a smile toyed at his lips. "You know better, Blume."

She took one step past him when his phone chimed with a text.

He pulled it from his hip holster and saw it came from Finn.

Weather says it looks like rain today. WTF, man.

His gut clenched. That was a code phrase the brothers used for bad news.

He caught Whitney's bicep. "Wait. You got your phone?"

"Yeah. Why?"

"Check the news sites. Something's wrong."

"What am I checking for?" she asked, tapping in the security code for her phone.

"The shooting at Twisted Talons to start. That would have made the news considering the state of things when we were chased." He pulled up his own search. Rather than search the bar's name, he entered Dontrell's full name. A newspaper headline sat at the top of the search results.

He read it aloud. "Local restaurant burned down overnight. Police searching for arsonist."

"Oh no," Whitney sighed.

"Yeah. I'm calling Har. For once, don't argue. Our club lawyer is the shit and you might need her."

CHAPTER 9

LIGHT TO HIS DARK

WHITNEY

WHILE MENSA TALKED TO Har, my heart sank reading the news about Donny's restaurant. The whole building on Pass Road was a loss. According to the article, authorities had not determined if the fire was related to the shooting at Twisted Talons.

"We better roll, Whitney," Mensa said.

I glanced up into his brown eyes. No matter how much he'd warned me last night, feelings were taking hold. I forced myself to replay his words in my head.

This ends once we leave this room.

We'd had our fun, now we were done.

His 'protective instinct' spoke volumes, though. He cared, even though I drove him up the wall.

Even if I was the light to his dark. I still had to nip those pesky feelings in the bud. Bad boys weren't my thing, even if everything Mensa and I did a few hours ago had felt so damned right. Nobody knew what we'd done in that room last night, and it was better to keep it that way.

I clambered on to his bike after him.

Scanning the lot, the detectives weren't in sight. Seemed Detective Robinson kept Fortner from following us.

Maybe.

Mensa wasn't the only one who didn't trust Fortner.

While we idled at the end of the hotel drive, Mensa reached back, grabbed my hand so I had to wrap my arm around him. With that as my cue, I did the same thing with my other arm. Did I hang onto him like this last night? I hadn't thought so...but then again, I had definitely stuck close while we were being chased. Him making it so I was pressed this close to him certainly sent a mixed signal, but maybe it was another 'protective instinct.'

In short order, he guided the motorcycle onto I-10 headed back to Biloxi.

Being on Mensa's bike wasn't my first time on a motorcycle, but it was the first time I found my mind clear in the past forty-eight hours.

My thoughts of Fortner fell by the wayside as I considered the situation.

I didn't know Dontrell Barlow well, but over the past fifteen months, we'd developed a friendship. He had four locations, and his seventeen-year-old son worked with him at the Pass Road location that had burned down. He had a younger brother managing his first restaurant because, as Dontrell said, "it ran like a well-oiled machine." I didn't know much about the other two shops because we didn't get to chat much during my visits, since he had other customers.

Small businesses couldn't afford setbacks of this magnitude.

A tiny voice asked me what Aunt Nadia would do if something like that happened to her. The expense and headache of that kind of loss was one thing, but I wasn't sure Aunt Nadia would survive the heartache of losing her business. Something told me Dontrell was the same way, even if he operated three other locations.

Then I wondered about the other workers he employed. What would they do without a job? Or would Donny send them to one of the other locations?

That was a silly question. Donny had a heart the size of the Gulf of Mexico. He'd send those workers to the other restaurants.

I recalled what Rod said to Donny last night before pulling his gun.

If Dontrell's time was up, why pull a gun in the first place? Donny wouldn't be able to pay if he was dead. It was a helluva risk to open fire inside a bar.

Then again, people did hasty things when they were angry, and plenty of criminals didn't think before they acted.

We veered off the interstate and headed toward the police station.

This should be standard procedure. Part of me believed Mensa's insistence that I have a lawyer was over the top. But lawyers served a clear purpose in the system, and a stronger part of me believed Mensa had it right.

Something was wrong, and a good lawyer would help me navigate this situation.

Mensa parked his bike five blocks from the courthouse.

I hopped off the bike and took off his helmet. "Why didn't you park closer?"

He grabbed the helmet from me. "Parking here is free. The police station is three blocks on the other side of the courthouse, and I do my best to stay away from LEOs. Do I need to drop you at the door, flower?"

My head reared back. "Flower?"

He opened the saddle bag and tucked his helmet inside. "Are you too delicate to walk?"

I shook my head, turned on my heel, and headed off toward the courthouse. No question, what happened at the hotel was over. I twisted my head to call over my shoulder, "Far from it, Ragstone."

He hurried up to pass me, pulled an about face, and blocked my path. "You need to understand something."

I stopped and crossed my arms. "What is that?"

"Club lawyer sent me a message. They're looking for an arsonist."

"That was clear from the news article."

I loved and hated how he could say so much by simply lifting an eyebrow.

He kept quiet.

I tossed my hands out in question. "What?"

"Our lawyer didn't confirm this, but my hunch is they're looking at you and me both for this fire."

"That's insane."

"No, you're insane if you aren't thinking two steps ahead of these people. Why not call you with info about your car? For that matter, how would they even know where you were?"

"I mentioned it when I reported the car stolen."

He tilted his head back and sighed. "Shouldn't have done that." He brought his gaze back to mine. "If the police had your car, they could have called. Sending those two detectives out reeks of a sneak attack or a scare tactic depending on how you reacted."

One of my eyes narrowed. "Elaborate, please, because I don't recall having any reaction since you stepped in before me."

He dipped his chin. "Yeah, and that's why I did it. They didn't have much to go on, and Fortner wanting to follow us... no."

I shook my head. "It doesn't matter, Mensa. We're here now. They're gonna ask me standard procedure questions, get our statements about the shooting last night, and then we'll be done."

With care, he put his hands on my shoulders. "That's what I'm trying to get through to you, Blume. Don't expect this to go according to procedure. Either one of us could be getting set up right now."

My head tilted. "That's crazy, but I'll keep it in mind, Mensa. Seriously. We didn't go anywhere near Donny's restaurant when we took off from Twisted Talons."

His eyes widened. "Another damn thing that rubs me the wrong way. We fled from a biker who didn't take pains to keep up with us on I-10. I get that he caught some traffic mid-way, but that's no excuse for not gaining on us when we hit that bottleneck. He could have caught up once he made it onto the Interstate."

"You think he gave up?"

"I think him falling back makes us look like we were on the run from a crime. The only thing that *might* work in our favor is the fact you paid for your snack stash with your credit card."

My stomach sank. "I used cash, had to dig out my two emergency fifties."

"Are you shitting me?" he demanded.

I shook my head. "No, but you paid for the gas with your credit card, right?"

He sighed. "I didn't want anyone to ping my card so I paid with a twenty."

I sucked my bottom lip between my teeth. "So there's roughly forty-five minutes to an hour where we can't prove where we were."

His eyes slid to the side and back to me. "Not unless that cashier remembers who we are."

We stared at each other for a moment.

Then a calculating look crossed his face. "Though... how many people buy pajamas at a fuckin' truck stop?"

I laughed.

He didn't. "You remember the cashier's name? Or better yet, you got a receipt?"

My eyes widened – and then my whole body deflated. "I did, but I threw it away when I brushed my teeth last night."

As his head twisted, he ran a hand through his hair. "Fuck, Blume."

I stood a little straighter. "Shoe's on the other foot here, Kenneth. Did you get a receipt for your gas?"

"Not quite the same thing. You get a name for the cashier? I paid a black man with dreads, but don't remember his name, and odds are damn good he won't remember me for shit because his whole day is filled with people telling him twenty-dollars on pump ten."

I stared off to the side for a beat. "I know she was blonde and it looked like she had a really great color-melt job done recently."

His eyes closed and his mouth dropped open as if he were painfully confused. He opened his eyes. "Don't know what the fuck a color-melt job is, but if you remember anything else about her – maybe I can get a prospect or someone to go out there and see if she remembers you."

I stepped past him because we were cutting it close on that thirty-minute time frame. Mensa fell into step beside me. I glanced up. "Yeah, I remember she had a Betty Boop tat on her inner forearm. She was younger than me, and it seemed odd, but I figured these days young people are into all kinds of things."

He nodded. "Good. I'll pass that along."

We kept walking, and I stayed quiet.

When we were a block away from the courthouse, I couldn't hack it any more. "Mensa, I don't want to question your gut, but seriously, they can't suspect us of this."

Mensa stopped and locked eyes with me. "You'd be right, except for one thing. Corrupt Chrome came to town just over a year ago. The other brothers weren't concerned, but I did my research. These assholes... they're scum. Not a damned thing they won't do for money, and the fact we were both there when Rod threatened Dontrell... my guess is that gave him the idea to make us the scapegoat."

Call me a nerd, but I loved people who did their research. The way Mensa didn't let anyone else's complacency keep him from being vigilant made me admire him anew. His road name made even more sense now, even if the brothers may have had different reasoning. By my definition, geniuses were smart people, and smart people looked into things so they showed up well prepared.

No matter how much I admired him, I gentled my tone when I spoke. "The scapegoat thing could be true, but you also sound paranoid, Mensa."

The way he tipped his head, I wasn't the first person to say that to him. "If overkill is better than being killed, then I'd rather be paranoid than *annoyed* that I'm sitting in jail."

I grinned. "Can't argue with that, Mensa. You have a name for this lawyer? Let's get in there, and get this over with."

Chapter 10

Incomplete Heathen

Mensa

Mensa spotted Monica Wright pacing in front of the police station. A man stood to the side watching her, and Mensa wondered if he was a junior partner or possibly an intern.

Before they got too close, Mensa said, "That's Monica, our lawyer. Not sure who she brought with her."

Monica smiled at him. "Mr. Ragstone. From what Mr. Walcott shared on the phone, I brought Todd Morton along because you and Ms. Blume have to be questioned separately about the events from last night. I can be with you or I can—"

"Stick with Whitney. She's former FBI and believes this is all standard procedure. No offense to your colleague, but my gut says they're banking on her playing by the rules."

They went into the police station, and found Robinson and Fortner waiting for them. Fortner deserved an award for his irritated scowl.

Monica introduced herself and Todd Morton to the detectives. With the formalities over, Robinson led them toward the rooms for questioning.

Fortner opened a door and looked at Whitney. "Ms. Blume, if you don't mind."

Whitney peeled off from the group, stepped into the room, and Monica followed her.

"This way, Mr. Ragstone," Detective Robinson said, opening the door across the corridor.

It bothered him much more than it should have that he and Whitney had been separated.

He sat down in one of the uncomfortable chairs in the cramped room, and Todd Morton settled next to him.

For almost an hour, Mensa endured a litany of repetitive questions about why he'd left Twisted Talons after the shooting began, why he fled the scene of a crime, why he hadn't returned after losing the motorcycle chasing him, and why he hadn't felt it was safe to take Whitney back to her home.

Any doubts Mensa had in Todd Morton were quickly dispelled over the course of the hour.

"Are you holding my client?" Morton asked.

Robinson took a deep breath and stared into the one-way mirror for a long beat as if he could read the minds of the people sitting back there. Finally he said, "No. He's free to go."

Robinson opened the door for them, and to Mensa's dismay, the door to the adjacent room stood open. He looked back to Robinson, but Todd Morton gestured for him to move forward.

They walked three paces before Mensa asked, "Where's Whitney?"

"I would think she's with Ms. Wright, but since I've been with you the past hour, I honestly don't know."

They stepped into the lobby and he saw Monica sitting in a chair with her phone in hand.

"Where's Whitney?" Mensa asked, his tone not just demanding, but borderline menacing.

Monica looked up at him with a gleam in her eyes. "She left with Finn and Riley. I'm confident Finn is capable of keeping her safe, though I doubt there's a threat to her any longer."

With effort, Mensa kept himself from glowering and instead gave a single nod. "Right. Thank you for your help, Ms. Wright."

She smiled. "It's what you pay us for, but it's always a pleasure, Mr. Ragstone. Tell Mr. Merino an invoice will be sent this week."

Mensa's lips tipped up a touch. "Will do. That should make Block's day."

Monica stood. "I'm sure." As she gathered her attaché case, she threw a sharp look at Mensa. "One more thing, if you talk to Whitney, be sure to mention that her brother's friend, Phil, hurried back looking for her before she left."

That was the last thing Mensa expected her to say. He leaned forward an inch. "What was that?"

Monica shook her head. "Sorry. Ms. Blume and I came out here after her questioning. A public safety officer, who's friends with Whitney's brother, saw us. His name is Phil. He was called away for a moment, but he came back hoping to see Whitney again before she left."

"She's not from here," Mensa said on auto-pilot.

Monica grinned. "No, but this man mentioned being friends with her brother... so I'm guessing that's how they knew of each other."

Jealousy stormed through his veins, but he refused to acknowledge it. In fact, it had to be something else because why would Mensa be jealous? She wasn't his.

Hell, he didn't want anything to do with her. Or so he thought.

The fact Finn and Riley came to take her home should have been a load off him... but it wasn't.

Being separated from her for questioning shouldn't have bothered him, but it did.

He should have felt free as a bird now that he didn't have to take her home... but he didn't.

Fuck. What was his problem?

Mensa nodded to Ms. Wright. "Sure. I'll let her know that Phil's looking for her. Thanks for the heads up. Hopefully, I won't need your help in the near future. Later."

Mensa checked his mirrors more frequently as he left downtown. He wouldn't put it past Fortner or even Robinson to follow him. For that matter, they'd probably have someone else follow him. When he approached Beach Boulevard, he hadn't spotted any sort of tail. He wasn't sure if that was good or bad.

He'd wanted to ask Ms. Wright what sort of questions they'd asked Whitney, but he also didn't want to have that conversation in the police station lobby.

As much as he needed to hit the clubhouse for some food, a shower, and a nap, he detoured to Dontrell's first restaurant instead. He hoped Dontrell would be there, but after having a location burnt to the ground, he might be dealing with insurance adjusters and other people.

Mensa had barely put his kickstand down before Dontrell came out of the restaurant.

"What the fuck do you want?"

Mensa swung off his bike. "I'm not your enemy, man."

Dontrell's face filled with outrage. "No, but the other bartender shooting at that asshole last night didn't do me any fuckin' good. Hell, it's probably why they burned my place down."

Mensa's mouth opened, but he kept himself from responding in anger. After a deep breath, he asked, "How long have they been pressuring you?"

"That shit don't matter."

Mensa squared his shoulders. "Two detectives came for me and Whitney, and for some fucked-up reason they asked plenty of questions about last night's fire – as if we had something to do with it. If you give a damn about 'Houston,' then tell me, how long has the Corrupt Chrome MC been after you to pay them for 'protection'?"

Under any other circumstances, Dontrell's overly-dramatic confused look would have been comical. "Thought you couldn't stand her?"

He stared at Dontrell. "Just because I don't like someone doesn't mean I want to see arson pinned on them. I'm not a complete heathen."

With a finger pointed at him, Dontrell nodded. "Damn right, you're an incomplete heathen. Figured you or one of those other boys woulda been watching my place."

Mensa's brows furrowed and he turned his head a touch. "You thought the Riot would be there? Why? The confrontation happened at Twisted Talons. How could we know that your restaurant would be targeted?"

Dontrell tipped his head back and to the side as if Mensa had lost his mind. "You brought at least five of those boys to the Pass Road location. I figured that was the only reason those assholes held off so long. They knew I was in with you Riot motherfuckers."

Mensa took a deep breath. "We aren't motherfuckers, and you aren't 'in with us'. Back to the issue – how long have they been after you for money?"

Now Dontrell inhaled sharply through his nose. "About a year now."

Mensa's eyes narrowed. "Fuck, man. They've only been in town for roughly a year. You mean to tell me they've been after you for protection money since they got here?"

Dontrell's head reared back. "What was I supposed to do?"

Mensa blew out a breath and turned his head sharply to the side. "Fuck."

"You can say that again. Now, what's goin' on with Houston? She's good people, and it takes a lot for me to say that, since I pegged her for being a cop from the moment she walked in my restaurant."

His jaw clenched. "I don't know yet. We were questioned separately about the fire. You got any camera feeds or some sort of security service?"

Hardness had settled over Dontrell's features at Mensa's explanation. His tone reflected the same. "You damn right I got a security service. I called them earlier, but I'll call again and ask for a copy of the feed."

Mensa nodded. "Appreciate it."

Dontrell gave him a chin lift. "You need a gyro?"

For the first time in twenty-four hours, Mensa smiled at the thought of food. "You bet I do."

After a ninety-minute nap in his bed at the clubhouse, Mensa couldn't stop thinking about Whitney.

No, he couldn't stop thinking about what questions Fortner asked her. It wasn't like he could demand that from Monica Wright. Perhaps he could have, but it wouldn't have been right.

For that matter, he couldn't beat back the thought that she was being set up for something. What that could be, he didn't know.

Maybe everyone was right… he was paranoid after all.

Calling Whitney would put his mind at ease, but he had promised himself he would never use the number Finn had programmed into his phone months ago. Hell, he still didn't know why he hadn't deleted it the first chance he had.

With a self-loathing groan, he pulled out his cell, found her contact, and called.

"Hello?" she answered on the fourth ring, her voice full of trepidation.

"It's Mensa. You at home?" he asked.

"Yeah."

"They find your car?"

"Not yet, but I also have anti-theft service on the car, so I should hear back soon."

"What else did they ask you?"

"Nothing out of the ordinary, Mensa. They don't think I had anything to do with the fire."

Or they're keeping that card close to their chest.

"How did you get my number?" she asked.

"Finn. He programmed it into my phone months ago just to fuck with me."

She chuckled quietly and he wondered if she had tried to hide it from him. Then she said, "I should drop by one of Dontrell's other restaurants. Make sure he's all right."

"Other than being pissed as hell, he's fine."

"How do you know?"

"I paid him a visit after I left the police station."

She scoffed. "I should have done that, but I was wiped out."

A small smile curled his lips at the thought of last night. "Yeah," he whispered.

"Who could that be?" she asked.

"What are you talking about?"

"Hang on, someone's at my door."

There was a pause, and then she whispered, "Oh, Geez. Let me call you back."

"No, I don't like that tone. I'm staying on the line unless it's someone you know."

She sighed. "It's my brother's friend, Phil. I—"

"You ran into him at the station. Yeah, Monica said he hurried back to see you, but you'd left already."

"Let me call you back."

There was another knock at her door and he heard it over the line. Something about that bugged him.

"Do you want him there?"

"Mensa, it doesn't matter. I can take care of this. Have a good night."

She ended the call, and the bad feeling he had grew.

His lack of sleep had to be fucking with his head. She had FBI training. She'd be able to get rid of that guy. That didn't change the fact that *he* wanted to be the one to get rid of him.

He had to shut that feeling down.

They fucked last night. It was the best he'd ever had, but she wasn't the right woman for him. No matter how much he loved kissing her, or how great she tasted.

Shit.

He had to stop thinking about last night.

Ten minutes later, he sent a quick text to her, asking if Phil had left.

Her reply was almost instant.

Not yet.

That sealed it.

He knifed out of his bed, tugged on his boots, grabbed his keys and wallet off the dresser, and stormed out to his bike.

Whitney's apartment was fifteen minutes away from the clubhouse, but Mensa made it there in ten. His instincts were on high alert as he climbed the stairs to her apartment. Standing outside her door, he heard Whitney's voice, but couldn't make out her words. The tone of her voice was clear though; she was getting impatient.

He knocked on her door and shifted foot-to-foot while he waited.

After a moment, she opened the door with a confused expression. "Mensa?"

"Hey, can I come in?"

A stocky man with olive skin walked up behind her. "No, you can't. We're in the middle of something."

He glared at the man, then directed his gaze to Whitney. "His name on your lease?"

In a resigned tone, she said, "You know it isn't."

He grinned, and locked eyes with Phil. "Then it's up to her if I can come in."

Whitney did a long blink, but that sweet smile on her face said it all. She opened the door wide and glanced up at him. "By all means, Kenneth, come right in."

Mensa prowled into the apartment.

Phil widened his eyes at Whitney. "Seriously, Whit? This is exactly what I'm talking about. You need to distance yourself from him. What were you thinking having his lawyer there today?"

CHAPTER 11

YOU REALLY DON'T SHARE?

WHITNEY

I CLOSED THE DOOR and put my hands on my hips as I faced Phil. "To be fair, legal fees add up fast, Phil. At this point, I'm not averse to someone else picking up that bill. I've asked you to leave, what? At least four times now. It's time for you to go."

"You lied. I asked if you'd texted someone — and now this bonehead shows up."

I hated being called a liar. Between that and the fact Phil wouldn't listen to me, I snapped. "I've had a rough twenty-four hours, Phil, and I've asked you to leave *repeatedly*. The only bonehead in this room is you. It's time for you to go."

He looked at me like I'd slapped him, then he blew out a sigh. "Right. I'm sorry, Whitney. I'll go, but please think about what I said."

I shook my head and shifted my gaze to Mensa. "I appreciate you coming over here, but it'd be a good idea for you to leave, too."

I opened the door, but of course, Phil didn't move until he'd given Mensa a long glower. He grabbed the knob and closed the door behind himself.

I turned to Mensa. "Thanks, but you didn't have to ride all the way over here."

"Fifteen minutes isn't a big deal."

Everything about this felt like a big deal, but I kept that to myself.

I shrugged. "He's gone, you've done your good deed for the day."

He turned and looked around my living room, then he sat down on the sofa and settled in like he'd stay a while. "I still want to know what they asked you."

I folded a leg under my ass, sat on the opposite end of the sofa, and then I ran down all the questions they asked.

His lips twisted for a moment and he cocked a brow. "Did you know Dontrell's been puttin' off Corrupt Chrome for almost a year?"

My head reared back. "A year?"

He nodded. "Yeah."

"That sucks," I muttered.

"Don't know why he didn't say something sooner."

We stared at each other for a moment. "Do you want something to drink? Or are you just here to compare notes?"

He ran a hand along his scruffy jaw. "You eat dinner yet?"

"No."

"Then we'll go get some food."

I propped my elbow on the back of the sofa, and leaned my head against my upturned hand. "What are we doing here, Mensa? At the hotel, you said everything ended the moment we walked out of the room, but your 'we'll go get some food,' almost sounds like you're taking me out on a date."

He slid his arm along the back of the couch and scooted next to me. "I don't fuckin' know, Blume. What I know is that I got this urge to protect you. I don't trust you being here alone, even though logically you can take care of yourself. And I'd like to take you out to eat, get you back to my room at the clubhouse, and see what happens."

I grinned. "So, you're asking me on a date."

"I don't date."

I narrowed my eyes a touch. "Is it because you're jealous of Phil?"

He leaned closer. "You know better. It's because you're the most annoying woman I've ever met, and for some fucked-up reason you're also the best lay I've had in years. I want more of that, all of it."

"Even me annoying you?"

"Especially that, because if I can determine that you're *always* going to annoy me, that ought to extract my head from my ass."

My head tipped back and I burst with laughter. My hilarity was cut short when his lips landed on my neck. I drove my fingers into his hair and he pulled away. My eyes danced between his. "Every word you just said should piss me off, but I love how freaking honest you are."

"Good. Now get your shoes on."

I still had my hands in his hair. "Aren't you going to kiss me?"

"Not a fucking chance because I don't want to fuck you on this couch."

My head shook. "You can't just give a girl a kiss?"

"You aren't a girl, and it's never just a kiss with you."

That made my whole body tingle.

And it made me want to kiss him even more.

I pushed forward, took him by surprise, and climbed on his lap. The moment my lips touched his, he groaned and took control of the kiss. His hands grabbed my ass, and wanton as I was, my hips bucked.

Okay, he was right. It was never 'just a kiss' with us.

I pulled away and he glowered at me, but it was half-hearted. I smirked. "What can I say? I had to find out if you were right, big guy."

He squeezed my ass. "Fuck. Now I gotta ride with a fuckin' hard-on."

"I think you'll survive. But if it's really a problem, I have food here."

"I got allergies."

I dipped my chin. "You think I don't know that? It's the very reason I hated that you came into Bayou Moon. Mick has enough dairy on hand, I figured you'd steer well clear."

He laughed. "You thought I'd avoid a place where my brothers routinely hang out just because I got a fuckin' allergy?"

His hands rubbed the cheeks of my ass, and I resisted leaning into his hands. "To be fair, you hardly ever showed up when I was there."

He looked at me askance. "So you were investigating me."

I shook my head. "Nope. Riley was my assignment, but I didn't trust your squeaky clean reputation."

His jaw shifted for a moment. "What about you? Why'd you resign? I got a feeling you didn't give me the full scoop on that."

My stomach growled. "Are we eating here? If so, I should start cooking."

After a long moment, he shook his head, leaned forward, and set me on my feet before he stood. "No, we're getting out of here. I expect your brother's friend, Phil, will come back when he thinks the coast is clear. Pack a bag so you have fresh clothes for tomorrow."

There was plenty there that I had questions about, but reflexively I asked, "How do you know he's Wyatt's friend?"

"Monica shared when I got done with questioning, but you also mentioned it on the phone earlier."

"Oh, that's right. Where are we going? Feels like you're getting short-changed since I'm not even dressed up for a date."

He rolled his eyes. "Not a date, and what you're wearing is fine, but no flip-flops on my bike."

<hr>

"Are you serious right now? You really don't share?" I asked, my voice loud enough to be heard over the breeze along the Gulf.

Mensa had taken me to one of his favorite places for Chinese food. After we loaded the take-out containers into his saddle bags, I expected to go to the clubhouse. Instead he guided his bike to the beach, pulled a blanket from the other saddle bag, and we had an impromptu picnic.

He aimed his plastic fork at me. "It's force of habit, Whitney. I'm so goddamned sensitive to dairy, and the fuckin' by-products like whey, that just dipping your fork or mine into something could make my throat close up. That shit never feels good."

I pressed my hands out toward him. "All right. I stand corrected. I'm sorry. Really. I hadn't even thought about that, though... didn't you say this restaurant's food never contained dairy?"

His head titled as though he regretted his words. "Yeah, but they say 'never say never', and I don't feel like finding out I'm wrong today. Especially since I got plans with this blonde law-abiding citizen who annoys me as much as she turns me on."

"She sounds like a winner. I like anyone who annoys you."

He borderline snorted. "I bet you do."

I bit my lower lip. "Why'd you bring me here?"

He turned to me, some of his hair whipping into his face from the breeze. "Why not? Best part of living in Biloxi is coming out to the Gulf and staring at that gorgeous water."

I watched him for a moment. "You really believe that?"

"Yeah, why wouldn't I?"

I shrugged. "I don't know. Seems to me that the best reason to live here is your motorcycle club."

He swallowed some of his General Tso chicken and nodded. "Can see where you'd think that, but there are other chapters around the country. There's nothing like being in Biloxi though." He locked eyes with me. "Like you told me, the weather's 'nice.' Even in December, I can come down here and rarely freeze my ass off. Lake Michigan has waves every so often, but you damn sure can't have a picnic next to it in the middle of winter."

I grabbed a fried biscuit and held it in front of my lips. "Fair enough."

He stared at the gentle waves for a beat, then focused on me. "Why'd you get forced to resign?"

My lips twisted to the side as I mulled it over. "Can we talk about something else? Anything else? What drove you to join the Riot MC? Not to sound judgmental, but your parents seem pretty normal, so what happened to make club-life so appealing?"

He stared at me for a long moment, and I thought he'd avoid the question. Finally he said, "It's a couple of things. Maybe it's hindsight clouding my memories, but the first reason is that as a teenager, I knew something was wrong with Uncle Jack. When I was fifteen, I swore I'd never be like him." He shook his head. "It's been hard not to kick my own ass because I should have said something to somebody back then, even if I didn't know exactly what was wrong with him. "

I sipped my soda. "You can't beat yourself up over that, Mensa."

He twisted a hand up to concede the point. "That's easier said than done."

"True. What's the second reason?"

"I didn't have a car as a teenager. Dad wanted me to earn the money and pay for it myself. I had a friend named Jacob who lived in our neighborhood. He and I were really close, and we walked to school every day."

A nervous feeling gathered in my stomach. "Okay."

He ran a hand through his hair. "Jacob wasn't that athletic, but he was all about after school activities like clubs and shit. That meant we didn't walk home from school together every day."

The way he bit his lip when he paused, my stomach dropped and my heart ached. I tried to stay optimistic. "All right, that isn't exactly surprising."

He blinked three times and exhaled hard. "No, what's surprising is that during our senior year, Jake was fuckin' gunned down one afternoon as he walked home." His chest expanded with his deep breath and his eyes blazed at me. "He wasn't in a gang, wasn't in gang colors, and that stretch of sidewalk wasn't in any gang territory. I was pissed as hell."

I nodded ever so slowly. Whether he realized it or not, he was *still* pissed as hell. Not that I blamed him.

"Were the shooters caught?" I asked in a soft voice.

He turned his head to the side, and I wasn't sure he heard my question. "I wanted retribution so fuckin' bad."

I grabbed his hand. "Did you get it?"

His gaze met mine – his pain downright palpable. "No. The bastard was shot by a member of the Miscreants – which makes Jacob's death even more senseless."

I squeezed his hand. "You're absolutely right, Mensa. Since you weren't able to get retribution, what did you do? How did that encourage you to join an MC?"

He grinned, and it was so boyish it took my breath away. "Because by the time I graduated, Brute had spotted me. He was twenty-one or twenty-two at the time. He didn't have his own business yet, but he was running a small crew for a contractor and he offered me a job. When I showed up on a bike, he asked why it wasn't a Harley."

"It mattered that much?"

His eyes went steely. "You know it does. I told him I didn't have the money for a Harley."

"Okay."

His grin returned. "Har had a Harley he could sell me, next thing I knew they introduced me to Brink – the president at the time – I started prospecting, and the rest is history."

I nodded. What he said made sense, but I couldn't keep myself from asking, "And you didn't have any second thoughts? Nothing?"

He tilted his head. "Mom had serious concerns, but that only pushed me closer to the Riot."

"Right," I drawled. "What about your Dad?"

He chuckled. "He thought it was a phase, which—"

"Also pushed you away?"

"Yeah. It was insulting to me at the time."

"You were eighteen?" I asked.

"Barely. I turned eighteen the day before I met Brute."

"Wow. You've been a member for at least seventeen years."

He shook his head. "I prospected for two years... so it's only been fifteen."

I fought off a smirk. "You're splitting hairs, but that's damned impressive."

Unlike me, he smirked outright. "I'll take your word for it, but this *almost* brings us back to my original question: how long were you with the Bureau?"

"Just shy of five years."

He nodded. "You resigned without another job lined up?"

"Essentially," I muttered. Then, I added, "I need to decide if I'm really going to take over Hard Pressed. But I should have—"

"Stop," he demanded.

"Stop what?"

He shook his head. "Your next words were going to be where you blame yourself."

"You don't know that."

The pointed look he gave me could have pierced my skin. "Don't I though? Between my mom and Riley, I don't know who's worse. They both blame themselves for my uncle's behavior. They constantly say they 'should have' done something differently. Isn't that what you were about to do? Say you should have done something differently?"

I opened my mouth and closed it.

He was right, dammit.

"You might be the most annoying man I've ever met."

He raised his brows in question. "Anything else?"

I leaned forward and smirked. "Are you fishing for a compliment?"

He returned my lean and the smirk. "More like the truth, Blume."

"I need more data."

He laughed, but sobered fast. "So, you got screwed out of your job?"

"The signs were there for me—"

"Whitney—"

"No, Mensa. I'm serious. Ben said things to the review panel, raising questions about my judgment. Every six months, I had to go back to Virginia for a stress test and mental health eval. My results on the psych test weren't favorable. Signs were there before. Undercover work is difficult."

"So?"

"What do you mean?" I asked.

"It's difficult. So what? Lots of shit in life is difficult. I'm pretty sure there's something else here. And can't you take another test, or is there a program the government offers to help you get back on track?"

After a sip of my iced tea, I said, "There are programs, but it doesn't change the fact that it seemed to be time to hang it up."

"Seemed to be?" he pushed.

I twisted my hands up. "Aunt Nadia's offer seems like a sign, too."

He shoved a chunk of chicken into his mouth and stared at the Gulf.

"I'm surprised you're so concerned."

His Adam's apple bobbed when he swallowed, then he turned to me. "I hate the idea that your fellow agent said shit to superiors that led to you feeling compelled to resign."

I shook my head. "I should have passed that test. It wasn't just what Ben told our superiors."

He stared at the water again while shaking his head.

Something struck me. "Are you angry?"

He shot me some side-eye, but he couldn't deny it.

I laughed.

"What's funny?" he asked.

"You're angry for me," I said.

"I'm more than angry. The way you talk about him, it sounds like that fucker had a real shot with you."

My lips twisted. "I thought we were moving toward living together, but it quickly became clear that I was wrong."

That earned me his side-eye again.

"Wait, are you jealous, too?"

He arched a brow. "Yeah. And it sounds as though you like that."

I shrugged. "I can't remember anyone being jealous before, so... yeah, I do."

In a flash, he set his container aside and leaned toward me. "Nobody's ever been jealous or possessive of you?"

"Not like that."

The way he exhaled, I didn't want him to shift back and I cupped his jaw. Our eyes locked. I leaned in to kiss him. My tongue darted out to his lips, I caught a hint of his spicy chicken but he didn't open his mouth.

I pulled back with a questioning look.

"Thought you'd have learned back on your couch, woman. I let you kiss me like that, we're going to jail for indecency."

"You're crazy."

He stood and grabbed his food container. "Nope, but it's time to go. You can finish your food in my room."

I'd decimated my Cashew Chicken to nothing but a few baby corn cobs and a bunch of celery chunks. With a head shake, I grabbed my container and stood. "I'm done, big guy. You need help folding the blanket?"

I waited while Mensa stuffed the blanket back into the saddle bag on his bike. My cell rang and I saw the number for the Biloxi PD.

"Whitney Blume," I answered.

"It's Detective Fortner. We found your car."

My eyes lit up. "That's great news, but why do you sound disappointed?"

"Not disappointed. The vehicle's been found at your apartment complex."

I blinked. "What?"

"Yeah. If you want to come downstairs—"

I grimaced. "I'm not home right now. I can be back there in roughly ten minutes."

Mensa's brows arched and he mouthed the word 'car.'

I nodded.

"I have to leave in a few minutes, but there's a patrol officer here if you miss me."

My lips pressed together for a moment, and I kept my tone neutral. "Understood. Thank you for your help, Detective Fortner."

The way Mensa's face drooped at the mention of the detective's name, I almost laughed before Fortner ended the call.

Mensa crossed his arms. "Is he with your car?"

I gave a short nod. "Not for long though. He said a patrol officer will be there if Fortner leaves."

"Patrol officer gonna take you to your car?"

With wide eyes, I shook my head. "No. It's at my apartment complex."

Mensa turned his head to the side and muttered, "Motherfuckers."

He swung onto his bike, I scrambled up behind him, and we were off.

Mensa parked his Harley near the stairwell to my apartment, but I didn't see any sign of a patrol officer. I dismounted, took off his helmet, and waited for Mensa to swing off.

My head was on a swivel looking for any sign of my car or the patrol officer. It hit me that maybe the car had been parked on the other side of the building. I strode in that direction, but Mensa caught my hand.

"Let's check your apartment first."

My eyes narrowed a touch. "My car could have been here all along, Mensa."

His eyes went wide. "You don't believe that."

He had me there. I'd taken a walk around the complex after my questioning before going upstairs for a nap and hadn't seen the first sign of my car.

Still... if I thought my place were compromised, better to have an officer there when I went inside. My eyes locked with Mensa's. "You don't like him, but if Fortner is still here, he should come with us to my unit."

Mensa deliberated that. "No arguments here."

I tipped my head toward the office. "Let's see if we can find Fortner."

We found the detective sitting in an unmarked sedan parked in front of the office. My car straddled two parking spaces, which set my teeth on edge. The hubcaps were gone, and I wondered what else would be missing inside the car.

Fortner unfolded from his car and sauntered toward us. "In addition to the lousy parking job, they left the car without your hubcaps, the spare tire, and your sound system's gone."

Great.

"I don't want to take more of your time, but would you or the patrol officer mind walking to my door? If they were in my unit, I'd rather report that right away."

Fortner pinned me with a look full of skepticism before he nodded. "I'll send Officer Robinson up."

My brows drew together. "Officer... there's another Robinson in the Biloxi PD?"

Fortner gave a nod. "Detective Robinson's nephew."

Five minutes later with Officer Robinson at my side and Mensa at my back, I shoved the front door open and sighed. The scent of marijuana wafted out of my unit. "Those assholes," I hissed.

Officer Robinson glanced at me. "I take it you don't smoke marijuana."

"No, officer. I don't."

Inside, the kitchen appeared untouched, but my end tables and bookshelves had been tossed.

Officer Robinson used his shoulder-mounted walkie-talkie to radio in the home invasion.

I turned to Mensa. "You can go. Probably—"

"Not a chance, Blume."

"It's going to be a while."

"No shit," he muttered.

CHAPTER 12

FIGHT TO WIN

MENSA

CRIME TECHS WERE ALL over the place from the glimpses Mensa got every so often when the door to Whitney's apartment would open.

He texted Monica to let her know what was happening. Overkill, according to Whitney, but if *he* was with the Corrupt Chrome MC, he'd have done more than just fuck up her shit if he'd broken into her place. This was a prime opportunity to leave something there.

Possibly something to help frame her...and maybe him, too.

Last night, he thought she'd been pulled into this as a coincidence – wrong place, wrong time. Now, he had a feeling she'd have been targeted regardless.

He shared that with her.

She crinkled her nose. "That seems far-fetched."

"Do you have any ideas?" he asked.

"I figure there isn't a reason. They did it because they *could*, not to frame me."

Mensa's lips twisted as he considered it. "You still have an FBI badge or gun in there? Any sort of credentials?"

Her patient smile made his breath catch for a moment. "The Bureau has my badge and my weapon. I have a personal gun, but it's in a safe."

"Key cards?" he asked.

"Access is revoked electronically, but those were returned also."

"Okay."

She kept quiet much longer than he expected, given the firm press of her lips. "Mensa, it's not as far-reaching as you think it is."

"Maybe not, but I don't think they took the risk of ransacking your apartment for the hell of it, either. They want you to know they can get to you."

With a throaty hum, she nodded. "That's fair."

He dipped his chin at her. "You're staying at the clubhouse."

She shook her head. "I'll go to Aunt Nadia's."

He bit back a sigh. "We've done this song and dance, Whitney. I'm sticking by your side."

"Fine."

His phone chimed with a text. It was from Har.

> Church. Noon. Tomorrow.

That worked.

He caught Whitney's gaze. "You at Nadia's shop tomorrow?"

"Yep."

"I'll be there too, but you're coming with me at eleven-forty-five to the clubhouse."

Her nostrils flared with her inhale. "Mensa, I've already—"

"No arguments or I'll call Nadia and convince her you need the day off."

Her blue eyes widened. "You fight dirty."

He grinned. "No, I fight to win."

She scowled. "For the record, I'm *letting* you win... this time."

He smiled knowingly. "Whatever you say, Blume."

Whitney stood in front of his bed at the clubhouse, glancing around his room. "Wow. I can see why you'd give up an apartment. You got a full bar out there, someone apparently cooks, and your room is much bigger than I expected."

Mensa cocked a brow at her. "It's the exact same size as that hotel room."

She threw her head back with laughter. "Far from it."

He wrapped his arms around her from behind, inhaling her intoxicating floral perfume. "Very same square footage, woman."

She settled her hands on his forearms. "Well, this is much better than a hotel room from what I can see."

He unfastened the button on her shorts and made fast work of the zipper. "So much better because nobody here slams their fuckin' doors at three-forty-five in the morning."

She twisted in his hold before he could shove her shorts down. "I don't know why you sound bitter about that."

"I like my sleep," he lied.

In truth, he owed that person huge. If it weren't for that door waking them up, they'd never have admitted to wanting each other, they'd have gone their separate ways, and then... he shut down that line of thought.

They were here now, and he'd never felt such strong feelings about a woman.

He couldn't tell her any time soon, but he was falling for her.

It wasn't just the physical attraction between them, either. He loved how she didn't take his shit, even when they both claimed to despise each other. The backbone and spunk she showed appealed to him. She surprised him at every turn, and he admired how calm she was when shit hit the fan. Riley would have lost it if she came home to a ransacked apartment, but Whitney kept it together while her home was full of crime techs.

She slid her hands up his chest, cutting into his thoughts. "I've yet to meet anyone over twenty-five who *doesn't* like their sleep, but that look on your face tells me there's more to it."

He schooled his expression. "Nope. Nothing else to it, Blume. You gonna let me kiss you, or what?"

The glint in her eye captured his attention a split-second before she went up on her toes and kissed him. Much like when they were on her couch and when they were at the beach, it escalated fast.

He slid his hands around her waist and down to her ass. She arched into his hands making him hum his approval. A woman could say she liked what he did to her, but responding and showing him she liked it said so much more.

Whitney broke the kiss and nuzzled his neck. "How do you make me lose control?"

Stepping back from her, he yanked his shirt over his head. "I need to figure that out, so I can do it all the time."

She grinned and took off her shirt.

He blinked at the sight of her pink lace bra. Her hands went behind her back, and he stopped her progress. "Don't take this off yet. Your tits look fantastic in this bra."

He traced his fingers along the edge of one cup. It was faint, but he saw her nipple harden beneath the lace. He circled it with his thumb.

She bit her lip. "Mensa... you're driving me crazy."

His eyes met hers. "Welcome to the club, Blume. You do that to me all the time."

"Not intentionally," she whispered.

He pulled down the cup of her bra, lowered his head, and sucked on her nipple. She drove a hand into his hair – another way he knew she loved what he did to her.

Her body wriggled, she arched her hips, and she tossed her panties on the floor.

Her cool fingers skimmed along his abs as she went for his jeans. He straightened, and took his pants off.

She pulled the sheets back on his bed and laid down. He never thought he'd have her in his bed, here at the clubhouse. Yet, everything about her being there felt exactly right.

Shit.

Seemed he had it wrong. He wasn't falling for her... he'd already fallen.

"What are you waiting for, Kenneth?"

His hands grabbed her ankles, and he spread her legs before he climbed onto the bed. "Not a damn thing, Blume."

He dragged two fingers through her folds and found her as wet as he expected.

Her hips jerked. "Are you teasing me?"

He lined himself up and drove inside her. "What do you think?"

Her eyes danced over his face. "I think it could go either way with you."

He kissed her. Their tongues danced a gentle duel and Mensa's hips moved in a steady rhythm. He made love to Whitney, even if he didn't tell her how deep his feelings ran.

———

After she cleaned up, she came back to the bed, got under the covers, cuddled up next to him.

He thought she'd dozed off, and was on the verge of doing the same when she slung a leg over his thigh. "Have you extracted your head yet?"

He shot her a questioning look. "What?"

She arched a brow. "Am I annoying all the time?"

His eyes danced over her face while he grinned. "So annoying."

She twisted and climbed on top of him. "Really? Anything else?"

He smirked while trailing his hands from her breasts down her body and around to her ass. "Not sure... think I need more data."

She smiled. "What kind of data?"

He felt her sultry tone in his hardening cock and he licked his lower lip. "Physical data."

With a kiss to his shoulder, she murmured, "How physical?"

"Very physical," he said, thrusting his hips.

She reached down, lined him up, and sunk down. "I do like collecting data."

———

Two minutes after twelve the next day, the brothers fell silent to listen to Har recount the shooting at Twisted Talons.

"We need to let the cops handle this," Brute said.

Fire burned through Mensa's torso. "Did I hear you right, Brute? We're gonna let the Corrupt Chrome MC come into our bar and open fire? The way my questioning went yesterday, shit's getting pointed in my direction. We have to retaliate against that, and it's wrong that they've been threatening Dontrell for so long."

Brute locked eyes with Mensa. "We'll draw a shitload of heat if we lash out at them. As for Dontrell's problem, we can't police shit like that. We don't have anything to do with that restaurant," Brute said.

Mensa tilted his head. "No, but how long before they go for Bayou Moon Pizza? Or Tiny's meat market?"

"Or even Twisted Talons?" Cynic chimed in. "Hell, they could be behind those vagrants who've been setting off our alarms."

Brute sat back. "Fine. Point taken."

Har wobbled his head. "Brute's caution is well-intentioned. This will get ugly, and none of us are going to jail."

Block tapped a pen on the table absentmindedly. "What are we gonna do? Not like we're gonna ask for a sit-down after a direct attack."

Cynic shook his head. "Word at Bike Week was that they're more vicious than the Devil Lancers."

Roman, Gamble, and Tiny nodded their heads.

Cynic continued. "Hate to mention this, but I also heard they make in-roads with street gangs. Though the idea of the Miscreants giving them an assist is ludicrous."

Block tossed the pen onto the table. "That won't factor. Inch will stay out of a beef between two MCs – especially since we have nothing to do with drugs any more."

Mensa ran a hand through his hair. "Might be just the angle for us to use with Inch. He helps us, it could help him."

Har's lip curled up in disgust. "I don't want to owe the Miscreants in any way if we can help it."

Brute caught Mensa's gaze. "You said the asshole who opened fire had the road name, Rod. We got nothing on the asshole who came after you on his bike though, right?"

"Right."

"And the cops didn't recover any security footage before the fire at Dontrell's?"

Mensa shook his head. "Not to my knowledge, but I spoke to Dontrell yesterday afternoon. He's got a security service, and he's going to see what they can give him."

Brute's lips tipped up and a mischievous gleam hit his eyes. "Can your new girlfriend find out what the cops have?"

A few brothers chuckled and Mensa blew out a quiet sigh. "Not likely, but I'll ask. She resigned, so she doesn't have pull like she used to. I first thought she was in the wrong place at the wrong time, but my gut's telling me she might have been targeted no matter what."

Brute's brows shot up. "Why would you think that?"

"Rod offered to help her find her stolen car before all hell broke loose."

"What does Corrupt Chrome gain from targeting her? Seems like bad timing if you ask me," Cynic said.

"Somebody tossed her apartment, but it doesn't appear as though anything was taken. My gut says they might have done the opposite and instead *planted* something to frame her. And, if they did that, it could even implicate me depending on what their end goal is."

Har stared at Mensa. "Do the detectives suspect you or her still?"

"Not to my knowledge, but I'm supposed to stay in town."

"Do you have a plan?" Har asked.

Mensa grimaced. "I'd love to do unto them what they did to Twisted Talons and Dontrell's restaurant, but I'm planning to approach Rod."

Cynic's eyes went wide. "You're taking a brother with you, right?"

Mensa tipped his head in agreement. "My gut says Corrupt Chrome must have something to hold over Dontrell, though."

"Or they're threatening his weak spot," Block suggested.

"What do you mean?"

Block looked at Mensa. "I've been to the location on Pass Road. There was a kid behind the counter every evening and weekend who's Dontrell's spitting image. You know if that's his kid? Or maybe a nephew?"

Hollowness invaded Mensa's chest. "Yeah, that's his son. And *if* they got connections with street gangs... maybe that's the protection Dontrell's supposed to pay for – they'll keep the Miscreants from luring his boy into their gang."

Har sighed. "You don't know that for sure, and we aren't operating on speculation. Does this tie back to Whitney being in the FBI? Did she investigate another Corrupt Chrome MC chapter? Or possibly piss off a street gang?"

"She was assigned to a public-corruption squad, not organized crime," Mensa said.

"It's unlikely they'd know who she is, being undercover," Block added.

Brute shook his head. "Seems to me we got two separate issues here. We got a club-owned business that's shut down because of these assholes—"

Cynic pointed at Brute. "We got a tentative go-ahead to reopen tomorrow afternoon."

Brute's twisted his hands up. "That's tentative, though. I agree Corrupt Chrome needs to fuckin' pay for what they did. But all this talk about Dontrell – that's outside of our skill set."

Mensa twisted his hands up. "Maybe so, but if Block's suspicion is true about Dontrell's kid being threatened, he's gonna need some help."

"What about Scrap?" Block asked.

Scrap was the street name, and unofficial road name, of a kid who Tiny had taken under his wing and was now prospecting with the Riot MC.

"What about him?" Tiny asked, protectiveness threading his tone.

Block raised his hands. "He wanted to join the Miscreants not too long ago."

Tiny's eyes widened. "And they know he's prospecting with us."

Block's tone became patient. "Yeah, but he may still have connections he could reach out to about Dontrell and his son."

"Even if there's a threat, what can we do about it?" Tiny asked.

Mensa shifted in his seat. "We make it known we're Dontrell's protection."

"Cops ought to be his protection," Two-Times said.

Mensa fought rolling his eyes. "That's worked out real well so far."

"Did he report the other confrontations?" Two-Times pushed.

Mensa sighed. "Didn't ask."

Block snatched up his pen and tapped it against the table. "Not sure it matters, Two-Times. If he didn't, he probably doesn't trust the police to take him seriously. If he did report it, he's got every reason to wonder if the cops took him seriously. It's a catch twenty-two all around."

Two-Times didn't exactly frown, but the set of his lips made it clear he wasn't happy with Block's response.

Mensa shook his head. "Don't worry about it, Two. It's not like I'm asking you to stake out any of Dontrell's properties. We all know you got kids at home, and I wouldn't ask you to put yourself at risk like this."

"Yeah, but if you drop shifts at Twisted Talons it'll be me who has to carry your load."

"You don't know that yet," Cynic said.

Har cleared his throat. "Before you put word on the street that we're protecting Dontrell, have Scrap check with people he used to hang with – if they'll even talk to him. Give that a day or two. Also gives us more time to find out what's going on. A couple of men who worked with my Dad haven't retired from the fire department, I'll see if they'll share any details about the arson investigation. We'll meet again in two days."

CHAPTER 13

LOST YOUR TOUCH

WHITNEY

MENSA BROUGHT ME BACK to Hard Pressed at five minutes after two. Unlike this morning, he didn't stick around.

Aunt Nadia stared out the glass door after he left. "You best be careful, Whitney. No matter what either of you says, that biker looks at you like his world revolves around you."

"That's dramatic, Aunt Nadia. Besides, that's only because right now, I'm tied up in something that's turned his own world upside down. Keeping me safe benefits him in a big way."

She laughed her high-pitched, gravelly laugh. "You go with that, sweetheart."

The double-beep of the alarm sounded. I twisted my head to the front door and saw my brother, Wyatt, striding inside.

"Well, hey there, handsome boy," Aunt Nadia said.

Wyatt gave her a look that said only she could get away with calling him 'boy'. "Aunt Nadia. You think you could go to the back? Maybe rustle me up a glass of your tea?"

Aunt Nadia's lips twisted into a slight pout. "You're standing right there, which means your legs aren't broken. Go rustle up your own glass. I'm not giving you two a second of privacy."

Wyatt closed his eyes and heaved a deep breath. I fought laughing because he knew better. Aunt Nadia was as nosy as could be, and even when people called her on it, she didn't give a damn.

My brother stepped closer to me. "Why were you at Twisted Talons when gunfire broke out?"

My head reared back. "How do you know—"

"I chased you out of there."

Once the words registered, my jaw dropped open. "You shot at me!"

He shook his head. "No. The asshole next to me shot at you, then he ordered me to chase you."

I put my hands on my hips. "But why chase us so far out of town?"

Wyatt crossed his arms. "Because I didn't want Mensa bringing you back to the bar or your apartment."

"He had no intention of going back to the—"

"I couldn't know that, but I *do* know you'd have pestered the hell outta him about it."

He knew me too well.

I crossed my arms. "Do you know who stole my car?"

Wyatt's posture relaxed and he shoved his hands in his jeans pockets. "Rod recognized you when you entered the bar. He called his road captain and ordered him to do that."

I straightened as I realized my focus was on the wrong thing. "Why the hell did you let Biloxi PD question us? You know Corrupt Chrome burned down DeeLight's."

He shook his head. "I don't know that. The fire's a local crime, which has to be investigated by the local authorities. I'm working a different case here. It doesn't overlap with Biloxi's case, at least not yet."

My head tilted. "If Corrupt Chrome didn't burn down the restaurant, then who did?"

His expression cleared. "I don't know."

"Sounds like BS," I muttered.

He pulled his hands from his pockets and put them on his hips. "No. It sounds like me doing my job. If you want any kind of future in law enforcement, you gotta take care of your reputation and stay away from Mensa."

"I got bad information, Wyatt. Hitting a bar for karaoke night isn't something a future employer will hold against me."

Wyatt's lips twisted to the side. "You know that he works there. That's more than enough reason for you to stay away."

I put my hands on my hips. "I should have stayed away from Twisted Talons, but at the same time, I should be able to let my hair down when I've been told his shift had been cut short. Believe it or not, the more I try to avoid him, the more I run into him."

My brother stepped forward and leaned into a hand on the counter. "Word is Fortner and Robinson found you two at a hotel."

I glared at him. "Yeah, because *you* ran us out of town and Block felt like my place was being watched."

Wyatt turned his head away so sharply, it was a tell.

"Why the hell were you watching my place? You've lost your touch."

He glared at me. "I haven't lost my touch, Whitney. I watched your place because Corrupt Chrome assigned me to it after I went back and said I'd lost Mensa."

I nodded once. "Did they get my address from my car registration? Were you the one who tossed my place?"

Wyatt's head moved as though he just stopped himself from shaking it. "You know better. When was it tossed?"

"Surprised you don't know about it, but it happened yesterday around dinner time."

Wyatt straightened from the counter. "And you slept there last night?"

"No."

He looked at Aunt Nadia and to me. "Her place?"

"No, sir," Aunt Nadia said before I could shrug.

Wyatt arched a brow. "You hit the hotel again? That shit gets expensive."

"Don't worry about that. I stayed away last night. I'll be in my own bed tonight."

"You got a gun?"

"Yes."

"You sure? Why didn't you have it Monday night?"

"I switched purses for the time being. Plus, why would I carry a gun on karaoke night?" I asked, though this conversation reminded me I'd needed to switch back to my Boho bag.

His eyes narrowed a touch. "That almost makes sense."

"That's a load off my mind."

"Whitney—"

"Why are you really here?" I asked, softening my defensive tone.

"I wanted to know about your connection to Mensa. And... let you know exactly how curious Rod is about you."

Great.

After a closed-lip smile, I asked, "Did you do anything to kill his curiosity?"

His lips tipped up. "I'm a hang-around, but I did what I could without blowing my cover. If you had plans to go back to Jackson – now would be a great time to do that. Let him forget about you."

I dipped my chin. "The heads-up is appreciated."

He shook his head. "Don't get stubborn. I'm trying to protect you from this."

"I heard you, Wyatt."

"Whitney—"

Aunt Nadia stepped closer to me. "Leave her be, Wyatt. She's got enough goin' on right now."

Wyatt's expression turned questioning. "She does? From where I'm standing, she's got nothing going on right now."

I glared at him for being so insensitive to Aunt Nadia. "Learning the ropes of Hard Pressed is *far* from nothing, Wyatt."

His eyes slid to Aunt Nadia. "I didn't mean it that way, Aunt Nadia."

She gave him a small nod. "I know you didn't."

He lifted his chin at her, then locked eyes with me. "Are you sure about this? You're giving up after almost five years?"

I pressed my lips together for a moment. "I put in my resignation. Been a long time since I had such clarity. As for Hard Pressed, I won't know anything if I don't get in here and see what I'm in for."

Wyatt pointed at me. "That's another reason to get back to Jackson. A decent amount of Aunt Nadia's business is with bikers. You don't need to run into the asshole here."

I turned to Aunt Nadia. "How often do you see actual members? Don't they usually send someone else? A woman?"

Aunt Nadia gave me a patient nod. "Normally, but on rare occasion, the bikers come in here themselves. I'd much rather see you be safe than sorry, Whitney."

My brows furrowed. "We don't know that Rod's gonna figure out I spend my time here."

"He knows where you live, but he doesn't know where you work. He told me and five others to keep an eye out for your car." Wyatt glanced out the windows. "Speaking of that, where is your car?"

I smiled. "I caught a ride. My car needs to be cleaned. It's gonna be a bitch to get rid of all that fingerprint dust."

People said twins often shared an almost telepathic connection. Wyatt and I didn't believe that very much. But I sensed he knew I was bullshitting him.

Seriousness filled his eyes. "Watch your back, Whit." His eyes softened when he turned to Aunt Nadia. "Love you Aunt Nadia. I gotta go."

"What? You don't love me?" I asked.

That earned me a dry look. "Got no choice where you're concerned," he said, then leaned in and gave me a cheek kiss.

Aunt Nadia and I worked quietly for two hours after he left.

She stood from her sewing machine, put her hands to her lower back, and arched for a stretch. "If that boy's right, you *should* go back to Jackson until this dies down."

I saved the spreadsheet I was updating and sat back in my chair. That would be sensible, but I hated the idea.

I sighed. "I'll keep that in mind, but for now, I can't stomach the idea of running away."

Aunt Nadia nodded. "I understand that, but it would only be for a little while. Far better to have wounded pride than a physical wound."

"That's very true. And, I'm sorry Wyatt was so insensitive to you earlier."

She scoffed. "He wasn't being insensitive, sweetie. He loves you and doesn't want to watch you do something you could regret. I suspect he believes you bailing out on law enforcement is a doozy of a mistake."

Hearing it put like that, my mouth ran away from me. "Do you think I'm making a huge mistake?"

Her lips curved into a patient smile similar to Mom's. "What I think doesn't really matter, does it? But ignoring your own safety isn't just a mistake, it's all kinds of foolish."

"I'm not ignoring my safety, and to be fair, even if I go back to Jackson, clearing out my apartment will only take a few days. Is that enough time? There's no telling how long I'd have to stay away to really be safe."

She nodded. "You're right, my dear. But you better keep your gun with you."

"Of course."

After a pause, she said, "How about you answer your own question."

I shook my head. "What do you mean?"

She gave me a sly smile. "Do *you* think you're making a huge mistake?"

I didn't even hesitate. "My gut tells me I'm not making a mistake at all."

She turned her hands out in front of her. "There you have it. Now, head back to Jackson tonight or tomorrow. All of this will still be here when you get back."

I contemplated that. Thinking about Jackson made me think about Ben, and how everything got twisted. That brought Mensa to mind, and it hit me that a big reason I didn't want to go back to Jackson was because he wouldn't be there.

What was that?

I never hesitated about going somewhere, and certainly not because of a man. That didn't change the fact that I wanted to take Mensa with me. Show him more of the real me because my apartment in Biloxi wasn't full of my personality. It was strictly a place to reside until the next case which could be anywhere in Mississippi.

Why did I want to drag Mensa up there? We were all wrong for each other and we both knew it.

Wyatt's concern for my safety couldn't be ignored. Jackson was the safest place for me right now, and putting some distance between me and Mensa would do us both good.

I stood and gave Aunt Nadia a hug. "You're absolutely right, Aunt Nadia. All of this will be here next week." I checked the time on my phone and smiled. "It's four o'clock. Think you can close up an hour early today, and take me to my place? If I get on the road by five, I'll be in Jackson by eight."

Her lips twisted. "Girl... I don't like you making that drive alone at night."

"I know, but what have you always told me? 'The sooner you start, the sooner you finish.' If I wait, I'm gonna have to convince a biker to let me be on my way."

"That's another reason for you to hold off. Maybe take Mensa with you."

"He was told not to leave town."

Her eyes widened. "And wouldn't *you* have been told the same thing?"

I shrugged. "Funny thing is, I wasn't told that. This keeps me and Mensa *both* safe."

She sighed. "As good as you are at manipulating me, I'd say you ought to consider politics for your next career, but this little shop won't give you the mountains of money needed to get elected."

I chuckled. "That really isn't a compliment, Aunt Nadia."

"I know."

I laughed. "Will you help me?"

"Yes, but for the record, I'm doing this begrudgingly."

"So noted."

Chapter 14

My Woman

Mensa

MENSA ROLLED INTO THE parking lot for Hard Pressed at five minutes to six. He noticed Nadia's Honda Civic wasn't in the lot, but that wasn't surprising. The woman closed the shop at five every day, and left at five-forty-five on the nose.

As he swung off his bike, he sensed he was completely alone, and that didn't compute. Whitney should have been in the shop, and would have heard his bike in the lot. At the door, he saw the lights were off except the one security light in the back. He pulled on the door. It didn't budge against the deadbolt lock.

Using his knuckles, he gave a light rap on the windowed door, then pulled out his cell and called Whitney.

"Hi there," she answered, her tone a blend of fake chipper and weariness.

The background noise told him she was driving.

"Where are you?"

"I'm on US49 and probably half-an-hour outside of Hattiesburg."

His free hand clenched into a fist. "What the fuck?"

"It's not a big deal, Mensa. Wyatt came by the shop, and he mentioned Rod with Corrupt Chrome is interested in finding out more about me.

More than he was before, which isn't ideal. Wyatt suggested I go back to Jackson and let this guy forget all about me."

He clenched his teeth and took numerous deep breaths to get his temper under control.

"You still there?" she asked.

"You didn't think to fuckin' call me?" he bit out.

"Mensa, this works out for both of us. You can't leave town. I need to pack up my apartment at some point, and this keeps us both safe. Two birds, one stone."

He shook his head. "How in the fuck does this keep me safe?"

"Leaving town would put you at risk of being arrested."

"Why didn't you call me?"

She paused. "What would you have said?"

"I'd have said my woman doesn't run from her problems."

A lengthy silence ensued. Even he couldn't believe he admitted that, but there it was. She was his. If he were honest with himself, he'd been thinking of her that way since the break-in.

"I'm not your woman, Kenneth."

That made him even madder, which shouldn't have been possible. But she did that shit to him. Made him feel more than he ever thought possible.

He stalked back to his bike. "You fuckin' are, and if you'd have called me or better yet, *waited* to tell me in person what you were planning, I'd have fuckin' shown you."

"When did this happen?"

"Maybe when I fucked you inside my room at the clubhouse, but you know it happened sooner than that." He ran his free hand through his hair. "When are you comin' back?"

"Next week."

"What the hell? Next week?"

"It's going to take time to pack up my place. Why are you so mad about this? Rod will forget all about me by then."

"He fucking will *not*. But I'll make sure he does."

"Mensa. Don't do anything stupid. And seriously...he'll move on to some other chick by then. I'm perfectly forgettable."

"Whitney, you aren't a woman any man forgets. He isn't going to forget about you in a fuckin' week."

He heard the smile in her voice. "That's sweet, but you're wrong, my..."

She trailed off and he knew he had her.

"My... what, Blume?"

She paused. "My friend."

That stubborn resolve of hers annoyed him, but it also made him smile. "Right. Keep telling yourself that, woman."

"I'm sorry I didn't call you sooner, but you don't need to make a trip to Aunt Nadia's shop."

"Yeah, it's a little late for that. I'm standing outside her shop right fuckin' now."

Her tone became more regretful. "Sorry. Really, I am, but I didn't want to interrupt you on your 'club business.'"

He dragged a hand down his face, fighting his anger and his perverse urge to laugh. "Right. I'm gonna let you focus on driving. I'll call you later tonight."

"Why?"

"Why the fuck not? But really, Blume...we got more to discuss. Later."

Mensa sat at a high-top table sipping a gin and tonic while watching Roman and Tiny shoot pool. He had his temper under control for the most part, but after he hung up with Whitney, he'd put a call into Monica Wright about whether he could make the trip up to Jackson without giving Fortner or Robinson a reason to bring him into the station. With any luck, she'd get back to him tomorrow morning.

Bottom line, he and Whitney had to have a conversation, and he didn't want to do it over the phone.

The front door opened and Scrap came inside.

"Yo, Tiny! How's it hanging?" Scrap asked, wandering toward the pool table.

"What the hell? Are Roman and Mensa invisible to you?" Tiny demanded.

Scrap's teeth flashed with his grimace. The effort to not roll his eyes was obvious. "Sorry. Roman. Mensa. What's up?"

Every so often, Mensa hated how they gave prospects so much shit just to earn their patch, but then it would quickly fade because he knew this 'shit' strengthened the bond between the brothers.

Roman gave Scrap a chin-dip and Mensa did the same.

Tiny lined up his shot.

Scrap waited until the cue ball rolled across the felt before he spoke. "I talked to one of my friends who's still trying to get in with the Miscreants."

Scrap's situation with the Riot MC was unique. He was eighteen, and old enough to prospect, but he was still in high school (for another two weeks), which normally would have forced him to be a hang-around for another year. Tiny and his woman, Sierra, had taken Scrap under their wing because of his awful home-life and the spiral that was taking. Proving how much he cared about Sierra, when her life was threatened, Scrap stepped up in a serious way. That meant once Tiny suggested he'd sponsor Scrap as a prospect, all of the brothers had been on board.

The seven ball dropped into the corner pocket, and Tiny straightened from the table. "That friend still in school?"

"Basically."

Tiny arched a brow. "Define basically."

"He's at school enough not to be truant, but he's failing all his classes except ICT." Scrap took in the puzzled looks from Tiny, Roman, and Mensa. "That's a computer class. Anyway, he said Demetrius Barlow is snubbing the Miscreants."

Mensa caught Scrap's attention. "If your friend is trying to get in, then how would he know that the Miscreants are getting snubbed?"

Scrap's eyes widened. "Because Dee's been snubbin' them for like almost a year now."

Mensa stared at Scrap for a beat. "When you say 'Dee,' are you referring Demetrius?"

"Yeah," Scrap said with a slight head shake. "Who else would I be talkin' about?"

"Dontrell, his daddy," Mensa said.

"Oh, yeah. Sorry, I forgot about that."

"Does your friend know why the Miscreants still want Demetrius to join them?" Roman asked.

Scrap shook his head. "I didn't get to ask that. He hardly wanted to tell me what he knew because the Miscreants are pissed I'm prospecting with the Riot."

"Are you gettin' threats?" Tiny asked.

"No. I'd tell you about that shit."

"You sure about that?" Roman asked.

Scrap nodded. "Certain because otherwise Tiny would throw me out of his apartment."

Tiny shook his head. "It ain't mine anymore, Scrap."

Scrap chuckled. "Not my name on the lease, and you remind me of that every chance you get."

Even with his head turned away from Scrap, Tiny couldn't hide his smug smile. "Gotta get my jollies where I can, Scrap."

Roman set his cue stick on the pool table. "Why are the Miscreants set on this kid? Seems like they could focus on your friend who wants to get into the gang."

Scrap frowned. "When I was trying to join, it was all about what you could offer them. My guess is they see the restaurant as a good place to deal or some shit."

Mensa took a sip of his cocktail. "Did your friend say where the Miscreants are spending their time these days? My understanding is that they haven't been in their usual spots."

Scrap shook his head. "No. He shut down after saying what little he did, but he probably thought I was going to try to talk him out of hanging around them. You need anything else?"

Mensa shrugged a shoulder. "Not right now. When you're back in school ask your friend, or better yet, ask Demetrius if he's feeling pressure from the Miscreants. We need to know if they're threatening

Demetrius, which by extension is a threat to Dontrell, and that would explain a lot of shit swirling around me and Dontrell."

"Demetrius doesn't go to my school, but I'll see what I can find out," Scrap said.

"The other thing that'd be good to know, is if the Miscreants are working with Corrupt Chrome, but my guess is no matter how much info your friend has, no way he'll know the name of the club the Miscreants might be working with."

Scrap shook his head. "They aren't working with them. There's no way, man."

That adamant tone got Mensa's attention. "How do you know?"

Scrap's eyes slid to Tiny and back to Mensa. "Because of the way they talked about the Riot MC last year. Inch doesn't like bikers. Why would he work with some other MC that's actually in competition with him?"

Tiny caught Mensa's gaze. "That might also explain Corrupt Chrome offering their so-called protection. If there's word on the street that the Miscreants are getting snubbed and pissed about it, then they got reason to make Dontrell pay to protect his kid."

"I still don't understand why he wouldn't have said something sooner."

"Pride makes people lose sight of logic," Roman said.

"Yeah, it sure does." Mensa whispered.

CHAPTER 15

WHAT'S CHANGED?

WHITNEY

THE TRAFFIC BETWEEN BILOXI and Jackson was better than usual. After swinging by the Taco Bell drive-thru, I got home at eight-fifteen. I ate my tacos at the breakfast bar of my apartment, willing the A/C to work a little faster.

My phone conversation with Mensa kept replaying in my mind. He took my news somewhat well. I hadn't expected him to be so gruff, or so... alpha about it. But calling me his woman threw me for a loop.

'But, Blume we got more to discuss.' Why did those words thrill me?

It had to be my hormones talking, and I needed to get them under control.

Logic said we would never work. Even if I took over Hard Pressed and turned my back on law enforcement, it didn't change who I was. A straight-arrow. A goody-two-shoes... legally speaking.

So far, though, I didn't have any evidence that Mensa routinely broke the law. In my limited free time, I had put some effort into catching him doing just that. But, it seemed that wasn't who he was, not deep down.

I had to stop thinking about this. Overthinking it wouldn't help one bit. I grabbed my nightie and fresh underwear and hit the bathroom for a shower.

As soon as I had donned my nightie and stepped out of the bathroom, my cell rang.

I grabbed it off the charger, Mensa's name on the display.

"Hey, Mensa."

"Sounds like you made it to your place."

"I did. Are you at the clubhouse or still dealing with club business?"

His voice lowered an octave. "I'm at the clubhouse, in my room, on my bed, and wishing you were here."

My eyes slid to the side. "That was rather precise."

"Where are you right now? Your living room? Guest bedroom, packing boxes?"

"I'm in my bedroom."

"Are you packing a box right now?"

"No. I just got out of the shower a few minutes ago."

His hum sounded appreciative. "What are you wearing?"

"My nightie."

"Take off your panties."

"What? You're joking."

His tone turned authoritative. "Take off your panties, Blume." He paused. "Now."

The way he said 'Now,' sent a jolt of heat straight to my vagina.

I chuckled. "Mensa. We're not having phone sex."

"Why not?"

"It doesn't do it for me."

He chuckled. "Baby, that just means you aren't doing it with the right person."

"Oh, really?"

"Yeah, really. Think about it... if you take the phone out of it, it's just sex. If sex doesn't do it for you... then, doesn't it stand to reason you're having sex with the wrong person?"

I laughed. "Your logic seems sound, but there's something to be said for physical chemistry between me and the other person."

"You're right, but considering our chemistry... give me a shot. Wanna know what I'm wearing?"

For some reason, I decided to play along. "What are you wearing?"

"A smile, and that's it."

My head tilted. "That's all? You're naked?"

"Yeah. Really wish my woman was here to take care of me."

I ignored the 'my woman' comment, even though it sent a warm sensation through me. "Like you can't take care of yourself."

"Seems I'm gonna have to, but you could help me out."

"By taking off my panties?"

"Yes, because you're gonna want to touch yourself while you get on your knees and suck my dick like a good girl."

At his words, without thinking, my hand went to my center.

What was I doing?

"Mensa," I whispered.

"What?"

"This is insane."

"You're right. The size of my hard cock is insane. Your fingers always feel so good wrapped around it."

"I bet my hot mouth would feel better."

"Yeah, it would. Did you take your panties off?"

I stood and shoved my underwear to the floor. "Yeah."

"Yes, sir, you mean."

My lips quirked. "Yes, sir."

"Is your nightie silk or satin?"

My nightie was actually soft cotton, but he didn't have to know that. "Silk."

"Are you lying to me?"

"No."

"I think you're fibbing, woman. What color is it?"

"It's purple with little pink roses."

"Are there spaghetti straps?"

"Yes," I said.

"Put me on speaker, so your hands are free. Then pull your tit out so I can suck on your rosy nipple."

His last words riled me up, but I wasn't good at working solo. Another reason I didn't engage in phone sex. "Mensa—"

"Whitney, you gotta relax so I can get you off."

I pulled the phone away, and hit the icon to put him on speaker. "I thought I was getting you off since you wanted me to suck your cock like a good girl?"

A dark chuckle came through the line. "If you're good, you might get that as a reward. First you're gonna help me glide my finger through your pussy. Is it wet?"

"Yes," I said.

"Are you sure? How do you know?"

I knew because of his earlier words, but I traced my slit. "I know because I felt it."

"You felt it when, baby? Were you so wet for me that it covered my finger and yours?"

I closed my eyes. "Yes."

"Do I do that to you?"

"You know you do."

"Should I drive one finger or two inside you right now?"

I chuckled. "Two, but why not three?"

"So greedy, baby."

"For you, always."

He made a satisfied hum. "Mmm, your pussy is always ready to go. Let me see what happens when I suck on your tit and finger you at the same time."

"Mensa," I wheezed.

"Yeah, that's what I thought. You need me to pinch that nipple, don't you? Or would you rather I bite it?"

Dammit. I'd never done anything like this before, but my fingers found my taut nipple and I pinched and rolled it with more force, imagining it was Mensa doing it.

"You're breathing pretty hard there, Blume."

"I'm gagging for your hard cock, Mensa."

"Good things come to those who wait, baby. You want me to rub circles on your clit, or flick it? Maybe with my tongue?"

It was like his words were a direct instruction to my fingers, and I flicked my clit. "Flick it," I breathed.

"That's what I thought. You like it like that don't you?"

"Mmm," I hummed.

"I'm throwing your legs over my shoulders, dragging your sweet pussy right to my mouth. Yeah, your clit needs some attention."

With his words, I rubbed at my clit like never before. I felt it building, and moaned.

"What do you want, Whitney?"

"Suck it, lick it, do whatever you want. I need your mouth."

"Damn right you do."

I pictured Mensa going down on me. Seeing as he'd done it roughly fourteen hours ago, the picture was pretty fresh in my mind. My body tensed, and an orgasm came over me.

"Oh my God," I moaned.

"That's right, baby. Come on my tongue. Lapping all of that up, while I jack my cock."

"You gonna let me jack your cock?"

"Only way you're jacking me, is if you take me in your mouth."

"Done, baby," I murmured.

"You sure?"

"Certain. I love running my tongue around the head of your dick."

"Yeah, what else do you love?"

"Catching that first bit of pre-cum... is your cock weeping?"

"Definitely."

"Poor guy. I better take you deep and suck you dry."

"Shit. How are you gonna do that, Blume?"

I kept working myself, though a second orgasm was highly unlikely. "Gonna use my hand to squeeze that monster cock of yours just how you like it."

"You gonna go faster?" he asked, his voice exceptionally husky.

"Show me how fast you want it, baby."

He went quiet for a moment. Then he grunted and hissed out, "Shit."

I kept quiet for a moment, and thought I heard him moving around. "Everything okay... sir?"

He chuckled. "Yeah. Haven't come on my stomach like that in years, and it was never quite that satisfying. Only way it could be better is if you were fuckin' *here*."

I stretched out on my bed. "I know, but things need to happen here... and this seemed like the right time."

"I'll have to take your word for it about the timing. Did I change your mind about phone sex?"

I laughed. "Let's just say, the jury's still out, but I definitely prefer the real thing."

"No shit. Most people do."

"How many boxes did you get packed tonight?" he asked.

I heard background noise, like clothes rustling. I shook off the thought of him pulling on his underwear. "Are you crazy? I rolled in here at like eight-fifteen, Mensa. So, I've packed zero boxes because I had enough time to scarf down my Taco Bell, then hit the bathroom, and now I've been on the phone with you, having phone sex of all things."

He laughed. "Not sure what this says about me, but I love hearing the outrage in your voice. Don't sound so disgusted about the phone sex, Whitney. You came and from the sound of it, I suspect you might have gone twice. If I'd been there, you would've definitely gone twice."

I groaned. "Don't remind me, honey."

"I'm coming up there tomorrow," he said.

"What? You can't do that. Biloxi PD told you not to leave town."

"I've left word with Monica and she's gonna see if that's still true. There's no reason to call me a person of interest in this thing. It's bullshit that they said that."

"It isn't necessarily bullshit, Mensa. Don't get yourself into more trouble because of me. It doesn't make sense."

"Why not? Give me one good reason why I should stay here."

In reality, there weren't any, so I glommed onto the only thing I could. "We're total opposites. We will never work as a couple."

"Nope. Now you don't make sense. Gamble and Vickie are total opposites. She's a lawyer for fuck's sake."

"Yeah, she mentioned she practices family law at Riley and Finn's wedding," I muttered.

He chuckled. "When they met, she was a public defender. We all thought Gamble was crazy for being with a lawyer, but they work. Really well, seeing as they're getting married later this year."

I nodded and sat back on my bed. "Oh, that's right. I heard about that. Her situation was extreme from what Riley told me."

"It was, but you haven't given me a good reason to stay in Biloxi. Two people will get the job done quicker, Blume."

I sighed. "That logic is true, but you *don't* want to leave town before you've heard from your lawyer. Going against a police order only makes you seem more suspect."

From the tone of his voice, I thought he might be smiling. "I'm aware, woman. I'll wait, but you better expect my company tomorrow."

I let silence fill the line as I debated posing a question. "What happened to what you said when I was driving? You were going to make sure Ron forgot about me?"

"I've learned some other information, and I've tabled that."

"Really? What kind of information?"

"Not anything I'll share over a cell."

I rolled my eyes. "Oh, please. Do you know the amount of paperwork involved in getting a phone tap?"

He still sounded like he was smiling. "It's not the government I'm concerned about, Whit."

I chuckled. "My point stands. Do you have any idea how hard it is to bug someone's phone?"

"Whatever. I'll tell you when I see you, woman."

"Are you coming on your bike?"

"That was the plan. Why?"

"I was going to ask you to bring me some boxes, but don't worry about it."

"You're definitely moving?" he asked.

"I'm definitely not keeping two apartments," I said.

He went quiet for a bit, and I wondered if me moving was the thing to push him away.

"I'll see if Har needs his truck this week. If he doesn't, I'll borrow that and bring some boxes with me."

"I don't want to cause any prob—"

"It's not a problem, Blume. I'm gonna let you get some rest, sweetheart. Later."

The following afternoon, I was kneeling on my bedroom floor, taping up a moving box when my cell phone rang. My place looked almost empty, seeing as Mensa had arrived four hours ago and had hauled away the items I knew I wouldn't take to Biloxi.

Now he was in the shower, and if things went well tomorrow, I'd have the rest of my stuff packed in no time.

I grabbed my phone off the nightstand, Wyatt's name on display. I answered and pressed the button to put the call on speaker so I could continue to pack another box. "Hey, Wyatt. Surprised you have time for me."

"I made time. Did you go back to Jackson?"

My lips quirked in a half smile. "Yeah, for once I listened to you. Did you have a change of heart or something?"

"Not really. I'm giving you a heads-up. Rod asked other members to Google your name. They find it real sketchy that you didn't have a single listing. I diverted them by pointing out that plenty of women protect their privacy. "

I grabbed a box that was half-full of my winter clothes and stacked it on top of another box. "So, I still need to watch my back. Got it. And just to say, that's pretty flimsy."

"That's why you're getting a heads-up."

"Thanks, I guess," I said with a chuckle.

"What's the deal with Phil?"

My head reared back, and I heard the shower turn off. "What?"

"He said he paid you a visit after your questioning."

I nodded once. "Yeah. I asked him to leave and he wouldn't take the hint. Which reminds me, did you give him my address?"

Wyatt hesitated. "I mentioned you were living in that complex."

My unease grew. "But you didn't give him my unit number?"

"Shit, Whit. I don't know. Not that hard to find your apartment number on a police report. That doesn't make him a creeper. He's a great guy. Why are you leading him on?"

My eyes widened. "Wyatt, that's way out of line. I don't lead people on."

Mensa leaned toward my phone and I wished I'd taken it off speaker, but I hadn't expected this turn in conversation.

"She asked him to leave and he wouldn't. That makes him pretty suspect If you ask me," Mensa said.

Wyatt's tone went dry. "If I'm talking to Mensa, Phil says she told you the same thing."

Mensa cocked a brow. "He told you that, and you still accuse your sister of leading on your friend?"

"Why is he there, Whit?"

"Don't answer that," Mensa whispered in my ear.

I grinned. I wasn't planning to answer, but he couldn't get used to bossing me around either. "What's it to you, Wyatt? I don't ask about every woman you spend time with. Besides, many hands make light work... especially when it comes to moving."

"What about your job?" Wyatt asked.

"What job? We went over this, I resigned. There's no getting my job back."

My twin sighed. "I was hoping going back to Jackson would make you rethink that and rescind your resignation."

"What's done is done."

"Bullshit. There have been agents who come back as long as it's within a quick time frame."

I shook my head. "You're right, but I'm not doing that, Wyatt."

My twin was undeterred. "If you want a decent job outside the Bureau, you've got to take care of your reputation."

"Wyatt, I appreciate your concern, but I'm due for a change."

"But with a biker?"

I pressed my lips together in a humorless smile, grabbed my phone, took him off speaker, and put my cell to my ear. "I thought we were talking about my work life"

"We're talking about both. How could you give up the job? It took so much just to get into the Academy."

I took a deep breath. "I hate to say it, but things change. *I've* changed."

Wyatt sighed and something struck me. "You seem more disappointed than I am."

"Yeah… it won't be – hell, it already isn't the same without you."

I shook my head because we didn't work the same cases together. "You'll adjust. You should get back."

"Sure, but when you get back, we're having a chat about Mensa being in Jackson with you. How long has that been going on? It seems like you just split up with Ben."

I opened my mouth to answer, but Wyatt kept speaking.

"Don't answer that. I'm glad you got rid of Ben. Hear me when I say, you're too good for either one of them. Remember that. Later."

The phone gave a double beep and with a seething breath, I put my phone back on the charger.

"Take it that last part was about me," Mensa surmised.

I glared at my bed, then softened my expression to meet his eyes. "That was about my brother being bossy."

Mensa scratched his jaw. "Noticed you don't like that. It's odd that you don't take authority well."

"That's 'odd'? I don't know many women who like being bossed for arbitrary reasons, Kenneth. And definitely not by their brother."

He chuckled. "All right. Chill out, woman."

"Yeah. Do you drink wine? I got a bottle of Conundrum calling my name."

Mensa grinned. "With a name like that, how could I say no? You aren't drinking on a empty stomach are you?"

I stared at him. "I suppose not. It won't make me very productive tomorrow."

He nodded. "I'll grill those chicken breasts you took out earlier. You make a salad or whatever vegetable you want."

I wandered to the kitchen. "The things I have to do for a glass of vino."

"You'll thank me later," he said, from behind me and giving my ass a squeeze.

***

An hour later, Mensa forked up a piece of chicken, but didn't put it in his mouth. "Heston said you weren't cut out for duty?"

I took my time swallowing some white wine. "He didn't say it quite like that, but even before my psych evaluation, he raised concerns about my focus, ability, and mentality."

"Why?"

I shot him a sheepish grin. "He thought I was obsessed with you."

He nodded. "So...what's changed?"

"What do you mean?"

"You said, things change and you changed. What's different?"

My jaw clenched as I thought about it. This would put a damper on things... but if this scared Mensa off, then that's the way the cookie crumbled.

"I want a family and even though I knew moving would be part and parcel of being an agent, the older I get the less I'm at one with uprooting my family." I shrugged. "That's a big strike against the FBI and with Aunt Nadia offering me the chance to take over Hard Pressed... it seemed like life stepped in for me."

Mensa stared at me for a long moment. "There are other agents with families, I'm sure."

"Yeah, but being undercover puts a different strain on me and my family."

"Then drop the undercover work."

I sipped my wine. "Yeah, but that thrill wouldn't be there any longer."

He mulled that over while he chewed a bite of chicken. "I can see that, but Hard Pressed isn't going to give you that thrill either."

I put my glass down and speared a cherry tomato with my fork. "No, it won't. But it will give me a sense of purpose, and it's actually a better income than I'd expected."

Mensa's head reared back. "Really? I'd think those Cricut machines have hurt Nadia's business."

I shrugged a shoulder. "Sure, for the smaller orders, but you'd be surprised how many orders she gets for jerseys, t-shirts, and the like."

We ate in silence for a few minutes.

Mensa finished his chicken. "How many?"

My brows drew together. "How many what?"

He drank some wine. "How many kids do you want?"

A bizarre, but enjoyable, thrill shot through me at his question. Nobody else had bothered to ask me that.

"Two, but I'm not opposed to three if the timing's right and all goes well."

The way he nodded, I suspected he approved.

The ensuing silence between us felt comfortable... even normal.

Finally, I said, "You look like you approve of my answer."

His head tilted for a moment. "Yeah. If I settled down, that would be what I'd want too."

If he settled down.

There it was.

In a playful tone, I said, "But you aren't settling down any time soon, I take it."

His eyes locked with mine. "I didn't say that. You don't normally put words in my mouth. Don't start now."

"I was only trying to lighten the conversation, but that's fair."

He stared at me for another moment. "This keeps on, I don't know if I could handle two of you."

I laughed. "Works both ways, Mensa."

He stood and picked up his plate. "So, how many more?"

I aimed some side-eye at him. "More? I told you three."

He chuckled. "I meant boxes. How many more have you got to pack? Are you aiming to head back tomorrow or the next day?"

I rubbed the back of my neck. "Definitely the next day. I have to handle some things tomorrow, like arranging a moving truck with a car trailer."

His focus shifted to my neck. "And it's stressing you out?"

"A bit. I'll be—"

He set his dish on the breakfast bar and stalked back to me. "Nope. Don't say you'll be fine. I'll give you an orgasm or two, and *then* you'll be fine."

I stood and grinned at him. "Pretty sure I'll be better than just fine."

"Damn straight."

I started my Friday by having a ninety-minute, heated conversation with the office manager. Thankfully, I'd had the presence of mind to take a copy of my original lease with me and I had already highlighted the language waiving the penalty for breaking my lease. Still, this woman tried to argue that the FBI clause in my lease wasn't binding since I didn't have any of my credentials on me. It wasn't until I repeatedly pointed out where her manager had initialed the changes that she finally relented.

Not the best start to my day.

Last night – and this morning – Mensa had relieved my stress in the most delicious way. Following my encounter in the leasing office, his magic had worn off.

"Jesus, you look ready to hurt somebody," Mensa said when I walked inside.

"Violence doesn't solve anything," I muttered.

He grinned. "Don't knock it, until you try it."

"It wouldn't be worth it on that lady."

"How long before we have to leave to get the moving truck?" he asked.

I glanced at the microwave. "Is that time right?"

He pulled out his phone. "Yeah."

"We have an hour."

His expression was easy to read. Part calculating, part mischievous, part hungry.

The next thing I knew, he hauled me over his shoulder and spanked me hard. "Then it's time to relax you again, Blume. Can't have you all wound-up and shit."

I laughed. "Put me down, Kenneth."

"I'm gonna put you down, all right. Put you down on my face."

If he weren't so talented, I'd refuse, but Mensa had ruined me for other men. I couldn't get enough of him.

"That sounds fun."

"Yeah. Since we gotta be quick, you gotta do some work too, sucking me off."

"Even better," I murmured.

He put me on the bed and undid his belt. "Help your man out, and get naked."

I did as ordered.

CHAPTER 16

HIDING YOUR TEMPER

MENSA

"YOU NEVER SHARED THAT new information you mentioned on the phone last night," Whitney said, handing Mensa a bottle of Sam Adam's and sitting next to him on the couch.

He didn't want to hide anything from her, but he was a big believer in the less she knew the better. However, a woman who once investigated crime for a living wasn't going to accept being kept in the dark.

"I've been told that Dontrell's son, Demetrius, has been ignoring the Miscreants and not just recently, but for nearly a year."

She raised an eyebrow. "Same amount of time Donny's been putting off Corrupt Chrome."

"Yeah. There's also a rumor that Corrupt Chrome goes out of their way to make in-roads with street gangs."

"That's hard to believe," she muttered and sipped her beer.

He shrugged a shoulder. "Stranger things have been known to happen, but it would also give Corrupt Chrome more leverage over Dontrell."

She shook her head. "But a group like the Miscreants can just move on to the next wayward teenager who wants to join."

Mensa nodded. "Yeah, that's the thing that bugs me, and a few others, too."

Whitney put her beer bottle down. "Seriously, why burn down one of Donny's restaurants? That doesn't indicate that they can protect the kid, it proves the very opposite. For that matter, why pull a gun on Donny at your bar?"

"Not that I'm giving that asshole the benefit of any doubt, but I really think the shooting was unplanned."

"Or it's two birds with one stone," Whitney suggested. "Pulling the gun puts real fear in Donny, and by opening fire Rod goaded your brothers into bringing out their weapons. Plus Twisted Talons had to be shut down for what? Two days at least, maybe two-and-a-half?"

"Yeah. Don't say that shit around Cynic, he's already salty as fuck about it."

She twisted her hands up. "Exactly. Cuts down on your club's income, makes you all look bad, and may keep others from coming back."

In the back of his mind, Mensa knew all that but had buried it. He took a deep breath and ran a hand down his face. "Okay, don't say that shit around me because I'm getting really fuckin' pissed all over again."

She stared at him for a beat. No, she examined him. "You're good at hiding your temper."

He did a long blink and locked eyes with Whitney. "I suppose that's the by-product of the few times I was around Uncle Jack. He could be volatile, we just didn't think he took it out on his family. Dad made sure I understood how to keep calm in almost any situation."

She nodded. "That's an important life skill."

He finished his beer and stood. "We should hit the sack. Tomorrow's gonna be a long day."

———

Moving across town sucked, but moving two and a half hours across the state while following his woman sucked even worse. Whitney had rented a moving truck with a trailer to tow her car, which was an excellent call since she didn't want to come back to Jackson. It still led to a squabble since Whitney refused to drive Har's truck, but Mensa pointed out that she'd never driven a vehicle that was towing another car.

"It can't be that difficult, Mensa."

He slowly dipped his chin. "Yeah, but do you really want to take that chance? I've had to tow trailers before, it's not something you're used to. Besides, Har won't care that you drove his truck... unless you put flowery air fresheners in it or some shit."

"Who would do that?" she asked.

He arched a brow. "Stephanie, but seriously, please drive his truck. It will make me feel better."

She stared at him for a lengthy moment. "Okay, but only because you're so insistent."

By his calculations, the two of them would be unloading the truck for a good five hours. Before they hit the interstate, he called Finn.

"Yo, where are you?" Finn asked.

"On my way back. Can you help me unload Har's truck in two hours?"

"Just Har's truck?" Finn asked.

Mensa chuckled. "And a small moving truck. See if Gamble can help. If it's just me and Whitney, we'll be at it for hours. Between you, me, and another brother, we should be able to do this shit in two hours, tops."

"And I want to do this, why?"

"Because I need a solid, jackass. And there will be beer."

"Since you asked so nicely... I guess I'll call Gamble."

Two hours later, Mensa unfolded from the moving truck. Whitney stood right by his door.

She tipped her head to where Gamble and Finn stood under the breezeway. "You called in the cavalry."

"Sweetheart, you and I make a great team, but those fuckin' stairs are gonna be a killer. This will help us get done much quicker."

Her expression turned wistful. "Four months ago, I never would have thought the Riot MC brothers would be helping me move. Who knew?"

Mensa shook his head. "All right, smart ass, let's get your car off the trailer."

CHAPTER 17

YOU AREN'T SAFE

WHITNEY

FINN, MENSA, AND GAMBLE brought in my sofa, setting it against the wall opposite my flat screen television.

"How is this the last thing to move?" Gamble asked.

I smiled. "Because it was the first thing we moved out of Jackson. First in is the last out."

"Yeah," Gamble whispered.

I held up a six-pack. "All I have is Sam Adam's Summer Ale. Or I can go buy a twelve pack of whatever you like."

"No, Sam Adam's is great," Finn said, grabbing a bottle and digging his key chain out of his pocket. I noticed a bottle opener dangling from the ring.

Gamble waved the beer away. "I gotta go." He winked at me. "Besides, you don't owe me for this, Mensa does."

"Riley dropped me here, she should be around soon," Finn said.

Gamble wandered out, and I looked around my living room. "I'm gonna need a bigger apartment."

Mensa chuckled. "You get rid of a piece of furniture, and it'll be fine."

I pointed at a small tweed love seat. "That can go. It was Wyatt's, before he went all leather."

Finn put his beer down. "Let's go, Mensa. We'll take it out."

Mensa nodded, but pinned his gaze on me. "After this, I'm gonna take Har's truck back and ride my bike over here. You can come with me."

I arched my brows. "I'll stay here. Get a box or three unpacked."

He shot me a hard stare. "Then Finn and Riley stay until I'm back."

I pressed my lips together. "I can take care of myself, Mensa. The door will be locked, too."

He shook his head. "I'm not taking chances here, Blume."

"I'd rather not keep Finn and Riley here. He's helped out plenty."

"Then we both go to Har's. Have you met Stephanie?"

I nodded slowly. "Briefly. I'm not trying to be antisocial, Mensa. Moving sucks, and the faster I unpack, the less it'll be on my mind."

Finn's eyes darted to Mensa for a second, then he cocked a brow at me. "Not that I disagree with you, but humor him. It's a twenty-minute ride round trip."

I offered him a wan smile. "Which means I'm looking at an hour if I have to make small talk."

Finn shrugged a shoulder. "He wants to keep you safe. Can't fault him for that."

Was I really going to be with a biker?

That was a stupid question. He called me his woman, and I'd almost called him my man. We were doing this, and the least I could do was appease his protective ways.

"Fine. I'll ride with Mensa."

Finn smiled – it was sexy, but it lacked the mischievous quality of Mensa's. "Good choice. Stephanie won't bend your ear too much anyway. Hell, she could be working tonight."

After Mensa and Finn hauled the love seat out to the dumpster, I grabbed my purse, and locked the door.

The moment Mensa drove his bike toward the Gulf, irritation coursed through my veins. I tapped on his shoulder as he put his Harley in a higher gear. "What are you doing? I need to go home!"

When he stopped at a red light a few minutes later, he looked over his shoulder. "Woman, you also gotta eat and we didn't hit the store. We're headed to Dontrell's for a gyro."

Funny how being hangry could sneak up on me. I'd been hungry when I brought in the last moving box, then I'd forced food out of my mind at Har's place.

"Fine," I muttered.

His body shook with laughter.

"Don't gloat," I said right when traffic started to move.

Minutes later, we walked into DeeLight's and I froze at the angry look Donny aimed at us.

"Houston, you aren't safe with him."

I laughed. "Not sure if I'm safe with any man these days – at least that's what my father tells me." Donny's expression softened and I smiled. "How are you holding up?"

The way he eyed Mensa, I suspected I'd get anything but a straight answer. "Been as busy as the first day I opened. Never realized how much people care."

His honesty floored me.

"Now you know," I said with a smile.

Donny exhaled through his nose. "The investigators think I did it. You believe that shit?"

My stomach plummeted and I kept myself from nodding. "It's unfortunate, but insurance companies often look at owners first. Sort of like how spouses are top suspects in domestic murders."

Mensa edged closer to the counter. "Didn't you tell them about the Corrupt Chrome MC and Rod's threat to you?"

Dontrell's eyes hardened. "You don't have kids. Not gonna do a damn thing that puts my son in danger."

"You being in jail puts him in more danger," Mensa countered.

They were both right.

"Be honest with the investigators, Donny," I said.

"Something happens to Demetrius, I'll never forgive myself."

"You got a decent lawyer?" Mensa asked.

"You gonna refer me to somebody?" Donny asked, aiming severe side-eye at Mensa.

"He might. His lawyer helped me out," I said.

Donny gave me a stern look. "You know that's different."

Mensa cleared his throat. "President of my club has ties to the Biloxi Fire Department. Good chance he knows someone who can help."

Donny ignored that. "You here for food or what?"

I nodded and placed my order.

We carried four bags of groceries into my apartment.

Straightening from the crisper drawer, and closing the fridge, I turned to Mensa. "Did you mean what you said to Donny? Har might be able to help him?"

"Yes."

The trepidation in his tone raised my hackles. "Why do you say it like that? Donny's already in a really bad position. The worst thing you can do is offer false hope."

Mensa set a box of pasta on the counter and faced me. "You can throw a drowning man a rope, but he's still gotta grab hold and help you help him."

"I get that, but—"

"If he's secretive, no lawyer or fire department contact is going to help."

"That doesn't answer my question."

Mensa twisted up his hands. "I'm pretty sure Har can help. But I get the feeling there's more we don't know."

"Like what? Demetrius is being threatened. Donny lost a restaurant. You think he's in a position to retaliate?"

"It has to have crossed his mind. I may not have kids, but someone threatens the people I love, I want my pound of flesh."

"Right," I whispered.

"Why are you so protective of him?" Mensa asked, coming closer.

I put a hand on my hip. "Do you have the slightest idea how hard it is to run a small business? Add in the hurdles of being a minority... it isn't right what's happened to him. He's a great man, Mensa."

Mensa's head tilted. "You haven't even known him very long, have you?"

"No."

"Then how do you know that about him?"

I shot him a pointed look. "Are you saying I'm wrong?"

"No. I'm surprised you know so much about him."

I shrugged. "He and I have chatted a little, but it's hardly ever small talk with him. I tend to be cynical after being with the Bureau, but I believe in my instincts. Mine tell me Donny's a great person."

Mensa nodded ever so slowly while stalking closer to me. He wrapped an arm around my waist. "Your instincts are right."

I slid my hands up his chest. "I'm glad you think so."

His other arm came around my shoulders and he drove his hand into the hair at the back of my head. "I know it's been one helluva long day. Moving sucks, and we're both tired."

All of that was true, so I kept quiet.

He lowered his face toward mine. "Know what I like the most about your apartment?"

My breasts were pressed up against his warm torso, and I stared into his heated, brown eyes. "I don't know."

He started walking us toward my bedroom. "The fact your bedroom doesn't share a wall with anyone else's unit."

I chuckled. "Okay... not what I expected, and that is rather specific."

His lips grazed along my jaw before he lifted his head. "That means you can be loud...and I can't wait to make you moan my name."

"I have neighbors downstairs," I breathed since his lips had hit that spot right behind my ear that felt really freaking good.

He pulled back and shook his head. "Nope. That unit's vacant. I checked."

CHAPTER 18

ULTIMATE REWARD

MENSA

FIVE DAYS HAD PASSED since Mensa helped Whitney move. The investigators were being very tight-lipped on both the shooting and the fire. Mensa had insisted on Whitney staying with him at the clubhouse to be safe. However, last night, they'd stayed at her place. He walked into the clubhouse on Thursday morning, and came face to face with Block and Har. That was odd since both of them had day jobs.

"What's going on?" he asked.

"The arson investigators are focused on Dontrell," Har said.

"Got that from him when Whitney and I talked to him last Friday."

The silence lingered, and his chest tightened. "Are they going to arrest—"

"Not yet; they're lining shit up so it's harder for Dontrell to post bail."

Mensa's eyes widened. "Did they even question the Corrupt Chrome MC?"

Block dragged a hand down his face. "If we were targeting somebody, and took such a drastic step, you know we'd have someone with either the fire department or police in our pocket."

He couldn't argue that.

Instead, he changed the subject. "What about the shooting? Sure as hell, the cops should be all over Corrupt Chrome for that."

Har tipped his head to the side. "You're right, but since no one was hurt, the news coverage is dying down. Police called 'Nic an hour ago. They're keeping an eye out for Rod. I don't put much stock in that though."

Mensa shook his head. "Detective Fortner claimed they couldn't find a Corrupt Chrome member named Rod."

Har nodded. "I don't doubt it. Seems Rod's gone AWOL."

"Convenient," Mensa said.

"Coward is more like it," Block muttered.

"Anybody know more about him?" Mensa asked.

Har hesitated. "Corrupt Chrome has a chapter in Memphis. I'm waiting on our Riot brothers there to get back to me."

"Fuck," Mensa hissed.

"Where's 'that woman'?" Har asked, grinning.

Mensa just kept himself from rolling his eyes. "At Hard Pressed until I go get her for lunch."

"Thinking you need to keep someone on her," Har said.

He nodded. "You're right. I'll get a prospect over to the shop while I take care of what I need to do here."

Mensa packed a duffel bag to take to Whitney's. Two minutes ago, a prospect texted that he was in place outside Hard Pressed.

His phone rang, and he expected to see the prospect's number, but his mom's name lit up the display.

"Hey, Mom."

"I know you're a grown man, Kenneth, but I shouldn't hear about a shooting at your workplace from your cousin!"

He bit back his immediate response – that the shooting had been days ago. That would only rile her further. "Sorry, Mom. I should have called, but it's been a little hectic around here."

"Hectic? Is that the term for dealing with police officers and being questioned downtown?"

His brows drew together. "Who said I was questioned downtown?"

"Are you saying you weren't?"

He sighed. "Mom, who told you that?"

She held out on answering for so long, he almost gave up. Then she said, "Finneas mentioned you were questioned."

His head reared back. "Finn told you that?"

"That isn't the point here."

It was totally the point, because his mom wouldn't have any reason to talk to Finn about Mensa going downtown for questioning. Mensa's cousin, Jonah, had moved in with Mom and Dad. He was an avid gamer, and he'd bonded with Finn. The two of them routinely played different games, and Finn probably would have mentioned Mensa's police questioning to Jonah.

That had to be how she knew. "Have you been eavesdropping on Jonah? He's twenty-three, Mom. Just because he lives at your house doesn't give you the right to listen in on his gaming conversations."

She sighed. "Jonah's had enough heartbreak in his life. He never tells me what's going on with him and Denver, so as long as he lives here, I'm going to do my best to protect him from a young woman hurting him."

He ran his hand through his hair. "Mom. He also deserves to live in a place where his privacy is respected since Uncle Jack damn sure had no respect for Jonah's or Riley's privacy."

"Don't you dare compare me to Jack," she said in a stern voice. "Have the police caught the shooter?"

He let her have the subject change. "Not yet, and to be honest, they're chalking it up to an aggravated bar fight. I'm safe, and you don't have anything to worry about."

At the familiar sound of her chuckle, he could practically see Mom's skeptical expression. "You ever have children, Kenneth, you'll find there's *always* something to worry about. I love you. Plan on coming to dinner on Sunday. It'd be nice if you brought Whitney along, too. Goodbye, dear."

With the double beep of his phone, he knew she'd hung up on him, but he'd also be having words with Finn. Making Jonah feel like he was one of the guys was one thing, but sharing serious shit while gaming with his cousin wasn't smart. His mom might have listened in physically, but who was to say someone couldn't hack into their feed... and he could practically hear Finn say Mensa was overly paranoid.

Security meant everything in their world – at least as far as Mensa was concerned. He thought Finn understood that, but it seemed he needed a reminder.

His phone chimed with a text notification.

> Your woman is getting in a car with Riley. Not sure where they're going, I'm following them.

He nodded and sent a text back.

> Good. Let me know where you end up.

He contemplated the last thing his mom said. *It'd be nice if you brought Whitney along.* If things were different between him and Whitney, he'd think it were too soon for a family dinner. But, the two of them were moving along at a rapid pace. He hardly ever helped his MC brothers move, and he damn sure didn't help a woman move.

He couldn't deny that something with her was different. The life or death situation with the Corrupt Chrome resulting in a shared hotel room, may have led to them getting physical, but it didn't explain him calling her his woman.

The last fifteen months of dancing around her, complaining about her presence, and busting his ass to make sure he avoided her - it was all a strange prelude to reality.

She was it for him.

Suddenly, he wondered why Ben hadn't taken more care. How could any man let a woman like her slip through his fingers?

He shook off that asinine line of thought. That man's ignorance resulted in Mensa reaping the ultimate reward.

Another text came through.

> They're at the mall. Do I need to go inside?

> **Are you allergic to the mall, prospect?**

> **No, but the fuckin' perfume gives me a headache.**

Mensa chuckled. With that information, he ought to insist that the prospect tail the women, but he didn't want them aware of the prospect's presence.

> **No, just watch Riley's car.**

Mensa couldn't stand the mall either, but he had the sudden urge to see his woman and ask her to Sunday dinner.

Chapter 19

Hard Pass

Whitney

Riley wandered into Hard Pressed with a grin. "How's it goin'?"

I saved the Facebook ad I was working on and looked up. "Good. Shouldn't you be at work?"

She smiled. "Har took a long lunch and told me to do the same. Wanna hit the mall?"

"Tempting, but I'd rather hit a Harley shop if you're up for it."

"What for?"

"Mensa should be wearing his helmet, but he makes me wear it instead. Figured I would get my own."

She shot me a reluctant smile as she nodded. "You ought to let Mensa handle that."

I blinked at her. "Why? Is it the cost? I priced some online, but I need to try one on."

Putting her wristlet on the counter, she leaned toward me. "I feel sure he'd want to provide for you. Besides, he might have a spare that he's—"

I'd switched back to my Boho bag and I grabbed it from under the counter. "Don't worry. I'll let Mensa know what I'm thinking. Let's hit the mall, I need some body wash and I'm craving some Snickerdoodles."

Twenty minutes later, I had downed three cookies while Riley sipped a smoothie.

"Are you happy at the shop?" she asked.

I lifted a shoulder. "I suppose. It feels like it's too soon to say. I have more to learn before I'll be certain." I tipped my head toward her. "What about you? Enjoying the paint fumes at the body shop?"

She chuckled. "Surprisingly, I don't smell them much. Probably because Har doesn't want his office to reek any more than it has to, but, yeah. It's good over there. It hardly even feels like work half the time."

"You can't beat that," I muttered.

"You got that right," she said, sipping her smoothie.

I sensed she had something on her mind. Rather than prompt her, I waited her out.

"It's new, but are you happy with Mensa?" she finally asked.

I laughed. "I am happy, but I didn't really want another man in my life right now."

She gave me a 'don't bullshit me' look.

"What? I didn't."

Her lips twisted to the side. "The way you and Mensa act around each other... no. You both wanted each other for a while."

I considered that for a moment. "Yeah, but I wanted him in custody at first."

"Are you serious?"

I cocked my head. "Those brothers have all done things. Something about Mensa never getting caught bugged me."

She laughed. "You bugged him too, that was clear."

"True. We're oil and water sometimes."

One of her brows arched. "Doesn't seem that way now. He helped you move, for heaven's sake."

I shook my head. "That was his way of keeping an eye on me."

She scoffed. "Okay, but word to the wise, I'd be honest with yourself no matter how much you lie to the rest of us."

We stepped outside the mall, and I paused to scan the parking lot.

"What's wrong?" Riley asked.

I turned toward her and pasted a smile on my face. "I have a strange feeling we're being watched. Stay calm."

She gave a single nod. "I'm pretty sure Har had a prospect follow me. I noticed him back at Hard Pressed. He's over there smoking a cigarette."

A tall man in a cut stood under an oak tree. That wasn't the direction from which I sensed the threat though.

The doors behind us opened and a couple wandered out while carrying on an animated conversation.

"Come on," Riley said.

A whoosh of cool air hit me from behind when the doors opened again.

A man stopped, right beside me. I smelled the pungent aroma of cigarette smoke before I saw he wore a cut.

"You find your car, sweet thing?"

His name patch caught my eye.

Rod.

"Yes. No thanks to you."

I stepped forward.

He grabbed my elbow. "Don't be a bitch."

My eyes locked with his, and I tamped down my urge to mouth off. I couldn't give away how much I knew or it would jeopardize Wyatt's cover. "Your offer at the Twisted Talons might have been nice, but shooting at people is a hard pass."

An insincere smile spread across his face. "That was just a misunderstanding—"

"Let go of my woman," Mensa ordered in a very deep and supremely authoritative voice.

Rod glanced from me to Mensa. "Your woman? She ain't claimed."

"Get your fucking hand off her."

Rod ignored him and looked at me. "You belong to him?"

I wrenched my elbow free. "Believe it or not, I belong to myself."

"Woman," Mensa growled.

I ignored Mensa growling at me and glared at Rod. "Why are you still walking free? You shot at people in a bar."

He looked at me like I was slow. "You don't need to worry about that, baby. What's your name?"

In a flash, Mensa had Rod in a choke hold. I caught the glint of a knife blade resting against Rod's throat.

"Did you hear anything I said, jackass? Her name isn't your business." Mensa bit out.

"What's she to you, asshole?" Rod asked.

"She's mine, motherfucker."

Rod scoffed so hard, he nearly spit on Mensa. "Not a fuckin' chance she's yours. Any bitch who doesn't wear a fuckin' cut is free game."

I opened my mouth to point out that I wasn't game of any kind, but Mensa shifted his body aggressively.

He pressed the tip of his blade into Rod's neck. "You ever been stabbed, Rod?" he demanded, his voice sinister.

"Fuck you."

"Focus, Roddy. Gettin' stabbed fuckin' sucks. I know because a coward stabbed me from behind."

He'd been stabbed? How had I missed that kind of scar?

"Mensa, we're in public," Riley said, pulling me from my thoughts.

"He needs to get my message," Mensa clipped out.

"You don't need to go to jail, though," I murmured. "Tons of cameras out here."

Finn, Cynic, and the prospect sauntered up behind Mensa.

"She doesn't exist to you," Mensa said, giving Rod one last shove before letting him go.

A security guard rode up in a golf cart. "What's the problem here? No loitering."

Mensa had tucked his blade away in a smooth motion I almost missed. He slung a heavy arm around my neck. "Not loitering, sir. We were just leaving."

Finn assumed a similar posture with Riley tucked under his arm. He aimed a good ol' boy grin at the guard. "Yeah, just needed to find our women. We never know which exit they're going to use."

The guard shot a skeptical look at Rod, Cynic, and the prospect, but they ignored it.

To my surprise, Rod hurried to the other side of the parking lot without another word.

Mensa led me to his bike.

"I rode here with Riley," I muttered when we were half-way across the parking lot.

"Yep. And you'll ride back with me, Whitney."

"Why? Just to prove to Rod that I'm with you? That's ridiculous."

He pulled my body flush to his. "That's my world, Blume. You're my woman and assholes like him especially have to respect that."

I stared at him for a long moment.

He frowned. "You got problems with that, tell me because that's not gonna change."

"What do you mean?"

"If I claim you, then I'll make sure people know it. And—"

"It shouldn't require a violent confrontation."

His eyes widened. "I don't confront that sort of disrespect, my claim on you doesn't mean anything."

I inhaled through my nose, calling on my patience. "You're aware that I'm a person with free will, right?"

"Yes, but an asshole like Rod doesn't fuckin' care. You heard what he said about you not wearing a cut. He'll fuck with you to fuck with me. *He* sees you as nothing more than something he can take from me."

"And the only answer to that is staking a claim and being a violent caveman?"

He dipped his chin. "Dial it back, Whit."

I squared my shoulders. "Tell me where I'm wrong with that, and I will."

He took a deep breath as though he were weighing his words. "We do this, you'll be part of my world. Shit works differently in an MC. Surely you know that."

"Yeah, but getting violent with him—"

"You were in the FBI and wanted to take me down so bad, but maybe you don't know how it works in my world. Violence is the only language Rod understands."

My lips twisted with skepticism. "Was the knife really necessary?"

He widened his eyes. "If I hadn't drawn my knife, he and I would have been in a fist fight instead. I prefer keeping the upper hand whenever I can with assholes like him."

Part of me could see that, but this wasn't the time or place for this conversation. I spotted the security guard driving his cart in our direction. "Let's get out of here. You don't need added attention from this guard."

Mensa handed me his helmet. "We're not done with this, Blume."

He was right. I needed to figure out if I could become one with my inner biker-diva or not.

No, I had to decide if I could become one with my inner *outlaw*, because I had a feeling that's where we were headed.

Chapter 20

Ask for Terrance

Mensa

THE CONFLICTED LOOK ON her face before she climbed onto the back of his bike wasn't one he'd forget any time soon.

Many of the brothers had been forced to acclimate their women into the MC life.

Only one of them had to deal with such a law-abiding woman.

He'd thought Gamble was out of his mind taking on Victoria as his ol' lady. Now he could see where it was out of Gamble's control.

Whitney had to understand what she was getting into, though. It didn't matter if the Riot MC brothers knew she had rights, other clubs wouldn't care unless she was claimed.

Mensa sped back to Hard Pressed. Knowing Rod was out and about, they had to be more vigilant.

By the time Mensa swung off his bike, Whitney had his helmet held out to him like an offering.

Also like it would be the last time she used it.

He took the helmet from her.

She smiled. "I'm buying my own helmet. You're breaking the law by not wearing one. Riley told me to let you handle it, but I'm capable of—"

"Have at it, woman."

Her blue eyes flared. "Have at... are you sure?"

He nodded. "Yeah, but hit the shop near the Interstate. Ask for Terrance. He'll set you up."

She arched a brow. "Should I tell him you sent me?"

He shrugged a shoulder. "You can, but I'm gonna tell him to expect you."

"Why would you do that?"

"He'll help you get what you need."

"You're being enigmatic."

"There's no mystery in those words."

She chuckled. "Sure there isn't."

He shook his head. "The timing sucks, but seems you're gonna learn in a trial by fire."

"Pardon me?"

"I called you my woman, and it threw us both. Thing is I meant it, and still do. Between that and Rod, you're finding out exactly what being mine will mean."

"And Terrance fits into this how?"

He smiled. "Terrance will help you with more than a helmet."

"I got that, Genius."

"Then I'm not being mysterious."

She growled before she spoke. "Fine. I got work to do, but thanks for the ride."

He fought off his laughter, then arched his brows. "You're always welcome, but you're forgetting something."

She leaned up and pecked his lips.

He dipped his chin. "Are you fucking with me?"

She chuckled. "No, but I'm not making ou—"

He pulled her to him and laid a heavy kiss on her. Then he cut it off just as fast.

"That's more like it," he muttered.

She sighed. "And now I gotta face Aunt Nadia."

"She'll be happy for you."

Her lips twisted with skepticism. "Yeah, if I kept that private."

"There's more to Nadia than what meets the eye."

Her eyes widened. "There you go again! What's that supposed to mean?"

Mensa ran a hand through his hair. "Normally, I keep my mouth shut about this type of thing, but she never married, right?"

Whitney's expression hardened. "Yes, but that doesn't—"

He grabbed her hand. "She had it bad for Brink – our last president."

"What?" she asked, her voice full of dismay. "That's... that's something she'd have—"

"Kept private?"

"Well... yeah. But Mensa, what would have kept them apart?"

"The daughter he had, possibly. His inability to stay faithful, definitely. Though to be fair, I don't know Nadia well enough to say. It's just that most women frown on cheating."

She cocked her head to the side. "Yeah. Most of us definitely do. Are *you* able to be faithful?"

He shot her a pointed look. "Why do you think I hadn't been laid since February? You in that fucking blue dress at Finn and Riley's wedding. Shit, I couldn't stop thinking about you."

She pressed her lips together to hide her smile.

He glanced to the side and back to her. "So noted, you enjoy my pain."

She shook her head. "Not at all. I'm just flattered."

He pulled her closer. "Good. Kiss me again. Nadia isn't going to have an issue with it. She knows how bikers are – more than you know."

"I guess you're right."

She kissed him, he took it deeper, then she pulled back.

"Do I have to keep this to myself?"

Mensa wobbled his head. "That's up to you. Nobody told me I had to keep it quiet."

Her head bobbed in three short nods as though she were deliberating it. "I'll be done here around five-thirty."

"Yeah. A prospect will be here if I'm not."

She didn't quite roll her eyes at him. "Mensa—"

"Rod's out there and even if he snuck off at the mall, he didn't get my message. You're gonna be covered, Blume. I don't care about your FBI training."

She pouted, but it was half-hearted. "Fine. You're wasting that poor prospect's time, though."

"It's my job to waste a prospect's time, baby."

"Am I dragging this prospect to see Terrance?"

He grinned. "Maybe. We'll see. When you're done with Terrance, let me know if you want to be at the clubhouse or your apartment."

"I can tell you that now: my place."

"Got it."

"What are you going to be doing?"

"Inventory at the bar."

She turned her head an inch. "Does that mean something else?"

He laughed. "No, Blume. Inventory is inventory and it's boring as hell."

Her eyebrows rose. "Okay. Please, don't go looking for Rod. Nothing good will come of it."

Mensa shut his saddlebag and heard another bike pull into the lot for Twisted Talons. The rider parked beside him and powered off his Harley.

Mensa's guard went up instantly when he recognized Whitney's brother. "Aren't you supposed to be—"

"I'm not here," Wyatt said, shoving his shades up on his head.

"Our cameras will dispute that, but sure. What do you want?"

"I want to know what you're doing with Whitney."

Anger welled up inside him, but Mensa kept his face stoic. "We're not doing this."

Wyatt cocked his head – almost the exact same way Whitney did. "Are you gonna fuck her over and toss her aside?"

Mensa glared at Wyatt. "*That's* why we're not doing this. If you weren't her brother, I'd have clocked you."

"And you'd be under arrest."

"I don't give a shit about that. I care about you insulting me *and* your sister."

Wyatt's eyes narrowed. "You're serious about her? After what? A week?"

Mensa scoffed. "More like fifteen months, since that's how long she's been a thorn in my side."

Wyatt gave him a hard-eyed stare.

Mensa withstood it for a minute before he said, "Your sister is the first one to tell anybody that she's her own person and she makes her own decisions."

"Yeah, but this is the most fucked-up one yet."

"Did you tell her that?"

Wyatt kept silent.

Mensa chuckled. "Yeah. Leave it at this, I'm not gonna hurt her."

"I don't trust you."

"Nothing I can do about that, but you should trust Whitney."

He shook his head. "I don't understand what she sees in you."

Mensa had wondered that on occasion himself. "You'd have to ask her. By the way, I'm not keeping this visit from her."

Wyatt's lips quirked. "I didn't ask you to," he stared at Mensa for a beat. "Don't fuck her over. She may not believe she deserves better than you, but she deserves better than being fucked over by you."

"Agreed. Is that all, Wyatt?"

He powered up the Harley and left.

CHAPTER 21

OVERZEALOUS

WHITNEY

A HULK OF A man smiled at me when I stepped inside the motorcycle dealership. His hazel eyes practically lit up at me. He had thinning, brown hair pulled back in a low ponytail.

"You have to be Whitney."

I returned his smile. "Yes, and you're Terrance."

He reached out and shook my hand. "In the flesh. Kenny tells me you need a helmet."

I couldn't hide my surprise at Terrance using that name. "Yes. Um, he let's you call him that?"

Terrance chuckled and his eyes twinkled. "Few people stop me from calling them what I want."

I nodded. "Right. I'm torn on a full helmet or something like Mensa's half-helmet. I've gotten used to it, but we haven't gone on a long—"

"I've got three picked out for you," Terrance interrupted.

It struck me that he had the personality of a salesperson, but him cutting me off raised a question.

"Okay. Is this a test?"

He shot me a quizzical look. "Now, why would a beauty like you expect a test?"

I shrugged. "Mensa mentioned that you would set me straight."

He tipped his head. "Right. You ever been to a rally?"

"No, but I've visited Sturgis."

After a patient smile, he said, "If it ain't when everyone's there, it don't matter. You gonna ride with him to Daytona? Or anywhere that's an all-day trip?"

"Maybe," I hedged.

"Helmets aren't a dime a dozen, Whitney. Your head is just as important as your heart. Gotta take care of both. Which is why I need to know how long you plan to ride behind Kenny."

Again, I thought we were talking about more than bike accessories. "Life can be unpredictable, but I plan to take a long ride with Kenneth."

He laughed. "Kenneth! Does he *let* you call him that?"

I cocked a brow. "Few people stop me from calling them by their given name."

He smiled, and it was bigger and brighter than any before. "I like you."

I dipped my chin. "If we're done with this crazy dance, and I've passed muster, I think I like you too."

He chuckled. "Yep. You're definitely what Kenny needs. No doubt about it."

———

Terrance bagged my Bluetooth-enabled helmet and sent me out the door at five minutes to seven. My stomach growled as I put my Elantra into gear. We had gyros last night, but Mensa admitted to never having tabbouleh. One of Donny's restaurants was on the way home, and I stopped.

A bike rolled in behind me, but it wasn't the prospect. That was strange since he'd stuck close to me earlier. I locked my car, and finally saw the prospect pull into the lot.

I settled down in a booth to wait for my to-go order. No sooner had I unlocked my phone, than someone slid in across from me.

"What are you thinking coming here right now, Whit?"

My head reared back when I took in my brother, Wyatt. It was strange seeing him wearing a patchless leather cut with his hair in desperate need of a good trim. "I could ask you the same thing. Do you want your cover blown?"

"Iron's out of town and left Rod in charge. And Rod only cares about one thing right now: finding *you*. He ordered the prospects to watch all three locations of DeeLight's, but he forgot that out of their four prospects, only two were available. You're lucky he asked me to come to this one."

I appreciated his concern, but this was getting out of hand. I couldn't let Rod dictate where I went or force me into hiding in my apartment. "Wyatt—"

He rested his forearms on the table and leaned forward. "You're asking for trouble coming here."

"I have to live my life, Wyatt. Besides, my order will be ready in five minutes."

He sighed. "You need to lay low. Whatever went down at the mall today only made Rod more determined to take you from Mensa."

"Great," I muttered.

"Yeah. And tell your biker, I'm sorry I didn't share that earlier this afternoon. I hadn't been given my marching orders yet."

I shook my head. "Repeat that."

My twin leaned back. "You heard me. I caught him outside Twisted Talons, but that was before Rod went on a tear about keeping tabs on the restaurants. What the hell happened at the mall?"

I narrowed my eyes. "Oh, no. You aren't going to redirect this conversation, bub. Why did you go see Mensa?"

He took a deep breath and stared at me.

We could stare at each other for hours without cracking – we were that stubborn.

Neither one of us had time for this, and I figured he had even less time since he was supposed to be working his case, so I broke the silence. "I don't need you to protect me, Wyatt."

"Tough. You're my sister, I'll do it anyway."

I fought a grin. "For the record, I'm gonna make you eat those words when the right woman comes along."

He narrowed his eyes. "Gonna be a long wait for that, sis. Back to my question, what happened at the mall?"

"Riley picked me up for lunch. We went to the mall, as we were leaving Rod came up behind us. Mensa showed and told Rod to get his hand off me—"

"He touched you?" Wyatt bit out.

My head tilted. "He grabbed hold of my elbow. Mensa wound up pinning him to the wall at knifepoint because I'm 'his woman.'"

Wyatt frowned and turned away for a long moment. Finally, he faced me. "It sucks that I'm so conflicted about that."

I laughed. "How can you be conflicted?"

He almost smiled. "As an FBI agent, I hate that you're with a man who pulls a knife on someone in broad daylight. As your *brother*, though, I'm pleased he'd do that in order to force Rod to leave you alone."

I rolled my eyes at that.

After years of me rolling my eyes at him, Wyatt ignored it. "You really want to be with a man like that? He's willing to pull a knife on someone for touching you... what else is he likely to do?"

I tossed a hand out. "I know where you're coming from with that question. But, he's damn sure got a sense of loyalty I've never experienced with another man."

"Loyalty—"

I grabbed Wyatt's hand. "He'd never do what Ben did to me."

His eyes widened. "No kidding, he's not an agent."

I shook my head. "No one's cared about me like he does."

"That's lust talking."

That didn't just rub me the wrong way, it put things in perspective. What I felt for Mensa went beyond the realm of lust.

I glared at Wyatt. "You need to stop."

"Or what?"

I didn't do threats. "Or you're gonna say something you can't take back."

"You'd cut me out for him?"

I knew I was falling for Mensa. It wasn't until that moment, I realized I'd fallen in love with him. But Mensa deserved to hear it first.

"It's serious. You know it or you wouldn't have gone to see him."

"Jesus. Do you love him or something?"

"He's not as bad as you think he is, Wyatt."

My twin shot me an incredulous look. "It wasn't that long ago, you wanted to convince a prosecutor to indict him."

My lips tipped up and I shook my head. "No. Get it straight. I wanted to be the one to arrest him."

"And now you say he's not as bad as I think he is?"

I nodded. "Yes. Wasn't it you who said, if law enforcement is doing their job, then his record would reflect his crimes and I needed to get over my obsession?"

His eyes traveled toward his eyebrows. "Yeah, but that didn't mean getting involved with him."

The girl at the counter called out my order number. I slid to the end of the booth, but kept focused on Wyatt. "I hate to mention this, but Aunt Nadia said fate had put Mensa in my path. I'd love it if you could just try to be happy for me."

He leaned forward. "It isn't that I'm not happy for you, sis. It's that if you make a life with him, and he is caught up in something illegal, you know damn well they'll come after all the assets. You could lose your home, and if you got kids—"

I matched his lean. "You're right, Wy. I do know all that, so you don't need to remind me. The moment I catch wind he's doing illegal shit, I'm out. Especially if there are kids involved."

Wyatt sighed. "Promise me you'll be careful."

I stood. "I promise."

"I never thought I could eat that much parsley," Mensa muttered before sipping his beer.

We were sitting on the floor around my coffee table eating picnic style because I still had boxes on the dinette table. I swallowed some wine. "But did you like it?"

"It was... a change of pace."

I leaned toward him. "I shouldn't tell you this, but you sound just like my dad."

He choked on laughter.

I put my wine glass down. "Speaking of family, I'm sorry my brother cornered you this afternoon. That was uncool and uncalled for."

He tucked a lock of hair behind my ear. "He cares about you, so it wasn't uncool at all."

"Still uncalled for."

"Not if he's worried about you. A man like me in a woman's life makes certain men worry. It's all good, Whit."

"I don't know what Wyatt said to you, but most men would run after that kind of invasive visit."

"Baby, I'm not most men, and if I had a sister – you can bet your sweet ass I'd be just as protective."

My eyes slid to the side. "Pretty sure holding a man with a knife at his throat proves that."

He had one leg stretched out straight, and he pulled his other leg up, propped his arm on his knee and tipped his beer bottle at me. "That still bothers you?"

I gathered up a couple napkins from the table and stuffed them in my to-go box. "It didn't... until Wyatt pointed some things out to me."

Mensa took a pull from his beer and set it down on the table. "When did he call you?"

"He was watching the location of DeeLight's that I stopped at. Rod ordered the prospects and Wyatt to watch all three restaurants."

"Really?"

"Yeah, he wanted me to apologize for not sharing that with you since he hadn't been given that directive by Rod when he saw you earlier."

"You're not going there until this shit gets settled."

"Now you sound like Wyatt," I said, pushing up from the floor, grabbing my to-go box, and meandering to the kitchen.

"Whitney, you don't need to walk into a trap from these assholes."

I shoved my container into the garbage. "I agree, but that club can't force me to become a shut-in."

"Not forcing you to do that, woman."

"Sounds a bit like it. Besides, you've got a prospect trailing my every move."

He rose from the floor and tossed his beer bottle in the recycle bin. "Yeah, I'll be tearing that prospect a new one because I should have been called the moment Wyatt sat down with you."

"He's my brother."

Mensa widened his eyes. "The prospect doesn't know that. The whole fuckin' point of having him on you is so that I know if someone approaches you."

I closed the distance between us and slid my hand along his t-shirt clad chest; he'd taken his cut off and hung it in the foyer closet when he came inside. "Calm down, Kenneth."

He dipped his chin and grabbed my hand. "I'm perfectly calm, Whit. What else did your brother tell you?"

I shrugged a shoulder. "Just that the incident at the mall only spurred Rod's determination to take me from you... so it seems you're right on that count. He only wants me in order to fuck with you."

"That's not the only reason he wants you," Mensa muttered.

I shook my head. "Whatever. He also said Iron, their president, is out of town and left Rod in charge."

Mensa nodded. "Then he's a bigger fuck-up, because why send prospects and a hang-around to watch Dontrell's restaurants when he could have sent patched members?"

"He definitely has a screw loose."

He wrapped an arm around my waist. "You done in the kitchen?"

I nodded. "Why?"

"Been a long day, I'm making us both a gin and tonic, while you cue up some music, and then it's time to hit the bedroom."

"Woman, why are you running those hands all over me? We both just came not ten minutes ago, but you keep this up, you're gonna need to focus your efforts a little lower."

Laying beside him, I stared up into his eyes. "I want to find your scar from where you got stabbed. Don't think that little tidbit was lost on me when you confronted Rod."

"Don't mention that bastard's name in bed, and the scar is on my back."

"Roll over," I ordered.

He laughed. "Not a chance I'm rollin' onto my belly when you're making me hard." He paused. "Not unless you're beneath me."

I leaned up on an elbow. "I want to see your scars."

"It's just the one, and seriously, Whit, it's healed. Why are you so determined to inspect it?"

I sat up. "When I love someone, I get a little overzealous when I find out they were stabbed."

In an instant, I was on my back and he'd settled his weight on me. Mensa's gorgeous brown eyes flashed at me. "What did you say?"

"You heard me," I breathed.

He settled himself between my legs and bucked his hips. "So? I want to hear you again."

"I get a little overzealous about people being stabbed," I murmured.

"Whitney," he said, his tone laced with authority and his gaze locked with mine.

I ran my hand along his scruffy cheeks, wondering when he found time to shave because I'd yet to see him do it. "I love you, Kenneth."

He dropped his lips to mine and kissed me long and hard.

Sadly, he cut it short, but his serious expression captured my attention. "Been waiting for you to catch up with me, Blume."

I tilted my head. "Catch up with you?"

He nodded. "I fell for you the night I took you to the clubhouse."

"Are you serious?"

"Very."

With my hand at his neck, I pulled him to me for another kiss. He took control of it, and I let my hands rove his body.

He reached down and slid a finger inside me.

I broke the kiss on a moan. "Yes."

"Say it again," he whispered, withdrawing his finger.

"I love you."

His forehead rested on mine. "I love you, too, Whitney."

I spread my legs, reached down, and guided his cock toward me.

He stared into my eyes as he drove inside me. "Your pussy feels so fucking good. Every single time, woman."

"I aim to please," I breathed, and ran my hands along his shoulders.

His free hand palmed my breast, giving it a squeeze. He lowered his lips to my nipple. Pure heat scored through my body when he sucked me in deep. My hips rose and the angle allowed him to surge further inside me.

"You like that," he murmured against my chest.

"I like everything you do to me, honey."

A deep chuckle rumbled through him as he slid his lips to my other breast.

His free hand found mine, and he pinned my hand to the bed. He repeated the maneuver with his other hand. Holding me down, he lifted his head and stared into my eyes.

"Love working your body, Whitney."

"Yeah," I breathed, feeling my orgasm building.

"Love making love to you," he said on an inward thrust.

"I love it, too," I whispered.

He pulled back and hammered into me. "And I love you."

"Yes, Mensa," I said.

It was the last thing either of us said, but we communicated so much more with our actions.

CHAPTER 22

NOT OFFICIALLY

MENSA

MENSA TRUDGED OUT TO Whitney's kitchen, the smell of sausage permeating the air. Thus far, they'd had a lazy weekend. Whitney had wanted to focus on unpacking boxes on Friday night and Saturday, but Mensa convinced her to go to the movies with him, then spend Saturday binging *The Brothers Sun* on Netflix.

Whitney put a plate on the breakfast bar for him. "Eggs, sausage, and home fries. I went with over-easy on your eggs, and cooked yours first because I'm having mine scrambled and I didn't want the milk to cause you problems."

He dragged a hand down his face. "Yeah, over-easy works for me. But seriously woman, you don't have to knock yourself out to cook for me."

She wore pajama shorts and a skimpy tank-top. The way she cocked her hip to the side, he wasn't sure what made it sexier: the pajamas or her attitude. "I wanted to cook for you. I figure Sunday morning breakfast is one of the easiest things I can make for you."

He tipped his head back with a groan, then focused on her. "That reminds me, we're supposed to have dinner tonight at my parents' house."

Her eyes went wide.

"You don't need to freak out, Whit. Hell, I'm pretty sure Riley and Finn will be there. In fact, I'll make sure they are."

She gave three short nods. "Yeah, that'll help."

"Woman. I'm serious. Don't freak out. It's just my parents, two of our friends, and Jonah."

She leaned forward. "Exactly! It's your *parents*!"

He narrowed an eye at her. "You were in Riley's wedding party. Didn't you meet them then?"

Her mouth dropped open, but she didn't speak for a long moment. Finally she got it together. "That isn't the same thing *at all*, Mensa."

Two slices of toast popped up, and he pointed at the toaster. "Get your toast and eat with me, Whitney."

After a short stare down, she grabbed her plate, put her toast on it, and joined him.

"You ever meet Jonah?" he asked.

She hesitated. "He was at the wedding, but I didn't really meet him. Not officially."

"But you've met him unofficially?" he asked, unable to resist fucking with her.

She turned to him and gave him a look that said, 'very funny.' After she swallowed a sip of orange juice, she said, "No, but in addition to the wedding, I've seen plenty of photos and videos of him. Plus, the few times Riley would talk about him, it felt like I'd been introduced to him. That doesn't make sense, I'm sure—"

He shook his head. "No, it makes perfect sense. Riley loves him, and with the shit that happened to them both, she was forced into being his caregiver. Whenever she talks to anyone about him, her love comes through to the point it's almost like he's at her side, so I get it."

"What are you parents like?"

"Good humans," he muttered.

She laughed.

He shot her a stern look. "I'm not joking, Blume. Seeing as you were part of an investigation into Mom's brother, that's the best way to answer your question. She's *nothing* like my uncle."

She grabbed his forearm. "To be fair, that's clear because *you're* nothing like your uncle either."

He covered her hand with his. "You're right. So, that tells you everything you need to know about them until dinner. Trust me, you have nothing to worry about. They're gonna love you."

"You'd say that regardless."

"Probably, but you have to admit, you're the one putting pressure on here. My mom could care less if you show up wearing a burlap sack or an evening gown. She's heard I'm serious about someone, and she just wants to meet you."

She leaned back and pulled her hand from his forearm. "Oh, shit. I don't know what I'm gonna wear!"

He dipped his chin. "Are you fucking with me right now? Didn't you hear what I said? She won't care, Whit. Meeting you is the goal and you're putting too much emphasis on a meal."

Her expression cleared, and he thought her freak-out had passed.

He thought wrong.

"You only get one first impression, Ragstone. I need to make this count."

Nothing for it. He wrapped a hand around the back of her neck and pulled her lips to his. Once he felt her relax into his hold, he broke the kiss.

He waited until she opened her eyes before he spoke. "You don't need to do shit, babe. Nadia's shop is closed today. Want to hit the beach?"

Her eyes skated toward a stack of boxes. "No. I need to unpack at least half a dozen more boxes. Besides, it's supposed to rain this afternoon."

He nodded. "You want my help with that, or would you rather me get out of your hair?"

She paused. "It's up to you. If you leave me alone, I'll probably go shopping for something to wear. If you stay, you'll probably be bored to tears while I unpack shit... fair warning, I'm a bit of control freak about where things go."

That made him grin. "You think a toddler's gonna give a shit about your need to control where shit goes?"

She narrowed one eye at him. "You're not a toddler."

He leaned toward her. "No, but you said your clock is ticking. We love each other... if we're really doing this, you need to start thinking about how our first kid is gonna rock your world."

After a long blink, she leaned back, turned her head to the side, and then back to him. "I'm pretty sure *you* just rocked my world plenty, since I haven't even met your parents yet."

"Not trying to rock your world, trying to get you to loosen up, babe. Let me help you unpack. You don't like where I put your LeCrusette, you can move it."

That got both eyes narrowed at him. "I knew you judged my cookware back in Jackson."

He slid off his stool and grabbed both their plates. "I'd never judge you about that. Let's get this shit done. Then if it isn't raining, maybe we'll hit the beach after all."

Whitney wiped her forehead with the back of her hand. "There isn't enough time for us to hit the beach, and for me to get ready for meeting your parents."

He broke down the last cardboard box he'd emptied. "It's just dinner, babe. What you wear won't matter."

She shook her head. "Nope. It matters. Either way, it takes like twenty minutes to get to the beach from here, then you gotta find parking...we'd have to come back after like ten minutes."

He gave her a curt nod. "You're right. Let's hit the complex pool instead. We can swim for an hour, and the bonus is, we can shower together when we're done."

"Any other time that would be a selling point, but I need to figure out what I'm wearing."

"That red shirt you wore to karaoke would work."

Her eyes widened. "Are you crazy? I can't possibly wear that! It's obvious that's for hitting a bar. Your beloved family home is *not* the place for that top and those jeans."

He fought off a chuckle. "Go put your bikini on, Blume."

She shot him a pointed look. "It's a one-piece. What about you? Do you have swim trunks here? You can't skinny-dip in that pool."

Battle lost, his head tilted back with laughter. When he got control of himself, Whitney only appeared half-amused.

"I was being serious."

"Yeah, that's why it's so fuckin' funny. I'm not the type to skinny-dip in a community pool, woman. Hell, a couple of the brothers have pools in their back yards and most of them don't even skinny-dip in their *own* pools. I brought a duffel over here, and I packed my swim trunks."

Her tone became haughty. "Well, I learned something new about you."

"You puttin' your suit on, or what?"

"Yes."

Mensa parked Whitney's Elantra in his parents' driveway. He rested his wrist on the top of the steering wheel. "You over your snit?"

She turned her head to him. "I'm not having a snit, Mensa."

"You sure?"

Her chin went up an inch. "Very. I was nervous, and letting me drive would have kept me from—"

He interrupted her by wrapping his hand around her neck. "You don't need to be nervous."

"I said, 'I *was* nervous'. And I was quiet on the way here because it's weird being a passenger in my own car. Not to mention, I'm curious if you driving was just an alpha-male thing or if you don't trust my driving."

"I'll go with both."

"What?" she demanded.

He chuckled and let go of her neck. "I'm messing with you, though driving back from Jackson behind you, I noticed you got one helluva a heavy foot."

She sighed. "The interstate is different, Ragstone." She looked out the window. "Where's Riley's car?"

He followed her gaze. "Not sure. They might be on Finn's bike and running late."

She nodded, pulled down the visor, and inspected her lips.

He leaned toward her. "Whitney, you look great. Mom's gonna love you."

"You would say that. You're biased, and you picked out my dress."

He laughed. "After we showered, you laid out three dresses and *told* me to choose."

It had been a no-brainer, too. The short, purple, polka-dot dress showed off her legs and a hint of cleavage.

Finn rode his bike up the drive and parked behind them. Riley scurried off the Harley, put her helmet on the seat, and beelined it to the passenger-side door.

Whitney opened her door, smiling at Riley. "Hey, there."

"Hey, yourself. I love your dress. It's so cute."

Whitney nodded. "Thanks. Do you have Sunday dinner here often? Or just when I need moral support?"

Riley laughed. "About twice a month. You're gonna love Aunt Celeste's pot roast. The potatoes she makes to go with it are heavenly."

"Are you four gonna jack your jaws out here all night?" Dad called from the front door.

Mensa replied while moving to Whitney's side. "No, sir. We're coming inside."

With his arm around her shoulders, he led Whitney around the corner of the garage to the front door, where his Dad stood, leaning against the jamb. He was wearing a pair of faded jeans and a royal blue polo shirt. Mom had likely insisted that Dad look like he was putting in the effort.

Dad smiled at them. "Hello, Whitney. I'm Dean Ragstone, I'm not sure if you remember meeting me at Riley's wedding, but it's a pleasure to see you again."

She reached out and shook Dad's hand. "Mr. Ragstone, it's great to see you again, too."

Dad shook his head. "None of that formal business, call me Dean. Come inside, all of you."

Whitney hesitated in the hallway, and Mensa guided her toward the kitchen.

"Hey, Ma," he called, before they rounded the corner.

"Hi, Kenneth," Mom said, wiping her hands on a dish towel, then leaning up to kiss his cheek.

She smiled at him, and turned to Whitney. "I've heard nothing but good things about you, Whitney. I'm Celeste. Do you want something to drink?"

Mensa caught Whitney's gaze. "You want a beer? Dad only drinks IPAs – or do you want wine?"

She gave a short head shake at the mention of an IPA. "A glass of wine would be good."

Dad had the corkscrew twisted into the unopened bottle of wine. "Celeste, you want a glass, too?"

"I'll wait until the food's ready," Mom said.

"Do you need any help?" Whitney asked.

Mom shook her head. "Thank you, but I'm just waiting on the biscuits to finish, then we'll sit down to eat."

Riley handed Whitney a glass of wine. "Aunt Celeste is a one-woman show in the kitchen."

Whitney's smile seemed hesitant, and she glanced at Mom. "Nothing wrong with that. Too many cooks in the kitchen makes everything more difficult."

"You got that right," Finn said.

"We'll set the table. I'll show you where the plates are," Riley said and led Whitney to the cabinet with the plates.

Finn handed him an open bottle of beer.

He caught Dad's gaze. "Where's Jonah? Upstairs?"

Mom answered just as the timer went off for the biscuits. "He was in the shower when you got here, so he should be down soon, but he isn't staying for dinner."

Mensa cocked his head. "He isn't?"

"He and Denver are headed to a concert," Dad said.

Riley bustled into the room. "Do you want me to grab an extra chair? We're short one."

Finn chuckled. "You're off your game, babe. They just said Jonah's got plans."

Her expression shifted to realization. "Oh, that's right. 3 Doors Down is playing at one of the casinos tonight."

Whitney wandered up behind Riley. "Then I'll take the extra place setting off the table."

The stairs creaked and Mensa went to the foot of the stairs.

Jonah came down wearing jeans and a faded Ozzy Osbourne t-shirt. "Hey, cuz."

"Hey, man. I have someone I want you to meet."

"You do?"

Mensa nodded. "Won't take long. I heard you've been looking forward to seeing 3 Doors Down."

"I didn't know they were in town," Whitney said, sidling up to Mensa.

Mensa grinned at her. "Yeah, Jonah's a huge fan."

She beamed at Jonah and introduced herself. "I'm sorry you won't be here for dinner. I was looking forward to getting to know you, but I'm also jealous you get to see one of my favorite bands."

Jonah nodded, but Mensa sensed he was getting antsy.

There was a light knock on the door, and Mensa glanced that way. "Denver picking you up, J?"

Jonah laughed. "Yeah. She insisted."

Mensa clapped Jonah on the shoulder. "Have a great time."

Jonah nodded, called out goodbyes to everyone, and left.

Mensa caught Whitney's gaze. "Still feel like you know him?"

Mom hurried past them carrying a small pot, a trivet, and a spoon. "Time to eat. If you need to wash up, hurry."

Dad followed her with the heavy crock pot in tow. "Grab a beer for me, son."

"Since Jonah's not here and we put the leaf in the table, your father and I aren't going to sit at the foot and the head of the table. Besides, us sitting at either end of the table always seems too formal," Mom said, as everyone gathered.

Mensa made sure he sat next to Whitney. Dad took the center seat on the other side of the table, Riley sat to his left, with Mom on his right. That left Finn sitting on the other side of Whitney.

After they said grace, Mom aimed an inquisitive look at him and Whitney. "I couldn't help but overhear the two of you after Jonah left. Why would you feel like you know him? Besides Riley and Finn's wedding, this is the first time the two of you met."

Riley and Mensa started in at the same time, but Whitney lifted her hand up at them. "It's okay." Her eyes met Mom's. "I was part of the investigation into Judge Tyndale. My assignment was to befriend Riley, and being part of the investigating team, I saw and heard plenty of recordings that had Jonah in them. But mostly," she glanced at Riley, "I don't think it's possible to be friends with Riley and *not* know about her brother."

"I could argue that," Finn muttered.

Whitney smirked at Finn. "As I understand it, you weren't exactly friends since you ghosted her."

Riley chuckled.

Whitney glanced back at Mom. "The way Riley talks about Jonah, it felt like I'd already met him."

Mom shifted her gaze between Mensa and Whitney. "Riley told me that you were between jobs."

Whitney shrugged a shoulder. "My Aunt Nadia is retiring soon. She's either going to close her shop, or I'm taking it over. Right now, I'm learning as much as I can from her, so I'll know if Hard Pressed will be successful when I'm in charge."

Dad picked up his beer, but simply held it over the table. "You gave up a job with the FBI for this?"

Mensa sighed. In a low voice, he said, "Dad."

Whitney patted his leg under the table. "It's all right, and it's the same question my brother and other family members asked me."

He twisted his head to give her a look. "I understand that, but it doesn't make it 'all right,' babe."

CHAPTER 23

NO NECKING

WHITNEY

I LOVED HOW PROTECTIVE Mensa could be. From the tone of his voice to his words, he hated that I was having to deal with this uncomfortable conversation. But in all fairness, most parents would be concerned about their only son taking up with a woman who — from the outside — seemed to be making half-baked decisions.

I grinned at him. "It *is* all right, honey."

When I faced his parents again, they were looking at the two of us with disbelief. Since I didn't understand that, I powered past it. "Doing undercover work is tough, lonely, and for me, it was leading to burn-out. After a routine evaluation, I was encouraged to take some time to work on my mentality and learn not to be so engrossed in my cases."

"Engrossed?" Celeste asked.

I nodded once. "Sorry, that's the term the evaluator used. I was taking my work home with me, so to speak."

Dean narrowed an eye at me. "You mean, mentally."

"Yes," I said.

All the nerves I fought off earlier kept me from considering what his parents would say about my sudden change of careers. The room had gone eerily silent.

Celeste's eyes, so similar to Mensa's, darted between the two of us during the ensuing silence. "I have never seen him like this."

I looked at Dean, but quickly realized she was referring to Mensa. I turned to him and I fought rearing my head back at his fierce scowl.

"You should have seen them at Bayou Moon," Riley muttered.

"Or anytime she came to Twisted when he didn't want her there," Finn chimed in.

I shot him a dry look. "I don't think that's what she's referring to."

Riley grinned at me. "Oh yeah, it is."

Celeste pressed her lips together for a moment before her eyes widened. "Speaking of Twisted Talons, have you done anything to protect yourself against another shooting?"

Mensa sighed, but Finn spoke.

"Not much we can do unless we all wear Kevlar, and that ain't happening. That shit gets hot fast." Finn's body jerked ever so slightly, and I guessed Riley gave him a kick under the table. "Sorry, that stuff."

I chuckled silently.

"What's so funny?" Dean asked.

I looked up, wondering if I'd put my foot in it. Maybe Mensa's parents were more strait-laced than I thought. Well, if I'd made a bad impression, this would only seal the deal.

"I'm sorry. It's just that your son is a member of a motorcycle club. It's surprising that Riley expects Finn to keep his conversation profanity-free."

Celeste speared a chunk of pot roast. "There's no way to keep people from carrying guns into that bar?"

"Not really, Ma," Mensa muttered.

She gave a short shake of her head.

"I'm more concerned about the Corrupt Chrome member who chased the two of you," Finn muttered.

I squeezed Mensa's leg to keep him from telling Finn we knew who chased us. Even if Mensa's parents weren't going to tell anyone about Wyatt, I wanted to do everything I could to protect his undercover status.

Celeste aimed wide eyes at Mensa. "Chased? What's he talking about?"

"Sorry, man," Finn muttered.

"It's fine," Mensa said. "You don't need to worry, Ma."

Celeste's head tilt conveyed serious attitude. "Oh, I don't, do I? If I've told you once, I've told you ten thousand times, I will never stop worrying about you. Especially since you continue to ride a motorcycle and all these other people are in their cars *while texting*, and you tell me not to worry."

Mensa sat back in his seat, and I wondered if he was going to walk out the door. "Ma, we were chased, I lost them. Everything is fine."

Celeste raised an eyebrow. "*We* were chased? Who's we?" She tipped her head toward me. "Did you have her on your bike?"

Mensa nodded, but from the energy coming off him, he was struggling to keep his temper in check.

"Good grief. Why would you put her on your motorcycle? If you're being chased, you should have gone to a police station. For that matter, you should have loaded into Riley's car."

Mensa let out a long exhale. "The moment shots were fired, Finn was taking care of Riley." He tipped his head toward me. "Her car had been stolen, so we didn't have any other choice than my bike. If I weren't part of a club, I might have gone to the police station, Ma. But it doesn't matter. It's done. We're safe, and that's it."

Dean turned to Celeste. "He's right, honey. Let it go."

I couldn't stop my mouth from running. "To be fair, I told him we should have waited for the police to arrive."

Celeste looked at Dean as if to say, 'See?'

Mensa's stern tone stole my attention though. "And we'd have been shot, Whitney."

I gave him a closed-lip smile. "Not if we'd taken cover, but like your dad says, we should let it go."

"What'd you do to the potatoes tonight, Auntie Celeste? Did you use a different seasoning?"

Celeste glanced over to Riley and nodded. "I did." She looked at me. "Where are you from, Whitney?"

"Maryland, not far from Ocean City."

Dean's face lit up with his grin. "I love that area. The crab cakes can't be beat."

We continued to eat while I endured a variety of new-girlfriend questions from his parents. It wasn't the ideal 'meet the parents' dinner, but what could I expect? It wasn't every day I had dinner with people who were related to an investigation subject.

For some reason, the mundane questions felt like exaggerated small talk, and it drained me more than Celeste's pointed questions about the investigation or the bar. I don't know if he sensed my unease, but Finn jumped into the conversational fray and diverted the focus away from me.

In no time, I carried my plate to the kitchen, following Mensa. Celeste and Dean had stayed at the table chatting with Finn and Riley.

No sooner had I set my plate next to the sink, than Mensa whirled to me and wrapped his arms around me.

"What are you doing?" I whispered.

He kissed me, which answered my question somewhat.

Luckily he kept it brief. When he let me go, I peered up at him. "What was that for?"

The left side of his lips quirked. "You're something else, Blume."

"I still don't know what the big deal is."

He shook his head. "You'll deny this, but Mom wasn't cool with you."

"You're right, I would deny that since any parent would be concerned about their son bringing home a flake—"

"You are *not* a flake."

I dipped my chin. "I was going to say, 'flake*y woman*,' which, from the outside looking in, I appear to be."

He mirrored my chin dip. "You got a raw deal – no matter what you tell me – and you're taking care of a family business."

"Many might see that as selling myself short."

He shook his head. "Bullshit. You handed me a diatribe about how difficult it is to run a small business. In no way is that selling yourself short. Hell, I've heard Sandy mention what Nadia charges for a new cut.

If you take over and grow that business, you'll be successful and anyone who's got a problem with it can fuck right off."

My body shook with my chuckle. "Telling people that won't help me grow my business, honey."

He stepped back and rinsed our plates. "No, but it's the attitude you need to have so you aren't worked over by anyone in the future."

"Kenneth, are you bringing in dessert? I made your favorite angel food cake with the icing you love," Celeste called from the dining room.

"I'll bring it in, Ma," Mensa said.

Riley and Finn brought the dinner plates to the sink. While Finn rinsed them, Riley grabbed dessert plates.

"Do we need more forks?" I asked.

Riley shut the cabinet door. "Only you and Mensa. Auntie Celeste told us to save ours before we came in here."

I grabbed two forks and mentally prepared myself for more small talk.

Mensa wrapped his arms around me from behind and nuzzled my neck. "We'll be out of here soon, woman. Relax."

I exhaled. "I'm fine."

"No, but you will be. You need another glass of wine?"

With my head tipped back against his shoulder, I looked him in the eye. "Not if I'm going to drive us home."

He did a long blink and gave a short shake of his head. "You're *not* driving us home. Live it up, woman."

I pulled free of his hold. "Now you tell me to live it up."

"Take the wine bottle to the table. I gotta grab the cake."

I set a fork at Mensa's setting, poured more wine for Riley, Celeste, and myself and then sat across from Dean.

Celeste aimed a smile at me. "I'm sorry if I was overbearing earlier. Kenneth hasn't brought anyone to dinner... ever. Unless you count Finn and Gage."

My brows furrowed. "Gage?"

Riley grinned. "She's talking about Gamble. She won't use anyone's road names."

"It's clear my son cares for you a great deal."

"And you can leave it at that, Mom, because anything else isn't your business," Mensa said, setting the cake on the table.

"Mensa," I chided.

"No way, Whitney. I like that she apologized, but you aren't answering any more questions. This cake is too damned good for any of us to be uncomfortable."

"How about you cut the cake? Then all of us will be too busy stuffing our faces," Dean suggested.

The way he said it sounded exactly like Mensa, and I couldn't stop my chuckle.

"You find that funny?" Mensa asked.

I shrugged a shoulder. "Sort of. He sounds just like you... so I can see where you get it."

"Where are you goin?" Mensa asked, tagging me at my hip before I could get to the master bathroom.

I looked up at him. "The bathroom. Hate to tell you this, but my period started earlier so I'm putting on my pajamas and brushing my teeth."

He shifted so we were face to face. "You in pain?"

"Not right now."

He stared at a point behind me for a beat. "Do you always abstain during your period?"

My head tilted. "No, but you can't want to—"

"Woman, I'll leave you alone if it bothers you, but my guess is this is like phone sex. You said it didn't do it for you, but hell if it didn't work for you when it was me on the phone with you."

I twisted my lips to the side. "That's true, but this is different."

His eyes met mine, and they were warm. "You know how Mom said that angel food cake is my favorite?"

I nodded. "What's that got to do with anything?"

His eyes twinkled with mischief. "My three favorite things to eat are pussy, Skittles, and bacon. In that order. *Always.*"

I tipped my head back. "You are not serious."

With his thumb and forefinger at my chin, he tipped my head down an inch. "Always, Blume. I don't have a problem with it. We'll stop if it really bothers you. Otherwise, period schmeriod, baby. That's what towels are for."

I flung my head back with my cackle. "Says the man who doesn't have to do the laundry! And only you could get away with saying 'period schmeriod' to me."

He stared at me until my humor faded. "It's light right now, yeah?"

My hands came up in question. "How do you know all this? You're an only child!"

His chin dipped. "You might have noticed that Mom has a way of getting in your business, but she also has a way of oversharing her own business – though she said it was so I'd be a man with a real understanding of women because Dad could only give me a male perspective on women."

I nodded once. "That kind of makes sense in a weird way." And it probably had something to do with his ability to read me.

He wrapped his arms around me and kissed me thoroughly. When he ended it, I felt dazed, and I loved the look in his eyes as he stared at me. "Give me a shot, Blume. Might just rock your world... all over again."

I shoved my hands up and under his shirt. "You know, you would make a great sales person because you're very convincing, Ragstone."

He laughed and unzipped my dress. It fell and pooled at my feet. "That's funny, because I thought the *very* same thing about you that night in the hotel room."

"What? I didn't convince you to have sex with—"

His tongue slid along his lower lip. "Wasn't talking about the sex, babe. I'm talking about the wine and Skittles. Nobody else could have convinced me to do that shit."

I yanked his shirt up and he pulled it over his head. "I guess that makes us even."

The sight of his tattoos always stole my attention. His body was a work of art without them, but add in all of that intricate ink, and I was mesmerized. He had flames licking along his rib cage; a small Riot MC patch sat on his left pec.

My perusal of his tattoos was cut short when he dropped his underwear and laid on his back in the bed. "Hurry up, Blume. I need my second dessert, baby."

I climbed up on the bed, he hauled me into position, and to my surprise, he rocked my world all over again.

———

From behind the counter at Hard Pressed, Aunt Nadia held her coffee mug aloft, and shook her head at Mensa. "Why are you dropping her off?"

"No need for us to both drive, since I'm sticking around until lunchtime."

Aunt Nadia sipped her coffee and blinked at him repeatedly. "I need her to have a vehicle – today especially, Mensa. The beginning of the week is when I get orders shipped out, and she has to get to the UPS store."

"Can't she borrow your car?" he asked.

Aunt Nadia hesitated. "She could, but neither one of us likes that. "

"It's for her own good... in fact, having her in your car is ideal, since Rod's got people on the look-out for her Elantra."

I shot Mensa a dry look. "Those bikers have better things to do than search for me."

Both of them ignored me.

Aunt Nadia narrowed her eyes on Mensa. "How long are you Riot boys gonna let this go on? There was a time when this would have been dealt with and the dust would have settled."

Mensa's head dipped just a fraction. "That time is gone, Nadia. We went legit years ago now, and we're going to keep it that way. Police investigations don't move as swiftly as Brink did."

The immediate change in Aunt Nadia's demeanor made me brace. It only made Mensa grin.

"I ought to wipe that smirk right off your face, young man."

Mensa shifted his gaze to me. "You didn't tell her anything."

My eyes widened. "Don't you drag me into this. You dug your own hole, genius."

Aunt Nadia glared at me. "What did he tell you?"

I pressed my lips together and debated the most diplomatic response. "It doesn't matter, Aunt Nadia. It's your story to tell, or not, and I'll respect that either way."

"Damn straight you will."

I glowered at Mensa.

"Why are you mean-mugging me, Blume?"

"Because she's pissed at me, when you're the one who brought all this up in the first place."

Aunt Nadia pointed a bony finger at Mensa. "Get her mess taken care of. She can't be tip-toeing around town for months on end."

"It's been two weeks," I muttered.

Aunt Nadia glared at me. "Three, young lady, or did the four days you spent in Jackson, slip your mind?"

I peeked over her shoulder and into her mug. Two-thirds of it held black coffee. "Drink your coffee, Aunt Nadia." I lifted my eyes to Mensa's. "And you need to learn – never mess with her before she's had at *least* one cup of java."

That earned me narrowed eyes from both of them.

"Did you print those labels Friday afternoon?" Aunt Nadia asked.

I smiled. "Yes, and they're on the appropriate boxes already. I'll go triple check the orders, and seal them up."

Aunt Nadia nodded, then turned to Mensa. "You can go help her, so you're both out of my hair. And no necking back there."

I swallowed back my laughter, because I'd forgotten how ornery Aunt Nadia could be without her caffeine.

CHAPTER 24

LIKE TWO ACES

MENSA

HE FOLLOWED WHITNEY TO the back room. "How wrong is it that I want to make out with you just to be contrary?"

Whitney whirled on him. "Forget it. You've gotten me into enough hot water with her. Besides, I got work to do, mister."

He glanced around the room and spotted five boxes with labels on them. "This is it? If I help you check these, you'll be ready to leave in no time."

Whitney shook her head. "Oh, no, I won't. The website probably had at least one or two orders over the weekend. Aunt Nadia never checks that until Monday morning, so I won't be ready to go until well after lunchtime at the earliest."

He didn't know why, but down to his bones, he didn't like that.

"I won't be here if you go after lunch."

She gave him her big eyes and a cute chin dip. "Hence, Aunt Nadia wanting me to have my vehicle."

He chuckled and muttered, "Vehicle."

"That is what modes of transportation are called."

"Is there any way to do this before lunch?"

She closed her eyes and took a deep breath. When she opened her eyes, they were filled with patience. "I appreciate that you're concerned, honey. But it's a routine errand."

He fought against his rising temper. "Like the trip to the mall should have been a routine outing with Riley?"

She pursed her lips together and nodded. "You've got me there, Mensa. But what's the likelihood of him needing to go to a shipping store? And it being the same one Aunt Nadia uses?" She shook her head. "I don't think so. You mentioned their clubhouse is in Ocean Springs."

Her argument held logic, but he couldn't ignore his gut. "It's not like Ocean Springs is another state away. It's maybe fifteen minutes from here."

She turned her head an inch. "I'm carrying a gun, Mensa."

He sighed. "That's true, but it doesn't mean I want you to use it. Pretty sure your FBI privileges were revoked when you resigned."

"Am I taking a prospect with me to the UPS store? I'm guessing that will go over better than the mall."

He'd received a text from Har earlier that said the only prospect able to help that afternoon would be Scrap because he had a half-day at school, with graduation happening the following week. He trusted Scrap and was all for him earning his patch, but he didn't want to put him in the position of having to defend Whitney.

Finally he said, "Possibly. Let's get these boxes sorted and start on other orders while we can. I'll see what Cynic has happening at the bar and go from there."

Two hours later, Mensa assembled another box for Whitney just as Nadia wandered into the back area. He caught Nadia's gaze. "If I'd have known how many orders you processed in a weekend alone, I'd have told the brothers to start our own screen-printing business, four years ago. The hours would be better than working the bar, that's for certain."

Nadia shot him a saucy grin. "I get so many orders over a weekend because I've been doin' this a long time, Mensa. Did you think about that?"

Whitney leaned to the side toward Nadia. "It's also because eight years ago, your niece hooked you up with someone to build out a great website for you."

Nadia gave Whitney a conciliatory nod. "And that's why I know you're the best person to take over for me. You care more than you let on."

"How many more orders need to be processed? Or is this it?" Mensa asked.

Nadia met his gaze. "I have two embroidery pieces going out, but since Whitney hasn't mastered the sewing machine just yet, it'll take me another two hours at least."

Mensa sighed and rubbed the back of his neck. "You know, if you do so much business with UPS, why can't you open a business account and have them come to you? They pick up from all sorts of businesses before five."

Nadia opened the small refrigerator and pulled out a soda. "You're right, but most of the time that sort of service comes with a corporate account. I can't afford that, and I prefer working with the people at the store."

Whitney moved to stand in front of him and put her hands on his biceps. "It will be fine, Mensa. I love that you care so much, but I can take care of myself."

"Will there be a brother following her?" Nadia asked.

Mensa did a slow nod. "If I can't stick around, a prospect will, yes."

Nadia shook her head. "I didn't ask if a *prospect* would follow her."

"Most of the brothers have day jobs now, Nadia."

"Well, la-dee-dah," she muttered.

His phone rang and he pulled it from his back pocket, Cynic's name on the display.

"Hey, 'Nic. Everything coo—"

"No, everything isn't cool. Fucking Corrupt Chrome set a dumpster on fire and pushed it up next to the goddamn building."

He opened his mouth, closed it, and pulled his thoughts together. "Did the building catch fire?"

"Not the way you're thinking. The back door's compromised. I'm trying to get someone out here ASAP, and Brute's working a few contacts he has to see if some other company will get us in fast."

"What do you need me to do?"

"Need you to get your ass down here. I got distributors comin' in all fuckin' day. I can't deal with the door people. That'll be on you because Finn's got the whole damned bar and grill until Two-Times can get here, which won't be until after four because his sister can't watch his kids until she gets off work."

He blew out a breath. "Know this isn't your call, but can I get a different prospect over here for Whitney? I don't want to put Scrap in the position to get so violent before he graduates."

"Yeah. I'll talk to Har. How soon can you get here?"

He ground his teeth together. "Once I know someone else is here, I'll be there in twenty minutes."

"Where do you have to be in twenty minutes?" Whitney asked, as he put his cell in his pocket.

Glancing around the room, he noticed Nadia had gone back out front. He faced Whitney. "I gotta get over to Twisted Talons. Seems the Corrupt Chrome assholes set a literal dumpster fire, and shoved it up against the building to try and start a full-on fire."

Whitney gasped, and her eyes were wider than he'd ever seen them. "And did they?"

"No, but they damaged our back door. Cynic needs me to be there to meet with a repair company because Finn's manning the grill and bar while Cynic has his regularly scheduled meetings with distributors."

"He can't reschedule those?"

He turned his hands up in question. "I'm guessing he tried...but knowing 'Nic, he might figure that lets the Corrupt Chrome MC win since it would disrupt our business."

Whitney tried, but failed, to hide her outraged expression. "I could argue that with him, but okay."

She turned back to the order she was working on.

"Blume," he called.

Her hands froze and she turned her face to him. "Yes?"

"Come here."

"Mensa, I've got a deadline if these—"

He closed the distance between them and tugged her a few inches toward him. "I need two things from you."

"Just two?"

He grinned. "For now, yes. Go easy on the prospect. Don't speed out of the parking lot away from him—"

"Like I do that," she muttered.

"You know what I'm saying. If the light's yellow, stop, don't make shit harder."

She nodded once. "Okay. What's the second thing?"

"Kiss me. I don't care if Nadia said no necking. This shit will run right into my shift at the bar, and I won't see you again until after midnight."

She wrapped her hand around his neck. "I was going to mention, you might want to stay at the clubhouse tonight seeing as you'll get in late, and I'm—"

"Do you love me?"

"Yes, but I'm just—"

"No, Blume. If you love me, then we're doing this, and that means going through the thick and the thin together. I'll do my best not to wake you, but you need to kiss your man before the prospect gets here."

"You are incredibly bossy."

Mensa smiled. "Says the pot to the kettle. Guess I'll kiss you."

***

Har, Gamble, Cynic, and Block were standing around the back door to Twisted Talons when Mensa arrived.

"This shit doesn't make sense," Gamble muttered.

Cynic shook his head. "No shit, Gamble. Not sure who I'm more pissed at, the assholes who sold us this building or the fuckin' Corrupt Chrome."

"Why would you pissed at the sellers?" Block asked.

"Those bastards should have had a ninety-minute fire door back here at a minimum. From what the fire department told me, it was a twenty-minute door tops. Otherwise, this damn thing wouldn't be so warped and shit. Almost owe the Corrupt Chrome a thank-you because without this bullshit we'd have never known, and would've really been fucked in an emergency."

Mensa slowly stalked around the group, looking at the dark soot outline against the brick wall. "Why would they half-ass this, though?"

Cynic glowered at him. "This isn't half-assed. We got a smoke alarm right at the door and it kicked off a call to the security company."

Mensa held his hands up for a second. "Chill, Cynic. They burned down Dontrell's restaurant – I don't care what the fire investigators say. They leveled that building, but didn't bother to do the same thing here. Why?"

Block dragged his hand over his bald head. "Can see why you'd ask that, but Dontrell's security set up is probably different. The building they burned down was definitely older—"

Mensa's patience slipped. "Okay, but I'm not the only one questioning this, so what's their goal?"

Cynic glared at Mensa. "I don't fuckin' know, but I know we're shuttin' their shit down."

"We aren't rollin' out half-cocked, 'Nic," Har said.

Cynic turned his glare to Har. "We waited too long to fight back after the gunfire broke out here, Prez."

"That was out of necessity." Har glanced at Mensa and back to Cynic. "Corrupt Chrome has a narc – *they* don't know it, but *we* do. We go after them, we'll get taken down with them. Gamble's gettin' married soon. He isn't doin' that from prison."

Cynic put his hands on his hips. "I want some fuckin' revenge, Har."

Har's eyes glinted with anger. "So do I, and Corrupt Chrome will pay. You gotta be patient."

"Shit," Cynic hissed. "This is enough to start smoking again."

"Don't let Fiona hear that," Gamble muttered.

Mensa tuned out the rest of the conversation because something told him this was a diversion. He wandered toward his bike and called the prospect assigned to Whitney. It rang five times and rolled to voicemail. He willed himself not to worry about not getting an answer.

After a deep breath, he called Hard Pressed. Nadia answered almost immediately.

"It's Mensa. Did Whitney leave for the UPS store?"

"She did , and she told me why you had to split like two aces at a blackjack table. Nobody got hurt, right?"

"Everyone's fine, but I wanted to check on Whitney since the prospect isn't answering my call. They must be driving."

He could hear the smile in Nadia's voice. "Yes, in fact, they just pulled up. You want me to put you on hold?"

"No, ma'am. I'll call her cell."

"You should have done that to start. She's got that new fangled in-car—"

His lips tipped. "No, Nadia, she's in your car today."

"I stand corrected. I got a business to run, you have a good one, Mensa."

Rather than call Whitney, he hit Hummer's contact.

"Yo, I was on my bike when—"

"Yeah, Nadia told me. Did you see anything odd?"

"No."

"Did you watch for a tail?"

"Man, I did two tours overseas. I know what it feels like to be followed."

Mensa ground his teeth together. "Now you're cocky. It's a yes-or-no question: did you *watch* for a tail?"

Hummer hesitated. "Not like I should have."

"Cynic's gonna kick your ass," Mensa bit out.

"What?" Hummer scoffed. "Are you too much of a pussy to do it yourself?"

"No, Cynic has more anger to work off. Then I'll pour salt in your wounds. You got one fuckin' job. Make sure you do it."

He ended the call, moved back toward his brothers, and heard Gamble say, "...think Hummer's ready for his patch."

Mensa prowled closer. "The fuck he is. Admitted to not watching for a tail. Claims he knows what that feels like."

"It does have a feel to it," Gamble said.

Mensa widened his eyes at Gamble. "You gonna trust that shit if Vickie's got an asshole like Rod gagging for her?"

Gamble's expression turned stony.

"Yeah. I didn't think so." Mensa looked at Har. "Like I told him, he's got one job and he needs to do it. Hell, he's on his second chance since he missed Whitney's brother making an approach."

"You didn't mention that," Gamble said.

Mensa tipped his head at Har. "I told him and Block."

Har dug his phone out, but didn't engage it. "Lucky for you two, we aren't voting on any new patches for a while." He aimed his phone camera at the door and took a picture. "Gamble, we need to get back to the shop, let them handle this shit. We're having church in the morning."

Cynic turned to Mensa. "You can help me set up the dehumidifiers Block brought over here. Water was all over the back hall. We'll be lucky if we don't have to rip out the dry wall."

"You probably will anyway, but this might help hold it off for a week," Block muttered.

"Lead the way, 'Nic," Mensa said.

Mensa approached Whitney's door and realized his mistake: he didn't have a key.

A dim light could be seen behind the blinds. He knocked softly, then tried the handle. If he found it unlocked, he'd find a way to drive it home how important her safety was. The knob didn't turn and relief swept through him.

He heard the click of what he assumed was the security bar lock, then the deadbolt clicked, and she opened the door.

"Why aren't you sleeping?" he asked, closing the door and locking it.

She chuckled quietly. "It's only midnight, Kenneth. I'm used to getting only six or seven hours of sleep."

He wrapped his arms around her and kissed her. His tongue slid over hers and he tasted hints of dry white wine... and if he wasn't mistaken, Skittles.

With a groan he ended the kiss. "You been eating Skittles, Blume?"

Her coy smile went straight to his dick. "Maybe. Now when I pair them with wine, I can't help but think of you."

He walked her backward toward her bedroom, tagging the light switch as they went. "What else does it make you think of?"

She slid her hands under his shirt. "How I didn't get to do half of what I wanted to do with you that night."

He arched a brow while shooting her his own coy smile. "Pretty sure tonight's your night, baby. Gonna let you do whatever you want."

A gleam hit her eyes. "Even put cuffs on you?"

That stopped him in his tracks. "Why would you want to do that?"

She shot him a curious look which faded to realization. "I guess I never told you. For so long, I wanted to be the one who cuffed you and brought you down."

"Brought me down? You wanted to arrest me?"

She looked slightly contrite. "I did. It doesn't make sense, but—"

"Baby, you don't need to justify it. Hell, I wanted you gone every time I caught sight of you."

Her head tilted, even as he moved them into the bedroom. "Yeah, but that isn't nearly the same as wanting to arrest someone."

He leaned forward, forcing her to bend backward, and he turned on her bedside lamp. "I have to think about that, since I've never let anyone restrain me, Blume."

"Yeah," she whispered when she straightened.

"For now though, we're pressed for time since you got work in the morning and I've got church. So, I hope you got a plan B in mind."

She kissed a path along his jaw. "Pay closer attention, genius. 'I didn't even get to half of what I wanted to do'. ...So yeah, I definitely got back-up plans."

CHAPTER 25

BONUS POINTS WITH AUNT NADIA

WHITNEY

THE BUTTON ON MENSA'S jeans slid free, and I worked his zipper down. He was right – the cuffs should wait for another night, because I wanted to take my time if he ever decided to be restrained. The very thought of it made me shift foot to foot.

He helped me by pushing his pants and boxer briefs down while toeing out of his boots. I stroked his stiff cock and sank to my knees.

He slid a hand in my hair. "You got a whole bed here, and you want to get on your knees, baby? Are you sure?"

I licked around his tip and glanced up at him. "I'm sure."

His eyes smoldered, and I felt a thrill of power surge through me. I opened my mouth and took him as far as I could.

"Fuck, Whitney. Your mouth feels so fucking good."

Reflexively, I hummed in response.

Mensa hissed and fisted my hair. That tug sent a shiver through me from my head to my toes. I redoubled my efforts, adding more suction and gripping him tighter.

"Oh, hell. I'm not gonna last long, Whitney."

I released him long enough to whisper, "Good."

He stared down at me. "Are you sure about that?"

I traced my fingers around his balls. "Very."

His fingers in my hair relaxed. With that as my cue, I licked his length before guiding him deep into my mouth. I reveled in hearing his reactions. With my free hand, I reached around and squeezed his ass.

The moment he lost control, his other hand cupped the back of my head and his hips bucked wildly. I clutched his ass, not to still his movements, but to hang on for the ride. This was unlike anything I'd ever done before – raw and wild. He tipped his head back and hissed a lengthy sigh when his orgasm hit. I swallowed it down as my eyes watered.

After a moment, he reached down and tugged me to my feet. "Get naked, Whit. I'd help you, but your mouth is lethal. I don't think anyone's made me come that hard in years."

I pulled my clothes off.

Mensa guided me toward the bed, encouraging me to lay in the center. "Time to return the favor, baby. Then I should be recovered enough to make love to you."

***

We woke up after hitting the snooze on my alarm twice.

Mensa caught sight of the time and knifed out of bed. "Shit. I gotta get going." He dragged his jeans up his legs, then his face went slack and he did a long blink. "Dammit. I'm not gonna be able to drop you at the shop, babe."

I grinned and nodded. "It's okay, my man. I have a car and I'll be careful."

He grabbed a t-shirt from the duffel bag he'd left behind a couple days ago, then he pointed a finger at me. "Keep your gun on you."

"I will."

He sighed. "The prospect will be at Hard Pressed around noon. Try not to lose him."

I nodded. "So I'm not being followed or anything this morning?"

He came to my side of the bed. "No, and it makes me uneasy."

I got up on my knees on the bed and wrapped my arms around his neck. "It'll be okay, big guy. For what it's worth, you'll get bonus points with Aunt Nadia. She was grouchy about having to drop me off yesterday evening."

His eyes skated to the side. "Wasn't she the one who encouraged you to head to Jackson for your safety?"

I smiled. "Yes, but she gets crabby when her normal schedule is disrupted."

Staring at him, it hit me that he hadn't shaved yesterday, and he wouldn't shave this morning. His scruff no longer bordered on becoming a beard, it was one.

He kissed me fast. "Don't know why you're staring at me like that, but you gotta knock it off. I can't be late for church. Har never misses an opportunity to hit us with a fine."

I gave him another peck. "Okay, honey, but let's just say if you were contemplating shaving..." I cupped his cheek, "...don't. Your beard is sexy as all hell."

He groaned and touched his forehead to mine. "Woman, you can't say shit like that when I'm running late."

I sat back on my heels with a grin. "Just food for thought."

His hands came under my armpits and he hauled me off the bed and set me on my feet. He slid his hands down and back to my ass, then pulled me tight to him. "You're gonna pay for that, Whit. Tell Nadia you're taking a long lunch."

"Really? Why?"

"Because you've made me hard and I gotta ride to the clubhouse dealing with that and thinking about my face between your legs the whole fuckin' way."

I chuckled. "I didn't say anything about that last part."

He dipped his chin. "You think my beard is sexy, imagine what it'll be like when I eat you out."

Even though I fought it, I fidgeted.

"Yeah... that's why. I gotta run. Later."

Half an hour later, I walked into Hard Pressed and saw Aunt Nadia standing behind the counter. "It's about time you got here."

I was only fifteen minutes late, but telling Aunt Nadia that wouldn't help. It was an excuse and we both knew it.

"Sorry, I'm late."

She waved a hand at me. "We got two rush orders, and they both paid the extra fee, so you're headed to the UPS store again – before noon."

As I stuffed my Boho bag into a drawer, Mensa's warning replayed in my mind. I faced Aunt Nadia. "Okay. Do you mind if I borrow your car again?"

Aunt Nadia shot me a regretful smile. "Would if I could, but it's at the dealer for the sixty-thousand mile service. They toted me back here because it's gonna be such a long wait."

She set the order sheet in front of me, and I got crackin' on the order.

"Here's your receipt. The tracking numbers are listed and will be active later this afternoon," the clerk said.

I smiled and nodded, then headed for the exit.

The strip mall held two other businesses, one of them a popular sandwich shop. The small parking lot had twice as many cars in the lot than when I arrived. Luckily, I'd parked on the end opposite from the sandwich shop.

My purse bumped my hip as I walked, the weight of it reminding me I had my weapon. Even when I was an agent, I carried my gun in my purse so it wasn't as noticeable in public. My keys were tucked in a pocket next to the gun, and I dug into my purse to grab my keys and unlock my car.

The moment I had my fingers curled around my key chain, I heard footsteps approaching. Before I could shift my fingers to the gun, a man wrapped his arm around my shoulders and pulled me flush to his side. From the corner of my eye, I saw it was Rod.

"About time I found you alone, bitch," he hissed.

I stopped, which forced him to stop. The self-defense tactics I had learned in Quantico came back to me. Muscle memory kicked in and I planted my feet to push into him while twisting out of his hold, but another man wearing a leather cut came to my other side, locking his arm around my waist.

"Never thought your tracking device would pay off, Rod. Night-night, dumb bitch," the new man muttered.

I felt a pinch at my bicep. My head twisted and I saw a needle there. He'd pushed the plunger down before I could try to wrench my arm away.

Shit.

"What'd you give me asshole?" I yelled, hoping someone at the sandwich shop might hear me.

The problem was that we were headed the wrong direction for my voice to travel and whatever was in the syringe, it was kicking in fast. So fast I listed forward, and I vaguely noticed Rod and the other man caught me before I face-planted on the ground.

CHAPTER 26

HEAVY SENSE OF DREAD

MENSA

CYNIC STOOD NEXT TO his chopper with a saddlebag open when Mensa pulled his bike to a stop behind the clubhouse.

"Good morning, 'Nic," Mensa said, taking off his helmet.

"Not much good about this morning, man."

Mensa's head reared back. "Did something else happen? I know those assholes attacking Twisted Talons bugs you, but that take this morning is even more cynical than your norm."

Cynic narrowed his eyes. "Long-ass night. Got here early for church, and Har can't fuckin' make it for an hour, maybe an hour and a half."

He hung his helmet on the handlebar of his bike. "Then go take a fuckin' nap, man."

The frown on Cynic's face made him look almost cartoonish. "Not a fuckin' chance, Mensa. Haven't taken a goddamn nap in a long damned time. Worst part is that I can't even do anything worthwhile at Twisted because by the time I get there and start on something, I'll have to turn around and come back after half an hour."

Mensa sighed and realized it was the same for him, too. He could go spend time at Hard Pressed with Whitney, but he'd have to come right back here. Not to mention, he wasn't much help there and he'd be wasting his time.

It struck him that he hadn't been to the gym in over a week. "Gotcha. I'm gonna change clothes and lift some weights, if you want to join me. Might help you be a little less cynical."

Cynic's eyes went wide. "The fuck it will, but I'll keep it in mind."

"Why is the new door so expensive?" Tiny asked, following Block's run-down of the costs thus far from the fire at Twisted Talons.

Cynic leaned forward, his menacing energy almost palpable. "Because we got the three-hour fire door which should have been installed to start with."

Tiny tipped his chin up. "Take it that would have saved us money."

"Yeah," Cynic hissed.

"Is there a plan for Corrupt Chrome to pay for what they did?" Roman asked.

"Yeah," Har said, and cast his gaze across all the brothers at the table. "Tonight anyone who isn't working a shift at Twisted Talons is headed to the Corrupt Chrome MC clubhouse in Ocean Springs."

"Are we on our bikes?" Finn asked.

"No. Find a brother who has a cage."

Mensa locked eyes with Har. "Do you know if their hang-arounds will be at the clubhouse?"

"Why the fuck does that matter?" Tiny asked.

Har shot Tiny a serious look. "The less you know the better, Tiny. As for your question Mensa, hang-arounds won't be there, but prospects will."

"We're sure of that?" Gamble asked.

Block nodded. "Scrap and one of his buddies watched their clubhouse over the last week. The friend acted as a hang-around and found out that the four prospects they have are positioned along the perimeter when they have church."

Har sat back in his chair. "Scrap's friend found out that they have church every Tuesday night. That means they'll have church tonight. Scrap studied how the prospects were stationed. Cynic and Brute are gonna take out two prospects at the southwest corner, while Tiny and Roman handle the southeast. That gives us the best shot at their back door."

"After that, are we gonna torch their clubhouse?" Finn asked.

Roman hissed in a breath.

Har shook his head. "If it were up to 'Nic, we would, but Roman pointed out, we're more likely to get caught doing that shit."

Mensa's phone rang, and Cynic glared at him. He silenced it and cut his eyes between Cynic and Har. "Sorry about that."

"If we aren't setting anything on fire, then what are we doing?" Tiny asked.

Mensa's phone vibrated on his hip. After a moment it stopped, only to start back up again. He pulled the phone from his hip, tilted it under the table and saw Nadia's name on the display.

Shit.

"Are you listening, man?" Cynic demanded.

Mensa looked up, realizing he'd spoken aloud.

"Sorry. I have to take this."

He stood, and hurried out of the room. "Yeah."

"Mensa, have you heard from Whitney? Is she with you?"

"No, it isn't even noon, why would she be with me?"

"It's a quarter to noon, and she left for the UPS store well over an hour ago. She only had two boxes, and she's not answering her phone."

"Could she be in a long line?" he asked, even as his gut twisted.

"That wouldn't explain her not answering her phone, and I got an email saying the tracking numbers had been generated for those two orders. If she isn't with you—"

The alarm in Nadia's tone didn't help matters. "There's got to be a reasonable explanation, Nadia. Don't worry—"

"Boy, you get to be my age, you know exactly when to worry. You've been watching her like a hawk, and now she isn't answering her phone. I'm calling her brother."

His knee-jerk reaction was for her *not* to do that, but if Rod had taken her in broad daylight, they'd need all the help they could get.

"You aren't gonna ask me not to do that?"

"No. You call him. I gotta get back to church."

He ended the call, and went back into the conference room.

Har held the gavel over the table, but paused when he saw Mensa.

"You look pissed," Brute said.

"Whitney's not answering her phone. She went to ship two packages. The prospect wasn't following her yet because I expected her to be at the shop all morning. My gut says Corrupt Chrome got to her."

"You don't know that though," Block said.

"It's the most likely scenario given how Rod acted at the mall."

"Law enforcement should handle this, especially with her ties to the FBI," Two-Times said.

Mensa clenched his jaw and stared at Two-Times. "If it were one of your kids—"

Two-Times glared at Mensa. "I'd *especially* let the law handle it, so I didn't fuck it up."

"Leave the hypothetical situations out of this," Har said. "What about her brother?"

"Nadia's calling him," Mensa muttered.

His cell phone rang and he put her on speaker phone. "Yeah, Nadia."

"Wyatt's in Jackson testifying in court. His case manager is calling their informant to verify if Whitney's been taken."

Mensa swallowed his words; they would only make Nadia worry even more.

"Thanks, Nadia. If I find out anything, I'll call you."

He ended the call, feeling despair washing over him. "Rod could have taken her any-fucking-where."

"Brother, don't do that shit," Finn said.

Mindless of the phone being in his hand, Mensa cocked his fist back ready to throw it across the room, but Block stood and drew his attention.

"Don't fuckin' throw that phone. It's your only line to your woman, and busting it into a dozen pieces damn sure won't make you feel better."

Slowly, Mensa lowered his cell to the table and let out a guttural yell.

"I say we move the plan up. We roll out on their clubhouse, now," Roman said.

Block shook his head. "I'm not against that, but like Mensa said, that asshole could go anywhere. Since the fire, I called some people and dug into Rodney 'Rod' Lewis. He's got a place in Ocean Springs." Block glanced at Har and back to Mensa. "Iron will probably be back today, so if Rod took Whitney, I'm thinking he'd keep her at his place instead of the clubhouse."

"Since nobody's willing to call the cops, I have a crazy idea," Two-Times said.

"This oughta be good," Finn muttered.

"What if we send Hummer to the Corrupt Chrome clubhouse? He hasn't earned his patch yet, and since he's been watching Whitney the most... he could offer to help Rod—"

"That would have been a decent idea except that ship has sailed," Cynic said.

Two-Times arched his brows. "He's a prospect. He wouldn't know that she's been taken already and he also wouldn't know that we're aware she's MIA."

Roman, who sat next to Two-Times, shook his head. "Corrupt Chrome won't let him through the gates. They see a prospect patch on his cut, they know he's aligned himself with us, and it's no better than me or you trying to get through."

"I want Rod's address," Mensa said.

"You can follow me to that address," Block said.

"Give me the address, Block."

"No. We're your brothers. We have your back. From the thunder on your face alone, you need us at your back."

That tracked, and Mensa took a deep breath.

"Told you 'Thunder' should have been his road name," Cynic muttered.

Har looked around the table. "Block, Cynic, Mensa, and Finn are headed to Rod's address. Once we know he hasn't taken Whitney there, the rest of us will ride out to the Corrupt Chrome clubhouse."

"Earlier, I thought we wanted to strike when it was just prospects manning the perimeter. What changed?" Gamble asked.

"My woman going missing is what changed."

Gamble looked between Mensa and Har.

"He's right. All bets are off now. We're done," Har said, and swung his gavel.

Block pushed back from the table and stood. "You got your gun on you?"

Mensa shook his head.

Finn rose from his seat. "I need to grab my gun, too."

Cynic stood. "Hurry up."

As he leaned into the turn onto Halstead Road, Mensa wondered what the hell Rod did to afford a house in this sleepy neighborhood. The area wasn't flashy, but house prices were steep, and rents were high, too. Then again, dealing drugs and other crimes paid well... until the cops found out.

A Harley sat in the middle of one driveway, and Mensa knew that had to be the house.

Block pulled ahead of Cynic to lead the way up the drive. Finn and Mensa brought their bikes to a halt near the parked Harley.

Finn swung off his bike. "Why does this feel like a trap?"

Mensa took off his helmet. "It's not a trap if we don't do anything illegal."

Before either of them made their way up the sidewalk, the front door opened and a white-haired, elderly man stepped out on the front porch carrying a shotgun. A cigarette dangled from his lips and his arms were heavily inked, though the tats were hard to make out on his wrinkled skin.

He shuffled forward on his open-toed, leather sandals. "You assholes get off my property!"

"Sir, is Rod here?" Block asked loudly.

"I'm Rod, and I want you to leave."

"What the fuck?" Finn muttered.

Now the address made more sense...a decade ago, this house would have been affordable. If the house belonged to this old codger, Rod probably felt safe dropping her here. What better way to hide Whitney, than to leave her with an old man.

"Where's Whitney?" Mensa hollered, in part so the man could hear him from ten yards away and partly so Whitney would hear him if she were inside.

"I don't know any Whitley."

"Whitney!" Mensa yelled to correct the man and in an added effort to get her attention.

Cynic turned toward Mensa. "I don't think she's here."

Block had edged closer to the house. "Do you have a son named Rodney?"

"Not any damn more. He got caught up with assholes like you."

"Let's go," Finn muttered.

Cynic nodded and moved toward his bike.

Block hadn't moved yet, and Mensa wondered if this old man were putting on an act.

The sound of another motorcycle coming down the street grabbed their attention, and all of them turned toward the sound.

Scrap rolled up on his used motorcycle.

"What the fuck is he doing here?" Finn asked before Mensa could.

Scrap swung off his bike and prowled up the drive. Once he was near Mensa and Finn, he said in a low voice, "Har and Tiny sent me in case this doesn't pan out. He wants one of us to stick around. That's why I parked in the street. He can't make a complaint—"

Mensa shot Scrap some side-eye. "He can make a complaint; the cops won't be able to do much about it... at least not legally. Depends on the cops who shows up."

Finn nodded. "He's right. You're gonna have to wing that, so don't mouth off to the police."

"I told you assholes to leave!" Rod yelled.

Block held his hands up. "We're leaving, sir. Before we go, though, there's a missing woman. Her name is Whitney. If your son brings her by—"

"I ain't got no son!" Rod shouted.

Block gave a deep nod. "Understood, sir. If Rodney Lewis brings a woman here, please, for her sake, call 911."

The man acted as though he hadn't heard a word Block said. "Are you gettin' off my property or what?"

Block didn't respond, but gave Cynic a nod to mount up. Finn moved to his bike.

Mensa noticed Block heading toward him and Scrap. "Don't go anywhere yet, Scrap."

As soon as he was within earshot, Block said, "Scrap, you're gonna have to ride away, and figure out how you can watch this place without this old man knowing you've got eyes on him."

"Are you shittin' me?" Scrap asked.

Mensa fought a grin. "Surprised you're not up for it. There's another street, two blocks from here. I suggest parking your bike on that street and coming back on foot."

"In broad daylight," Scrap complained.

Mensa shot him a look. "Figure it out, Scrap. Whitney's missing, and we need your help."

That shut him up, and he moved to his bike.

Block sighed. "Let's head to the Corrupt Chrome clubhouse."

Mensa gave him a half-nod. "Right. Why do you sound doubtful?"

Block shook his head. "Not doubtful. Just really thought the asshole would have dropped Whitney here. She doesn't strike me as a woman who's easy to contain. If it were me, I wouldn't want her at my clubhouse."

"That doesn't help, Block. If anything, it makes me think he's taken her somewhere else that we don't know about."

Block turned his head to the side, and Mensa noticed a muscle twitch along his jawline. "You might be right, but we can't think like that. We have to stick to the plan, meet the others, and hit their clubhouse."

Mensa trudged to his Harley with a heavy sense of dread.

CHAPTER 27

EMPTY

WHITNEY

I WOKE UP WITH dry mouth. It took a moment before I realized it stemmed from a wad of fabric shoved between my lips. I opened my eyes. The room was dimly lit, and it appeared that I was alone. My wrists were bound to a chair with duct tape. With care, because my neck hurt like hell from my awkward position, I turned my head to see if any one was behind me.

Alone.

Thank God.

I took a closer look at the chair. It was a white, plastic outdoor chair. Whoever bound me made sure my forearms were flat to the armrests. Little did they realize that could work in my favor. I began to move my forearms back and forth to cut through the duct tape. It would take time. With any luck, there would be enough time for me to break free.

I noticed a windowsill a few feet away. When I went to move my legs, I found they'd been taped to the chair also. Trying to cut the tape on my legs and my arms would take more coordination. I started working my legs to break them free also, but free hands would do me the most good.

The blinds weren't completely drawn. The sun shifted enough to brighten the room, and I couldn't believe my eyes. Rod or his buddy was dumb enough to leave my purse on the floor.

With effort, I jerked my torso to scoot the chair forward. I expected to hear the chair scraping the floor, but no sound came. That was when I noticed the room was carpeted.

Could they be so stupid as to leave me in this room with my purse? Surely they searched it.

I shook my head. This was no time for assumptions. If there was a chance my phone or my gun was in that bag, I had to get to it. Who knew what Rod wanted to do to me now that he had me here?

My mind flooded with thoughts of all the things I wanted to do but hadn't had a chance: buying a house, marriage, starting a family, proving to Aunt Nadia I could keep her legacy going.

Mentally I shook off the thoughts, then I took another quick glance around the room because putting cameras in here wouldn't be that difficult. Another thought hit me: even if there were cameras, I had limited time and I had to make the most of it.

I scooted across the room as fast as I could – though with my arms and legs bound, it wasn't very fast at all. During my slow trek across the room, I debated the choice I'd have to make. I wouldn't be able to bend over and grab my purse – at least not until I freed an arm. If I really wanted to grab my bag, I'd have to tip myself over. There was no way I'd get upright again. That was a bridge I'd have to cross when I got there.

With all those thoughts running through my head, I propelled myself forward too hard. All my weight rested on the two front legs of the chair. Somehow I stopped the momentum before I fell on my face. Once I had the chair on four legs again, I took some deep breaths and kept working on the tape at my arms. To my surprise, I heard something tear on my right side. I examined my right arm, but it didn't appear any different than before other than my skin being red.

Still, that sound encouraged me to redouble my efforts to tear the duct tape.

After another seven scoots and what felt like at least twenty minutes, I was finally within a foot of my bag.

I clenched a fist and pulled up with my right arm. The tearing sound was music to my ears, but my arm was still stuck. On my third try, the tape finally tore loose. I pulled the gag out of my mouth and took a huge gulp of fresh air.

I tamped down my urge to shout with joy, then awkwardly bent forward and grabbed my purse.

Whatever minimal relief I felt was short-lived.

My purse was empty.

I blew out a quiet sigh and set to work freeing my left arm and both legs.

Once I broke loose, I went to the window.

Lifting one of the blind slats, I saw an empty field with nine motorcycles. The slat I'd lifted ran along the top edge of the window rail, and I noticed there was a sash lock. Carefully, I shifted the lock and lifted up to open the window. It didn't budge.

The room had three doors. Light coming through the bottom of one of the doors told me that led out to the rest of the building. Another door was close by with no light emanating from it. I opened it and found it was an empty closet.

I hustled across the room to the last door, and found a small bathroom. I turned on the light and searched the cabinet under the sink. There was a bottle of spray cleaner alongside an aerosol can of pest spray.

Giving Rod a face-full of pest spray was tempting, but I knew better. That could backfire and would only serve as a distraction.

As I backed out of the room, the ugly shower curtain caught my attention and an idea struck me. My junior and senior year of high school, I'd been on the track team, not for running but for shot put. I pulled down the curtain, wadded it up, tucked it under my arm, and grabbed the toilet tank lid. It wasn't an ideal shape, but the concept was still the same.

The plastic chair wouldn't bust through the window, but a toilet lid most likely would. If it didn't shatter along with the glass, I could use the lid as a weapon when I ran into someone preventing me from escaping.

At the window, I set everything down, and yanked on the cord to raise the blinds. The light flooding the room made me wince. My eyes were downcast and the glint of something metal caught my attention.

My cell phone was on the ground in the corner of the room. That was strange, but I had to guess they were more interested in my handgun than my phone.

I picked up my cell and my growing relief shriveled up. The screen wasn't just cracked, it was clear they'd stomped on it. I hit the power button, and nothing.

Nevertheless, I tucked it in my back pocket and picked up the toilet lid.

Before I could swing at the window, I heard multiple bikes outside. Outside the door to this room, I heard the commotion of footsteps pounding down the hall.

Through the window, I saw four bikes pulling into the backyard. All of those riders wore Corrupt Chrome patches.

So much for busting out of here.

"What the fuck are you doing?" a man demanded.

I whirled around, but the door to the room was still closed.

A gruff voice spoke on the other side of the door. "I'm gonna bring this blonde bitch out front. She's the type our brothers from Georgia like."

I'd left the plastic chair close to the door, and I quickly dragged it back to where I'd initially been situated. Whoever came in would expect to see me sitting there, hopefully with the chair in the right spot it would take them an extra second or two to register that I wasn't where I should be.

I moved to the closet door and pressed my back against it.

The first man spoke. "You're out of your mind. That bitch is Rod's. You bring her out here, he'll fuckin' kill you."

"No, he won't. He'll be pissed he didn't think to hand her over to them."

My eyes closed as I took a deep breath. The idea of being handed over to *anybody* didn't sit well with me. My hands were getting clammy.

I opened my eyes and shifted the lid to one hand while I wiped the other one on my shorts.

Nothing about this situation was ideal, but I sent up a prayer that only one man came into the room. One on one, I might stand a chance – especially if he were unarmed. Two on one, I had to hope my guardian angel came ready to tussle and kick some ass.

"You're a moron. Rod's been jumpy as hell all week. He'll slit your fuckin' throat you even go in that room."

The man with the gruff voice let out an annoying laugh. "Even better. Someone needs to show Rod his place. You want in on this action?"

"Fuck no. And why are you carrying a gun? She's tied to a chair in there."

"The gun is to scare her. I like it when they're scared. You gonna rat me out to Rod?"

"Should, but I won't, Scaler."

Scaler? What kind of road name was that? At least I knew this asshole had a weapon.

I heard a set of footsteps move away from the room, then I heard a key being inserted into the doorknob just before country music blared from the adjacent room.

Even if the tunes were annoying, they might drown out the sounds of me fighting with this asshole.

The door opened and an overhead light came on just as I heard the door slam shut.

With the door closed, I was able to hear him speak. "Hey, Blondie— what the fuck?"

I had to wait for him to step further into the room. As luck would have it, he had his gun in his left hand. I raised the toilet tank cover high and cleaved it down on his arm. It took more effort than I expected to keep hold of the lid after impact.

He yelled in pain, dropped his gun, and reached out to punch me. My reflexes kicked in and I blocked his punch by holding the lid out like a shield. He howled at punching the porcelain. Before he could lunge at me again, I threw the lid at him. It hit him in his sternum. I didn't watch what he did next, opting to scurry to his gun instead.

I grabbed the gun from the floor, turned, and saw him rubbing his chest and stalking toward me – his brown eyes enraged. I took aim and fired the gun. Blood bloomed across his chest. The music stopped and I opened the bedroom door.

To my right the hallway led to a common room, and to my left was a back door. I sprinted left and ran out to the backyard.

That guardian angel had to be working overtime today because nobody was in the back yard. I ran past all the bikes toward a chain-link fence.

In the distance I swore that I heard more motorcycles approaching, but I kept running away from the back door.

"Stop, bitch!" someone shouted behind me, and I zigged to the right.

Then there was a loud boom that most likely came from a shotgun. The ground to my left sprayed up. I heard the sound of someone approaching from behind, but I didn't dare look over my shoulder.

"Whitney!" someone shouted from beyond the fence line.

I heard heavy breathing just before a heavy weight hit me and a man tackled me to the ground. It wasn't a typical tackle, though. He sliced at my right arm, forcing me to lose hold of the gun.

We wrestled on the ground and he got an arm around my neck. I twisted my head and bit him on his exposed bicep.

"You fuckin' bitch!" he yelled and pulled his arm away.

I used the distraction to jerk out of his hold, but three pairs of boots blocked my path.

Grimy hands reached down, hauled me to my feet, and shoved me forward so I faced Rod.

"For a cunt, you put up a decent fight," Rod snarled.

It took all my willpower not to spit at him. I heard the faint sound of sirens, but there didn't appear to be any homes around the clubhouse. My every instinct said my luck had officially run out.

Rod cocked a brow. "You got nothin' to say... Whitney?"

"No," I said with a reflexive lip curl.

Movement over his shoulder stole my attention. Five men had climbed the fence, and one of them I'd know absolutely anywhere... Mensa. Roman, Brute, Finn, and Gamble were running behind him.

Sadly, I must not have hidden my reaction because Rod and the two men at his side shifted and looked behind them.

"Stop or she's dead," Rod yelled.

Mensa and the other Riot members stopped in their tracks. The concern on their faces cut through the adrenaline and sheer bravado that had driven me.

"Let her go," Mensa yelled.

Ever so slowly, I turned to glance behind me. The man holding me didn't appear to have a weapon. I hadn't seen where the gun went when I got tackled. I faced them all before they noticed I was looking around.

"I'm not letting her go, asshole," Rod hollered.

The man behind me pushed past me and yelled at Mensa and the others. "You fuckers are trespassing. We're gonna kick your ass."

With nobody standing behind me, I wondered if this was a decent time to make a break for it. I recalled there had been nine bikes parked out here and the four others that rolled up made thirteen. My eyes darted around the area and I only counted seven other men since there were three men positioned to the side of Mensa and the Riot brothers.

Without law enforcement here, this stalemate wouldn't end well. Five Riot brothers up against thirteen or more Corrupt Chrome members... the numbers were not in our favor.

I took a step backward and none of the Corrupt Chrome members noticed.

"She wants nothing to do with you, Rod," Mensa said.

With the men focused on Mensa, I moved back another two paces.

"Not yet, but she will," Rod said, turning to look over his shoulder to where I'd been.

His eyes locked with mine, and from the crazed look in his eyes I saw my mistake. Rod hadn't tackled me. Rod hadn't picked me up off the ground. Hell, back at the strip mall, Rod wasn't the one who stuck me with a needle. He'd let other people do his dirty work. That didn't mean he *always* let other people handle his problems though.

And I hadn't noticed if he had a weapon on his person or not.

Most likely it was five seconds that Rod stared at me, but it damn sure felt like five minutes. Whether it was a bizarre law of human nature or pure instinct, the moment I decided to flee, Rod also pulled a gun.

I took off at an angle, but it wasn't enough. The sound of Mensa shouting my name... no, the gut-wrenching plea in his shout was something I'd never forget.

White-hot pain sliced along my left shoulder blade. The ground looked and felt like it had tilted. I had a fleeting thought to stretch my arms out in front of me before the ground rushed up to greet me, then my vision went dark.

CHAPTER 28

YOU GOTTA FIGHT

MENSA

"WHITNEY, DON'T!" MENSA SHOUTED, the moment he saw Rod pull a gun. The sound of his voice was raw and foreign to his ears.

He heard the gunshot, and saw Whitney's body jerk on impact. His whole world fell out from under him. She took a bullet in her upper torso. Then he saw Whitney fall to the ground and uncontrollable rage engulfed him. He felt Finn or Gamble grab for his arm, but he broke free and ran toward Rod. He yanked Rod around by his shoulder. Before Rod could take aim with the gun, Mensa was tackled to the ground.

Mensa shoved against the man and found Brute had taken him down. "Goddammit, let me up! I'm gonna kill that asshole!"

Over Brute's shoulder, Rod hovered over them and laughed. "Typical Riot pussies. Won't let another brother fight because you're all pussy-whipped by your fuckin' women."

Sirens wailed in the air.

Two of the Corrupt Chrome members shuffled their feet. One of them looked toward the back gate. "We gotta move, Rod."

Rod lifted his chin. He moved toward the bikes, passing Whitney's body along the way, and the asshole stopped and kicked her in the ribs.

Mensa struggled against Brute's dead weight. "That asshole is fucking dead!"

"Let him leave," Brute muttered.

"Let me up. Whitney needs help. Get the fuck off me!"

Brute backed off by two inches and with herculean effort, Mensa shoved him away. Within seconds, he'd scrambled to Whitney's side. He found she had a pulse, but when he rolled her over, the amount of blood on her upper chest gutted him. In a flash he shrugged out of his cut, and tore his t-shirt off to put it on the exit wound.

"You gotta fight, Blume. Don't give up, baby," he murmured.

The sound of motorcycles roaring away enraged him anew. A huge part of him wanted to chase after them and wreak vengeance, but there was no way he would leave Whitney's side. He forced himself to remain calm for her sake.

She opened her eyes. He leaned forward in time to hear her whisper, "I love you."

He stared into her eyes. "I love you, too. Now, you fight this, woman."

She closed her eyes just as two EMTs squatted next to him. Their instructions for him to let them take over barely registered, but he found himself standing back shirtless, watching them move her onto a gurney.

One of his brothers handed him his cut, and he shrugged it on. He turned to follow the EMTs, but stopped short at the sight of police officers blocking his way. "I need to go with her, she's my fiancée and she was shot by a Corrupt Chrome member."

"You aren't going anywhere," the closest officer said.

Mensa focused on the gold name plate which read, Officer Wilson. He did his best to make his tone neutral. "She could be dying."

"We have to secure this crime scene, and question your involvement in her shooting."

"I'll answer all the questions you want at the hospital."

Another officer who seemed to be in charge sidled closer. "I'll question you and get someone to take you to the hospital."

Something told Mensa that was all hot air, but he nodded, and prayed what the officer said was true.

The sergeant who questioned Mensa took his sweet time about it... most likely because he knew Mensa desperately wanted to get to the hospital for Whitney.

"I think we're done here, Mr. Ragstone. I'll have a public safety officer take you to the hospital."

No doubt that public safety officer would be none other than Phil seeing as Mensa had caught sight of the asshole meandering the scene.

Mensa held back his lip curl. "Thanks, but I'll ride."

"You didn't ask which hospital."

Mensa's lips twisted. "Merit Health's the only one equipped for that sort of gunshot wound, right?"

The sergeant gave him a dry look. "Right."

Mensa hurried out of the compound. He called Nadia on his way back to his bike.

"Mensa," she answered, panic lacing her tone.

"Go to Merit Health. Have the prospect drive your car. Whitney's been shot. I don't know much more because the cops kept me from going with her."

"Oh, dear Lord above," she whispered.

"I'll see you there, Nadia," he said when he reached his bike and ended the call.

"I'm riding with you," Finn said from his right side.

Mensa hadn't even heard him approach.

Ten minutes later Finn and Mensa pulled into the hospital parking lot. He saw the prospect parking Nadia's car. Mensa found a spot, parked his bike, and jogged over to Nadia.

She grabbed hold of Mensa's forearm and walked beside him. It was the first time she'd shown signs of her age around him.

"Wyatt should be here in a little over an hour. He got a call from the EMTs when she was brought in – guess he's her emergency contact."

Mensa looked at her askance. "That's gonna blow his cover."

She shook her head. "He told me not to worry about it."

Mensa sighed. "Whatever. I hope they'll tell you what's going on."

"How did this happen?" she asked.

Mensa covered her hand on his arm. "I'll tell you right after we know how she's doing."

"Did they get the shooter?" Nadia asked as they went through the sliding doors.

"Not yet," Mensa muttered. What he didn't say was that he hoped they didn't because he wanted to rip Rod apart, limb from limb.

There would be time for that. In the meantime, he would strategize the best way to make Rod suffer.

The nurse behind the counter checked Nadia's ID, typed on her computer, and looked up at them. "She's in surgery right now. I don't have any idea how long that will take."

She directed them to the appropriate waiting room.

Mensa guided Nadia to a chair and she patted the seat next to her. "Now you tell me what happened, Kenneth."

Something about her use of his first name reminded him of how Whitney said it and he sat. Always a believer in ripping off the bandage, he told her what happened as fast as he could.

"And that fellow got away?" she asked.

He scoffed. "He's no fellow, he's pure scum. Assholes like him never stick around when cops are coming."

"Why did he want her?"

Mensa shrugged a shoulder. "Why does any lunatic fixate on a gorgeous woman?"

Nadia shook her head. "It doesn't make sense to me."

"The night her car was stolen, Rod interrupted her asking me about the security feeds at Twisted Talons. He'd apparently talked to her once at Dontrell's restaurant because he claimed to remember her car. I'm not sure I buy that, but he offered to help her find the car. She told him she wanted the cops to handle it."

"That makes sense," Nadia muttered.

Mensa nodded. "An asshole like Rod doesn't deal well with getting rejected. Finding out later that she's with me didn't help either."

"Don't blame yourself, now."

Mensa tipped his head side to side. "Hard not to, Nadia. I made a big deal about how she was my woman thinking that would get through to an asshole like him. All he did was point out she wasn't wearing a cut, and he'd recognize her as mine if she had a property patch. My guess is that upped the ante for him. Get the girl and fuck with me all at the same time."

She patted his arm. "Still not your fault."

He turned his face to hers. "At a minimum, I should have had her at the clubhouse with me. Or I should have had Riley, or someone go to your shop and be with her."

"Then why the hell didn't you?" Wyatt demanded from the entrance to the waiting room.

"This is no time for that question or that tone, Wyatt," Nadia said.

Wyatt's hard stare softened when he turned his gaze to Nadia. "Have they said how she's doing?"

Nadia stood. "She's in surgery. That's all we know so far. Come give me a hug. Did you call your parents? I should have done that by now."

While they hugged, Riley bustled into the waiting room. "Oh, my God, Mensa! I came as quick as I could. How is she doing?"

He stood, went to Riley, and gave her a hug. "In surgery. No idea when they'll be done," he murmured against the top of her hair.

She pulled back from his hold and rested her hands on his shoulders. "And you saw it happen?"

"Why didn't you stop it from happening?" Wyatt bit out through clenched teeth from the sound of it.

"Wyatt, I'm not gonna tell you again. That isn't going to help. He's already spoken to the police," Nadia said.

"Aunt Nadia, if he's as serious about her as she is about him, then he's gonna have to get used to me questioning him."

Mensa turned around to face Wyatt, but he and Nadia were in a stare-down.

Nadia's lips pursed. "Not at a time like this, he won't."

Mensa hated it when family members argued with one another. "If I could have taken that bullet, I would have."

Wyatt turned back to Mensa. "Sure, you would have. Getting shot hurts like hell."

"Strange. The surgeons told me after I got stabbed that knives are worse, but frankly, it doesn't fuckin' matter what hurts more. You're aunt is right, this isn't the time or place, and I'd rather spare Nadia from hearing this, but I've never been this goddamned worried about anyone before in my life. I saw her body jerk when she took the hit. My whole world fell out from under me in that moment."

"I almost believe you."

"Don't give a fuck whether you do or not. She has to pull through. If she doesn't, I'll be in jail because I'll make it my mission—"

Wyatt held up a hand. "Don't finish that. I'm an FBI agent, and I'll take action if you make a threat to kill someone in front of me."

Mensa dipped his chin. "There wasn't a damned thing I could do to keep that asswipe from shooting her. Not without having three or more Corrupt Chrome members shoot at her instead."

"He's right. Two other members had guns out when she took off, and there were two others at the edge of their clubhouse," Roman said from behind Mensa.

"Rod's known for demanding he gets the first shot," Cynic muttered from Mensa's other side.

"Christ, is your whole club here?" Wyatt asked.

Mensa looked over his shoulder to see Roman, Finn, Gamble, Cynic, Har, and Brute. He nodded at them, and slowly turned back to Wyatt. "Almost. The others are probably taking care of business at Twisted Talons."

Har, Brute, Roman, and Cynic moved to one side of the waiting room, while Finn and Gamble joined Riley, who sat close to Nadia.

Wyatt glanced past him and started forward when a man said, "Blume family."

Nadia stood and brought Riley with her, since she had a firm grip on Riley's hand.

Once Nadia was closer, the doctor introduced himself. "Ms. Blume is out of surgery. She's in serious but stable condition. The bullet missed her lung, but did nick her collar bone. We were able to remove the bone fragments. She's going to be in a lot of pain, and her range of motion will be very limited."

Mensa unclenched his jaw and pain flooded his tongue – he hadn't noticed he'd been biting it.

"Will she get that range of motion back?" Wyatt asked.

The doctor pressed his lips together as he deliberated it. "That's going to depend. She will definitely be in physical therapy for at least six weeks to rehabilitate it. The damage was done to her left side; if she's left-handed that—"

"She isn't," Mensa and Wyatt said at the same time.

The doctor's eyes darted between them. "That's good, but she will still be challenged with some activities. If she heals well, and is diligent about her therapy, I imagine she'll have a decent range of motion again."

"What about blood loss? Did she need a transfusion? There was a lot of blood coming from that wound," Mensa said.

"We gave her a transfusion. Now that we've stitched up the wound, as long as she doesn't get an infection, she should be fine."

"Can we see her?" Nadia asked.

The doctor met Nadia's gaze. "She's still under anesthesia and is in the Intensive Care unit for tonight – in case things deteriorate – even though they shouldn't. Family can see her, but only one at a time. I'll get a nurse to lead you back."

As soon as the doctor was out of ear shot, Wyatt looked at Mensa. "You can go now."

"Don't be a jackass," Riley chided.

Mensa fought laughing because that was very close to what he was going to say.

Wyatt arched his brows at Riley. "This doesn't concern you."

"Whitney was in her wedding, so don't you dare say it doesn't concern her. Furthermore, I was ready to say the same thing. Nobody's leaving, Wyatt. Your sister wouldn't want that. Keep this up, I'll have you tossed out of here," Nadia said.

"Aunt Nadia—"

She held a hand up. "Nope. You sit down and say a prayer. We have a lot to be thankful for from the sound of it, and I'm not gonna have you telling the man Whitney loves that he can leave. Not only does it make me angry, you know good and darned well it would infuriate your sister. Now, knock it off."

A nurse turned the corner, her eyes zeroing in on Nadia. "Are you Ms. Blume's mother?"

Nadia stepped forward. "I'm her aunt. Her mother will be here as soon as her flight lands."

The nurse nodded. "Very good. Come with me."

Mensa felt Wyatt staring at him, and he met the man's gaze.

"I'll tell you what I told her. She's too good for you. She can do better, and if I get half a chance, I'm gonna make certain she sees that."

Riley crossed her arms. "Have *you* seen how happy she is with him? Hell, before they got together, did you see the way each of them looked at the other when they *thought* nobody else was watching? Seriously. Everyone of us knew they were meant for each other. Give Whitney a chance to be happy with someone who isn't using her for once."

"Riley," Mensa muttered.

She dropped her hands to her hips. "Oh, no. I'm not breaking the girl code right now, though I'm pretty close. I knew the two of you were meant to be, but Finn wouldn't let me say anything. All that 'it's not your business' stuff that he says."

She'd dropped her voice an octave to imitate Finn, and Mensa would have laughed, except this wasn't the time or place.

Wyatt kept quiet for a moment. "Did *she* tell you her last boyfriend was using her?"

Riley shot a coy grin at Wyatt. "That's part of the girl-code I won't break."

"He wasn't using her."

Riley arched a brow. "He didn't help her, either, and that's shitty enough on its own."

Finn came to Riley's side and slung an arm around her shoulders. "Babe, let's go get some coffee for everybody."

Wyatt watched them walk away. "I'm surprised you have a woman who's so vocal on your behalf."

"She's my cousin, and everything she said is true. It'd be nice if you can open your mind and give me a chance to prove myself."

At five-fifteen, a nurse led Mensa into the ICU department. Nadia and Wyatt had already visited, and Mensa's time was limited to forty-five minutes because visiting hours for the ICU ended at six. He couldn't decide what alarmed him more: how pale her skin was or how frail she appeared.

"Is... this normal?" he croaked out.

The nurse tinkered with a monitor at Whitney's bedside. "I'm sorry, is what normal?"

"Her being so pale. The doctor said she had a transfusion."

With a patient smile, the nurse nodded. "Yes, sir. It's normal, so don't let it worry you. She's on the mend, even if it doesn't look that way to you."

Mensa nodded. "This will sound crazy, but with this kind of injury... is there anything she won't be able to lift?"

The nurse chuckled. "Well, I don't see her doing any weight-lifting competitions in the next year, but if she does what the doctors tell her, I don't really think so. Is there something specific you had in mind?"

"A baby? Really, more like a toddler or small child?"

A tender look stole over the nurse's face. "Yeah. If her recovery goes well, she should be able to pick up your children in a few months. I'll leave you alone. You don't have much time before I have to kick you out."

Mensa didn't get a chance to correct her, but the image of their children flitted through his mind. Whitney holding a little boy or a little girl with dark, wavy hair, but Whitney's striking blue eyes gave him something to hope for...something he knew he wanted the same way he knew he wanted to be part of the Riot.

He positioned the wheeled-stool close to the bed, perched his ass on it, and grabbed Whitney's hand. "You gotta get better, Blume. I love you, and I can't wait to marry you and get you pregnant – and I don't care which order that happens in either."

The bedside monitor maintained a steady rhythm of her heartbeat.

"Your brother really doesn't fuckin' like me. Gonna need you to help me out with that, babe," he murmured.

Beep. Beep. Beep.

He'd never been good at talking to himself, which surprised many people since he was an only child. Seemed everyone expected him to talk to himself all the time. He might be good with his own company, but he didn't like talking without any response from the person he was talking to.

"Love you so much, Whit. They're gonna kick me out of here soon, otherwise I wouldn't leave your side... no matter how much it would bug your twin."

He swallowed down a chuckle and muttered, "Then again, bugging Wyatt would only make it that much better."

The rhythmic beeping shifted ever so slightly.

A small smile curled his lips. He picked up her hand and kissed the back of it. "Sounds like I get to meet your parents tomorrow. I really hope you're awake when that happens, baby."

A different nurse slid the door to Whitney's room open and ducked her head inside. "I'm sorry, sir. You're going to need to head out now."

He nodded to the nurse, rose, and pressed his lips to Whitney's forehead.

⸻

The door to the ICU slammed behind him. Most of his Riot brothers had left when he was finally led back to see Whitney, but Finn and Riley had told him they'd stick around.

He wandered back to the waiting room and saw them sitting on either side of Nadia. Each of them held one of her hands. Their heads were bowed, and Mensa suspected they were praying.

Whether they were done praying or they heard him approaching, they lifted their heads.

"Sorry to interrupt. Nadia, do you need a ride home?"

She gave him a feeble smile. "Far from it, Mensa. Sandy's gonna be here in ten minutes to take me home. I had these two stick around because..." Nadia trailed off, emotion making her voice sound gravelly.

Almost as if she were a game-show host, Riley swung her arm out toward the windows. "It's drizzling out there. In light of everything that's happened today, she would like you to drive my car home and leave your bike here."

Mensa cocked his head to the side a touch. "What about you? How are you getting home?"

Riley grinned. "Back of Finn's bike, of course."

Mensa locked eyes with Nadia. "Nothing's gonna happen to me."

Fire lit behind Nadia's eyes. "The man I loved said the same damned thing to me on a night very similar to this one." Her head tilted just a touch. "And he was wrong because the worst possible thing happened to him and I've never gotten over it. I'll be damned if I don't prevent that for my Whitney."

Mensa swallowed against the emotion building in his throat. He hadn't thought much about Brink's accident since it happened. Hell, he'd only just earned his patch about three months before that awful night.

Mensa ran his hand through his hair and nodded. "All right, Nadia. I'll drive Riley's car since that will make you feel better."

"It will. Thank you."

CHAPTER 29

RAVAGED

WHITNEY

MOST OF THE TIME, I tended to be a light sleeper. Whenever I got sick, though, it took effort for me to wake up. The unexpected sound of my mom's voice had the power to cut through any sleep fog.

"Oh, I think she's coming around," Mom said.

I forced my eyes open against the bright light. "Mom?"

"Yes, honey. The doctor said you should wake up any minute, and he was right."

I scanned the room. My dad sat in a chair on the other side of my bed. "Hey, Dad."

He leaned forward and grabbed my hand. "Hey, sweetheart. This is quite a scare."

"Sorry about that," I croaked.

Mom handed me a cup of ice. "I knew I should have called you last week. You haven't been calling like you used to, but I know you're a busy young woman."

"Margo," Dad drawled.

"What, David? I don't know who to believe, Wyatt or Nadia. Obviously, I need to hear about her new man from her."

Dad's face set with an expression I hadn't seen since I snuck out of the house with my high school boyfriend. I had no doubt Dad had gotten an earful from Wyatt, but he usually listened to me. Hard to say if that would be the case this time. Catching a last-minute flight because I'd been shot probably skewed his views quite a bit.

"As far as I'm concerned, there isn't much I need to hear if he's the reason you were in ICU."

I looked at Dad. "It isn't his fault, Dad. He did everything he could to keep me safe."

We went into a stare-down.

Finally, Dad glanced at Mom. "I agree with Wyatt, her new man should be her old man."

I pressed my lips together to fight against my anger. My energy had been drained and I lost that fight.

"Dad," I said, waiting for his full attention. Once I had it, I continued. "You haven't even met him. He didn't shoot me, someone else did. Weren't you the one who told me to have an open mind? Weren't you the man who taught me that there's always two sides to every story? Now you won't wait to hear me out? Or even meet the man I love?"

"Love?" Mom asked.

My eyes met hers. "It's crazy. It's fast, but he's the one, Mom."

A knock came at the door and I saw Aunt Nadia there. She grinned at me. "Sorry to interrupt, but Whitney, I'm so thrilled to see you awake." She bustled over to Mom and gave her a hug, then did the same with dad and he offered her his seat. She glanced at me. "I couldn't help but overhear you, and you're wrong. It hasn't been that fast with Mensa. The two of you danced around each other for over a year."

Mom turned her puzzled expression from Aunt Nadia to me. "You never told me about a man you were dancing around last year. The only man you mentioned was the one you wanted to see get arrested."

I gave her a small smile. "That's the one."

"Are you having a nervous breakdown, Whitney?" Dad asked.

"William!" Mom cried.

"She resigns from a very good job, moves out of her place in Jackson, and is in love with a biker, who I'm not convinced didn't play a role in her getting shot in the chest. On top of that, this man is someone she once wanted to have arrested. Any one of those decisions sounds like a cry for help, and all of them together sound like she needs an intervention."

"I don't need help or an intervention. And I got shot in my shoulder, not my chest, Dad," I corrected.

His eyes widened with his 'Dad stare.' "A bullet came out through your *chest*. That's what the nurse told us."

I put a hand to my head because it felt like I had a migraine forming. "Dad, I love you, but I'm tired. If you can't have an open mind about someone you haven't even met, then I think you should head back to Wyatt's."

Dad sighed. "Sweetheart, I love you so much and I care about you far more than you'll ever know."

Aunt Nadia grabbed my hand. "When are they gonna let you outta this joint? Has anyone said?"

"She got shot, Nadia," Mom said.

Nadia glanced up at Mom. "You don't have to remind me, Margo. Good lord, the waiting took five years off my life, and I don't have five years I can lose."

"Aunt Nadia," I whispered.

She gave me a sly grin. "I'm joking... sort of, as you say. When do they start you on the therapy? They mentioned that yesterday, that you'd need help to get your full range of motion back."

"I don't know. I'm guessing it will be later."

Nadia widened her eyes. "You do all of it, you hear me."

I raised my chin. "I'll do my best. It's going to take a lot of orders to cover my medical bills."

She patted my hand. "Don't you worry about that. I'll help you out with whatever you need. Focus on getting better. I gotta get back to the shop."

"Bye, Aunt Nadia."

She stood, when she was half way to the door, she stopped. "Ooh! Look who's here. How's it shakin', Mensa?"

I looked to the door with a big smile on my face, but it dimmed when I saw how ravaged he looked.

He raced into the room, pausing long enough to squeeze Nadia's shoulders, then he came around the bed and propped his hip on it before sliding both hands along my jawline holding my face still.

His eyes closed as if he were saying a prayer, then he dropped his forehead to mine. "I love you, Whitney."

"Love you too, genius."

He pulled his head back, a mischievous grin on his face. "Thank fuck you're all right."

"You must be Whitney's new man. I'm Margo," Mom said, reaching a hand across to him.

Mensa stood and went through introductions with my parents. To my relief, Dad didn't seem to give him a hard time, though I noticed a muscle in his jaw ticked.

An awkward silence sat heavy in the room.

Dad's blue eyes were cold as they slid between me and Mensa. "How can you love someone you had every intention of arresting?" He tipped his head toward Mensa. "And you – if you wanted her gone every time you saw her, which is what I heard from her brother about your interactions – what changed? How are you two suddenly so serious?"

I'd never been so tired before, which had to be why I didn't know I could be this angry and tired at the same time.

Using my legs, I gingerly pushed myself higher up on the bed. "Dad! What kind of question is that? Can't you start with what he does for a living? How he got into motorcycles? Something like that?"

Dad shook his head. "Why go through small talk when what I care about is you? If he loves you and this lasts, I'll have plenty of time to find out what he does."

I sighed.

Mensa twisted his hands up. "What changed was tackling her to the ground and getting her away from danger when Rod started shooting at a mutual friend of ours. Then he shot at us, which forced us to leave."

Dad scratched his upper lip. "It took someone shooting at my girl for you to realize you were interested in her?"

I caught myself before I rolled my eyes. "There's a little more to it, Dad."

Mensa shrugged a shoulder. "Your son chasing us away from the scene to another town over, making us think there was a heightened threat, didn't help. Or really, it forced us together."

Dad shifted his gaze from Mensa to me, and I wanted to shrink under the scrutiny, but it hit me that Dad had part of our story wrong. "I never really hated him, Dad, and once I got to know him, things—"

Aunt Nadia lurked near the doorway. "For heaven's sake, Bill, for some of us when it happens it happens."

Dad shot Aunt Nadia a dry look, then focused on Mensa again. "If you're so protective of her, how'd she get shot yesterday?"

I grabbed Mensa's hand. "Don't answer that. This isn't the time, and I meant what I said, Dad, if you can't have an open mind, go back to Wyatt's."

Mensa stared at me and I couldn't figure out what was working in his eyes. He looked like he was trying not to smile, but the way things were going for me, maybe he was trying not to patronize me. After a beat, he dipped his chin. "Woman, I'm going to answer him because if we have a daughter, one day I'll be asking questions like that."

"You're pregnant?" Mom asked.

Mensa and I looked at her and said, "No."

"That's good to know," Mom muttered.

Mensa turned to Dad. "She got shot because I didn't know she'd have to leave Hard Pressed before noon. The earliest we could have someone watching her was twelve o'clock, and on top of that, she'd gone to the UPS Store the day before. It seemed highly unlikely Rod would find her, shipping packages."

"Then why did he?" Dad asked.

A memory hit me, and I recalled the words of the biker who jabbed me with the needle. *Never thought your tracking device would pay off, Rod.*

I caught Dad's gaze. "Nobody knew there was a tracking device in my purse, Dad. Mensa especially wouldn't have known that, Dad."

Mensa pulled my hand on to his lap and gave it a squeeze. "It's okay, Blume," he whispered.

"It isn't, Mensa. None of this is your fault or the prospect's or anyone else's, but Rod's."

Mensa widened his eyes at me. "The prospect didn't do much right by you, Whitney."

"Who's 'we'?" Dad asked.

"What do you mean?" Mensa asked.

"You said, 'the earliest we could have someone watching her was twelve o'clock,' I'd like to know who 'we' is."

A sideways smile twisted Mensa's lips, and it drew my attention to his sexy beard. "'We' is the Riot MC brotherhood. They know that even though I haven't put a cut on her, I've claimed her. And that means, every one of my brothers will sacrifice themselves for her."

I scoffed. "That's crazy. The police are the—"

Mensa whipped his gaze back to me. "The police keep the order out there, but the lawyers and judges – hell, my uncle was a prime example – they fuck up the order using the law, of all things. There are cracks in the system and my Riot family doesn't fall through those cracks, *because* we protect what's ours."

Dad sighed and stepped forward. "Your mother and I will be back later."

"When he's not here, isn't that what you mean?" Aunt Nadia asked.

"Nadia," Dad started.

"Oh, no, Bill. Don't you 'Nadia' me. She's asked you twice to open your mind to her man. It's the least you can do, and the best way to do that is to stick around. Not run away because you don't like what he's saying."

After a long, slow blink, Dad looked at Aunt Nadia. "I also need to cool down."

Mom leaned closer to me. "Well, I'm staying, so you can bring me an iced coffee when you've cooled off."

"Margo—" Dad started.

"No. I'm going to chat with Whitney and her friend."

Dad shook his head. "I'll be back."

"I'll walk with you, Bill," Aunt Nadia said.

"Your brothers sound very protective," Mom said.

Mensa moved off the bed and sat in the seat on my left. "We are. None of us likes when women are threatened."

"How long are you and Dad in town?" I asked.

"Your Dad's heading back in a few days. My ticket is open-ended, since I have no idea how much help you're going to need."

I nodded. "That's a good point. I don't want to cause problems for Aunt Nadia."

Mensa cleared his throat, leaning forward with his forearms resting on his knees. "Whit, you won't need her help."

I widened my eyes at him. "I'm not going to be able to shower or get dressed on my own for a while."

He tilted his gaze down to his boots, then raised his head. "I know, woman. You won't need *her* help."

"Why not?" I asked.

He cocked his head to the side. "Did they give you drugs recently? *I'll* be around to help you."

Mom crossed her legs. "That seems like an imposition. Especially since I can stick around for her."

"It isn't an imposition, Mrs. Blume. This is serious, and I'm not leaving her side when she gets released."

"You sound rather dedicated to her," Mom said.

"I am."

Mom stared at him.

Mensa gave her a boyish grin. "Don't worry. I'll prove to you how serious I am."

Mom nodded. "I don't doubt it. I'll talk to Bill. He's protective of her, and getting that call from Wyatt that our girl had been shot... it threw us, since we thought we didn't have to worry about that any more."

CHAPTER 30

IT'S A START

MENSA

MENSA STRODE OUT TO the hospital parking lot. He pulled his helmet over his head, and his phone rang.

He took the call, only to be interrupted mid-answer by Dontrell.

"What the hell is this I hear? Houston got shot on your watch! Is she okay?"

Mensa willed himself to stay calm because it was good for Whitney to have someone who cared about her like that. "Take it down a notch, Dontrell. How'd you find out?"

"Who cares how I found out?"

Mensa stayed focused. "Was it your son? Or Scrap? Or did Rod come in to tell you himself?"

"He won't last two seconds if he comes around here—"

"Don't say shit like that. You never know who might hear you."

"Like I give a damn," Dontrell muttered.

"Why did you call me?"

"To find out about Whitney."

Mensa gave him a quick summary of what happened and how Whitney was doing.

"Okay. That's a relief. What are you doing about that asshole?"

He shook his head. "No offense, D, but I wouldn't tell you if I knew."

Dontrell's tone went stern. "I want to help you."

"I appreciate that, but you don't need to give the cops another reason to question you."

Dontrell sighed. "Fine. I'm making a Greek combo plate for her. Come get it, so I don't have to leave. The assistant manager here is six months pregnant and I'm not leaving her alone."

"I'll be there in twenty minutes."

Half-way to DeeLight's, Mensa was reminded of how much he despised rush hour traffic. Cars wove in and out of the lanes, and it didn't matter how loud his pipes were, those distracted drivers rarely knew he was riding next to them.

He pulled into the Division Street location of DeeLight's, and parked his bike near the entrance. As he unfastened his helmet, he heard approaching sirens from his left. The restaurant wasn't far from a busy intersection.

He went inside the restaurant, and from the front window, he watched a motorcycle run a red light, turning onto Division Street, narrowly avoiding the on-coming traffic.

The motorcyclist picked up some speed, but then slowed to turn right into DeeLight's.

"Shit," Mensa whispered.

The last thing Dontrell needed was some speed-demon trying to hide out in his parking lot.

When the rider pulled to a halt, Mensa saw the Corrupt Chrome MC patch. He reached for his gun, but realized he didn't have it on him. He'd taken it off and locked it in his saddlebag to go into the hospital to see Whitney. He hadn't expected to need it for a simple food pick-up.

The sirens grew louder, and Mensa saw there were two police cruisers approaching.

"I'm startin' to think you bring the trouble with you," Dontrell said from beside him.

"Thinkin' that works both ways, D," Mensa muttered, keeping his eye on the rider who had swung a leg off his bike, but hadn't turned around.

For a moment, Mensa wondered if it was Whitney's brother. The rider took off their helmet, turned around, and Mensa recognized Rod reaching for his weapon.

The cruisers sped into the parking lot, both at angles to block Rod.

"We need to move," Mensa said.

Dontrell turned and led the way to the counter. He told two men sitting on the far side of the dining room to move closer to the counter.

Mensa backed away slowly. As he drew farther away from the windows, he saw Rod raise his gun and point it at the police cruiser closest to him.

The officers were out of their cruisers and crouched with their guns drawn.

Even from such a distance, Rod's resigned look couldn't be missed.

One of the cops yelled at Rod to drop his weapon. Mensa couldn't put his finger on it, but when Rod turned his head toward the street, he got the feeling Rod expected something – no, expected some*one* – to show up.

The officer yelled again at Rod, and rather than focus on the cops, Rod stared at the restaurant windows. He still had the gun raised, and Mensa shifted farther backward then crouched. The moment the shot rang out, two other shots followed.

A large windowpane shattered. Shards of glass scattered everywhere inside the dining area. Mensa rose and saw two officers crowded around the area where Rod had been standing.

Two more Biloxi PD cars showed up, blocking the parking lot entry. A minute later, an ambulance arrived.

Mensa wandered to the counter. "I don't think Whitney's getting that combo plate any time soon."

"What are you doin' here?" Wyatt asked when Mensa came out of DeeLight's.

Mensa lifted a cellophane bag with Whitney's food. "Dontrell heard about your sister and he insisted I get a to-go order for Whitney... only

I got stuck inside the restaurant when Rod pulled into the parking lot." Mensa looked Wyatt up and down and shrugged a shoulder. "I'd ask what you're doing here, but obviously your assignment has wrapped up."

Wyatt thumbed his Kevlar vest with the FBI patch across the chest. "This tends to give it away, if the arrest warrant doesn't first. While we served the arrest warrant, Rod managed to bolt. We chased him, but I have no idea why he stopped here."

Mensa tipped his head toward the ambulance. "Are they taking him to Merit?"

Wyatt nodded once. "He's been officially arrested, so he'll be under guard and cuffed to the bed once he's out of surgery."

Mensa ground his molars together.

Wyatt's lips tipped up. "Yeah, I'm not thrilled about that since Whitney's there, but I've let people know he's a security risk."

"Surprised you're still here. Seems Biloxi PD has this under control."

Wyatt nodded toward the restaurant. "I have to talk to Dontrell. There's enough evidence now, that he's no longer a person of interest in the arson investigation."

"That's good news. I won't keep you."

Wyatt stared at him for a long moment, then he lifted his chin and went inside the restaurant.

Mensa loaded the bag into a saddlebag, put on his helmet, and went back to the hospital.

Twenty minutes later, Mensa stopped in the middle of the hospital corridor at the sound of Whitney's laughter. He'd made her laugh before, but this... it was different. Unadulterated, no holds barred.

No matter how much he knew not to do it, he edged closer to the room and eavesdropped.

"Dad, it's not as bad as all that."

"No, it's worse because this guy's got your mother duped, too," William said.

"Are you serious? If you think I can be duped, then you've got another think coming, bub," Margo said.

"Margo, you know what I'm getting at."

Margo's tone became stern. "No. I know that you left when you should have stayed and tried to get to know him. How does your favorite saying go? A mind is like a parachute... it only works if it's open."

"My mind is open. The problem is that not too long ago she wanted nothing to do with him. Now she's talking about how he can take care of her getting in and out of the shower."

"Life's funny that way, Dad. Not to mention, you and Mom were pretty similar."

"Your mother never wanted to arrest me."

"Maybe not, but you've told me and Wyatt that you couldn't stand each other for the longest time. Then all of a sudden you didn't. I never did find out what changed, but at this point, I don't want to know."

A nurse approached from the opposite end of the corridor. Mensa rustled the bag and trudged into the room with a brief knock on the door. "I hope you haven't eaten yet, Whit. Dontrell wanted me to deliver this to you."

Whitney smiled at him, but her eyes lit up when she noticed the bag. "Ooh, is that my favorite combo?"

Mensa nodded. "Yeah. Hopefully it's still hot."

Whitney shook her head. "Hot tabbouleh doesn't sound that great, honey."

"Do you eat that stuff?" William asked, his eyes intent on Mensa.

Mensa huffed out a silent chuckle. "It's not my go-to, but I tried it for her. I'm more of a gyro man."

Margo laughed. "That's what Bill said the first time she brought it home."

Mensa moved the over-the-bed table so Whitney could reach it, and put the to-go container on it and opened it.

"I could do that," Whitney said.

He cocked his head. "It won't bother your stitches? Have you even started therapy?"

Margo hung her head for a beat, then grinned at Mensa. "She had a brief therapy session about an hour ago."

"Didn't seem to do much," William muttered.

"You have to crawl before you can walk, Dad."

Mensa ran a hand through his hair. "Have they said when you might be discharged?"

Whitney narrowed her eyes on him. "No. Why?"

Mensa leaned a hip on the bed. "Rod got shot today outside DeeLight's. Cops were chasing him across town, and for some damned reason he led them to Dontrell's restaurant."

William glared at Mensa. "That's the scumbag who abducted her, isn't it?"

Mensa nodded. "Yeah, and Wyatt notified people about that."

Whitney shook her head. "How do you know that?"

"Your brother showed up at the scene and spoke to me briefly before I left."

"You were there when it happened?" Whitney asked.

Mensa hadn't thought it possible with all the blood Whitney had lost, but her skin had paled.

He dipped his chin. "I was inside the restaurant. There's no way Rod knew that when he pulled into the parking lot. It seemed like he thought he could hide there or something, but the cops had been too close for him to lose them."

"Hard to say what his reason was for that, but I don't think he had any rational thoughts at that point," Wyatt said, coming into the room and around to the other side of Whitney's bed.

Mensa stood to give them some space.

Margo grabbed Mensa's hand. "You aren't going anywhere. Both of them need to get to know you better. This isn't the ideal setting, but it's a start."

Mensa arched a brow. "I can see where Whitney gets it."

"Gets what?" Margo asked.

"Her convincing nature."

To his surprise, everyone in the room erupted into laughter.

CHAPTER 31

GONNA LAST

WHITNEY

AFTER FORTY-FIVE MINUTES, WYATT took my parents back to his place. Dad seemed to be softening toward Mensa, but I wasn't getting my hopes up yet. If Wyatt still had reservations about Mensa (and being in law enforcement, he had reservations about *everyone*), then Dad would likely withhold any approval for a while.

Not that his approval mattered, but I loved my family and I wanted Mensa to feel accepted.

"Are you going to finish your food?" Mensa asked.

I shook my head. "My appetite hasn't been normal lately. You can eat it."

"I'll pass. Are you tired? Do you want me to leave?"

"Yes. No. I mean, I'm tired, but I want you to stick around – unless you have somewhere to be."

He grabbed my hand, leaned over, and kissed my cheek. "Whitney, I'll be here until they kick me out, if that's what you want. Only thing I need to do is call Har. I'd rather not text him about what went down today."

I caught movement at the door and Riley bustled inside. "I'm so sorry it took me so long to come visit today! It's been non-stop work at Har's shop and normally I have that place running on auto-pilot."

Mensa stood. "I'm gonna let you two chat and make a phone call."

Riley gave Mensa a knowing look. "If it's about Rod getting arrested, he already knows."

"Thanks, but I'm gonna call him anyway," Mensa said after a short nod.

Once he was gone, Riley sat in the chair next to my bed and leaned closer. "Now that he's gone, how are you really feeling? I can't even imagine how much pain you must be in."

I shrugged my good shoulder. "The pain meds they're giving me are working really well, though I'm probably due for another round."

She looked around the room as if someone might be spying. "I'm sorry – well, not really – but I ran my mouth in front of your brother while you were in the ICU yesterday."

"What do you mean?" I asked.

An abashed look stole over Riley's face. "Your brother was telling Mensa that you were too good for him. I got offended and prattled on about how he should have seen the two of you acting like you weren't interested in each other."

I dipped my chin, felt a pang of pain and straightened. "Well, we weren't, Riley."

Riley tilted her head. "Right. You can keep telling yourself that, but you're wrong."

Mensa stepped back into the room. "Why are you telling her she's wrong?"

"Don't be so protective, cousin. She was trying to say you two weren't pining after each other for so long."

Something about the big eyes, his arched brows, and the skeptical set to his bearded lips made me giggle.

"Neither of us pined for the other," Mensa muttered.

"Whatever you say," Riley said.

Mensa sat on the other side of the bed, but kept his eyes pinned on Riley. "Don't you have somewhere else to be?"

She stood, stooped over, then thought better of it and gave my hand a squeeze. "I'd hug you, but that's probably not a great idea right now. I'm so freaking glad you survived. If you aren't out by tomorrow, I'm bringing my laptop and we'll watch *Zoolander*."

I grimaced. "Ugh. Anything but that."

She grinned. "One day, Whitney, you'll see the light."

"Won't be a runway light," I said, tipping my head to the side and immediately hissed with pain.

Mensa's body stiffened. "Are you all right? You need the nurse?"

I straightened and shook my head tentatively. "No. It's fine. I think I'm due for another dose of pain killers. They'll be in—"

Mensa looked at Riley. "Go get the nurse."

Riley scurried out of the room.

"Honey," I said, in a low voice.

He turned to me. "No. You aren't going to be in pain, Whit. You've been through enough damned pain."

Those brown eyes said it all, and they said he felt deeply for me. "I'm not the only one who's been in pain."

He closed his eyes and shook his head. "Doesn't matter, Whit." He opened his eyes. "The sight of you taking that bullet is ingrained in my brain. I've been stabbed and it hurts like fuck. I can't even imagine the pain of a bullet tearing through you. If your meds are wearing off, then you're getting more pain medication."

The nurse came into the room. "I hear your pain is coming back."

"Yes, but if it's too soon—"

She shook her head. "Don't worry about that. Nobody earns a gold medal for enduring extra pain. Let's get you taken care of."

My nurse hadn't messed around. She'd brought me a fast-acting pain medication, that came with the side-effect of knocking me out.

I woke from a very bizarre dream and saw Mensa conked out to my left, but felt my someone holding my hand on my right.

"Hey," Wyatt whispered. "Didn't think you'd wake up until morning."

"What time is it?"

"Eleven-thirty."

"Surprised they haven't kicked either of you out."

Wyatt shot me a half-hearted smile. "It helps when you know some people."

"I'm gonna be okay," I murmured.

"Yeah," he whispered.

The silence between us felt unusual and heavy. "I know I shouldn't ask this, but what's happening with Rod? Was he threatening Donny's son? And did they figure out which Corrupt Chrome member burned down the restaurant?"

"Slow down, Whit," he whispered.

I grinned. "What can I say? I'm curious."

He nodded. "Rod is under arrest, and will be taken for processing once he's discharged. He threatened to hurt Demetrius Barlow according to what I gathered. I shouldn't share this with you, so you better keep it to yourself. As for the restaurant, the security footage from Twisted Talons pointed to three members of Corrupt Chrome. It's being reported in the press, that at least one of them confessed to the fire at DeeLight's. Your friend isn't a person of interest any more."

"Thank goodness," I breathed.

"Your purse was recovered at the scene. It's in evidence."

Between the drugs and the late hour, his words confused me. "Okay. Why are you telling me this?"

"There was a tracking device in your big-ass bag."

"It's a Boho bag," I said reflexively.

"Whatever. That's how he knew you were at the UPS store. This isn't the time, but in the morning, think back. Did you have that bag when he cornered you at the mall? That's good information to have."

"I did, but nothing was taken from my apartment after the break-in." I paused. "In fact, Mensa thought something might have been planted – the tracking device could be it. I switch purses for karaoke night, and I didn't switch back until the day I went to the mall. The same day Rod showed up again."

Wyatt nodded. "I'll pass that along."

"Are you headed back to Jackson?" I asked.

"In a couple days. Got some reports to finish." He tipped his head toward Mensa. "Are you really sure about him?"

I gave his hand a squeeze. "Yes, very. When I found myself taped to a chair, I didn't know what was going to happen next. My life didn't exactly flash before my eyes, but there are a ton of things I *haven't* done yet." I tipped my head toward Mensa. "He's the one for me, and he wants the same thing."

"Exact same number of kids?"

I stared at Wyatt for a beat. "You know that isn't something anyone can plan right down to the exact number. He wants a family. We're around the same age, and I really love it here. There are still some things I have to learn about Aunt Nadia's business, but at a minimum I can keep that going, and I believe I can make it grow."

Wyatt stared past me at Mensa. "He could get arrested at any time."

I resisted tilting my head since that caused me pain earlier. "If he breaks the law, you're right. But I've yet to see him do anything like that. I haven't seen any of the Riot brothers do that."

Wyatt leaned forward. "Thought he held Rod at knife-point in front of you?"

I twisted my lips and slid my eyes to the side for a beat. "You got me there, but you'd have shoved Rod up against the wall or done something violent to get him away from me, too. I distinctly remember you being pleased that Mensa did that."

My twin sighed. "Your memory is a real pain the ass sometimes."

I chuckled quietly. "Besides, weren't you the one who told me that if he'd broken the law, he'd have been caught by now?"

"Yeah. I'm gonna trust you about him. I'm just concerned."

My brows drew together. "What are you concerned about?"

Wyatt scoffed. "You were *very* sure about the FBI, and you resigned. He does it for you now... are you sure that's gonna last?"

"Nobody has a crystal ball, Wyatt. But love is entirely different from a career choice. Not to be all sappy, but he makes my heart sing. Plus, a relationship is a two-way street. You've been perennially allergic to those, but he and I work."

He nodded. "All right. Gonna let you get some sleep. If you're lucky, they'll discharge you tomorrow morning."

"From your lips to God's ears," I whispered.

He stood, leaned over, and kissed my forehead. "Goodnight, sis."

After Wyatt quietly closed the door behind him, I closed my eyes.

My entire body jerked when Mensa said, "We're gonna last, Blume because you're right. You're the one for me, too. Any relationship is a two-way street. Shit starts going bad, I'll put in the work to make that right again."

I smiled at him. "I love you so much. As much as I love having you here, you should sleep in a real bed."

He widened his eyes. "Not a fuckin' chance. I heard him say you might get discharged tomorrow. If that happens, I want to get you out of here as soon as possible."

EPILOGUE

MOSTLY LEGAL

Mensa

"I FEEL SO FREE now that I'm out of that arm sling," Whitney said, hanging her keys on the hook by the garage door.

Mensa pulled a foil tray from the refrigerator. "Did you ask your therapist about that? I think they took you out of it too soon."

She leaned her good shoulder against the kitchen doorway. "Yes, Kenneth. I asked twice just to put your mind at ease. Is that tray full of lumpia?"

He shook his head. "Not as far as you know."

She shot him a cute angry pout. "They won't miss just one."

He closed the distance between them and wrapped his arms around her. "You have one, then I'm having one, and two missing lumpia are much more obvious than just one."

"Too bad. And I thought this bash was the biggest one of the year because you open it up to so many people. Nobody's gonna care. Someone snoozes, they lose."

"We have to put them in the oven at the clubhouse to reheat them. You aren't eating cold lumpia, woman."

She pushed up on her toes and whispered. "That's why God made microwaves."

He kissed her quick. "We don't have time for that, woman. If you want to wear something different for the Fourth of July party, then you need to change."

She stepped back, glanced down at herself, and back to him. "Is there something wrong with what I'm wearing?"

She was wearing a pair of high-cut denim shorts and the sleeveless red blouse she wore at Twisted Talons that fateful night. He shook his head. "Not at all, but other women..."

She put her hand on his chest. "I don't care about other women, Mensa. Are we staying at the clubhouse?"

He nodded.

"Then I have to pack a bag with fresh clothes."

"Hurry up, babe. This party's important."

Whitney stared at the Riot brothers gathered around the grill. "I'm not sure what surprises me more. The fact there's a sneaky back gate to get in here, or that there are far more people here than I expected."

Mensa moved in front of her and grabbed her hands. "I should have had your cut ordered—"

"Mensa—"

He shook his head. "I know you don't like the idea, Whit."

"It isn't that I don't like the idea."

"Then what is it?"

She stared at him so long he expected her to keep quiet. Then she muttered, "It's that I don't get to claim *you* the same way."

He shifted her hands to his left hand and dug into his pocket with his right.

"What are you doing?" she asked.

He shrugged. "Having you wear a cut would be better, but I don't have one for you. With all these other brothers here, I have to stake my claim a different way."

He slid the ring onto her finger.

She gazed down and gasped. Her eyes were huge when she looked up at him.

"It's not very romantic, but—"

Her chin dipped and she took in the carat-and-a-half square-cut diamond before glancing back at him. "Mensa! How? When did you get this? This ring had to be really expensive." Her voice dipped an octave. "Did you use drug money for this?"

He laughed. "No. You thought I had an apartment, but I'd dropped the lease. Did you check how long I'd been there? I've lived at the clubhouse more than most of the others. No mortgage and no huge rent bill means I've got money saved."

She nodded. "Fair. I'm sorry I asked if the money was legal."

He grinned. "It was mostly legal."

She gasped. "Mostly? What the—"

He put his finger to her lips. "Listen, Blume. You know something? I'm tired of calling you 'Blume.' You need a new name, and Whitney Ragstone has a nice ring to it. Do you want to marry me or what?"

Her watery smile couldn't have been more gorgeous. "Yes, Kenneth. I want to marry you."

"Then, kiss me and make it official."

***

"Where is Two-Times going in such a hurry?" Fiona asked.

Mensa put his beer bottle on the picnic table. "He got a call from his sister earlier. She had to head into work due to a breaking news story, and she's watching his girls. I'm guessing there isn't anyone else to pick up the slack today."

Whitney doctored her cheeseburger. "It has to be rough being a single parent."

Fiona nodded. "You're absolutely right, and he's lucky are almost as easy-going as he is. For now, since Cheyenne's a teenager." She focused her eyes on Mensa. "Speaking of teenagers, did Scrap even prospect for a year?"

"He's shy by about a month," Mensa muttered.

Whitney looked from Mensa to Fiona. "Is that really a requirement?"

Mensa nodded. "Anyone else, yeah, a year or more. His situation was an exception. Not to mention we all voted unanimously."

Fiona squinted an eye at him. "The brothers vote on all new patches though... or at least they did when Dad ran this chapter."

Mensa grinned. "You're right, but she's asking about the requirements. "

Fiona stared across the forecourt to where Scrap was being given shoulder slaps and handshakes from other brothers. "That's true. He definitely looks happy." She glanced at Whitney. "You need anything? I'm going to hit the dessert table again."

Whitney tipped her margarita at Fiona. "I'm good."

The moment Fiona was far enough away, Whitney turned to Mensa. "Are you serious right now? Is she the daughter of the man Aunt Nadia—"

"Yes, but she doesn't know about Nadia being involved with her dad. I'd rather not bring that up to Fi."

"The way you all care about one another, it's like you all really are a huge family," she said.

He grimaced. "That's true for the most part. It sucks, but Fiona's relationship with her dad was strained at best."

Whitney sipped her margarita. "I'm sorry to hear that. You don't have to work tonight?"

Mensa shook his head. "No. We shut down the bar three times a year. Fourth of July, Thanksgiving, and Christmas."

"That's strange. I'd think today would be a high-volume day."

"Yeah, but people get over it. When you take over for Nadia, are you gonna keep her policy of closing Hard Pressed for the whole *week* of July fourth?"

She grinned and shrugged her right shoulder. "Too soon to tell, honey."

He put his arm around her shoulders. "After we get married, I'm taking you on a honeymoon, so... you might want to consider that in your decision."

Her blue eyes went wide. "What? Are you telling me I have to have a summer wedding?"

His fingers traced circles on her upper arm. "I've heard it takes a year to plan a wedding. Your parents strike me as the traditional type...so, yeah. Sooner would be better than later."

She aimed her coy smile his way. "See, I'd always wanted a winter wedding. Then we can get cracking on starting our family.

Someone yelled across the forecourt. "Houston!"

Whitney's smile brightened and she looked at Mensa. "Is that Donny?"

"Might be. I told him he was welcome to come by. He never believes me when I tell him we roast a whole hog."

Whitney waved a hand at him. "Yeah, no need to remind me. I'd rather not know that y'all do that."

Dontrell took a seat across from them. "Where is your sling, Houston?"

Whitney chuckled. "At the back of my closet where it will rest in peace. Yesterday, they told me I was done with it and I never want to see another sling again. Did you ever hear back from your insurance agent?"

When Dontrell grinned, it had a lightness to it Mensa hadn't seen since last May. "Yes, thanks to your brother. He recommended I send them articles about Rod's trial and how I was targeted by Corrupt Chrome MC and one of the members admitted to the arson. Last week they cut me a check. Construction begins next week."

"That's great news!" Whitney said, sliding out of her seat and rounding the table to give Dontrell a hug.

Hearing that Dontrell's troubles were resolved was great, but Mensa believed the best news was that Rod had been sentenced to twenty-five years in jail for that crime.

Dontrell nodded. "It sure is. Now, where's this hog I've heard so much about?"

Whitney shook her head. "That's all Mensa. I'm out."

Whitney

Five months later...

"Girl, it's high time for you to level up your leather game, before I retire in February," Aunt Nadia said from her sewing machine. She was working on a large piece of leather. For some reason I hadn't paid attention to what she was sewing.

Back when I was in my teens, I had my first experience stitching leather. I'd convinced my parents to enroll me in dance lessons. My ballet slippers were leather, and I had to sew the elastic band in place. I remembered how tough it was to get the needle and thread through the slipper. The sewing machine made working on leather cuts easier, but I wasn't at the same level as Aunt Nadia.

"What do you mean, level up? I've been doing embroidery now for three weeks, but those VFW members are picky about their patches."

She cocked a brow at me and grinned. "Yes, and you're never gonna be able to deal with those fussy ol' men if you don't try your hand at this more often. Now get over here."

I sidled up to her and she stood to give me her seat. Once I sat down, I focused on the leather. Aunt Nadia had already stitched a rocker at the top. It read 'Property of.'

"Now, here's the patch you need to put on and make sure it's centered just so," Aunt Nadia said, handing me a die-cut embroidered patch.

I flipped it over to put it in place. The wings caught my attention first, and I recognized the Riot MC emblem.

For a moment, I paused, then I centered the patch under the needle. "Who is getting their property patch? I know Riley already has hers, but is this for Trinity?"

Aunt Nadia didn't answer and I turned my face in her direction.

Mensa stood there, leaning against the counter. "You didn't read the bottom patch, did you?"

I blinked. "No. This is the largest patch I've ever had to sew."

He tipped his head to the machine. "The bottom rocker tells you every thing you need to know, babe."

I pressed my lips together as a warm sensation bloomed in my belly. Ever so carefully, I lifted the bottom hem of the cut and saw the large rocker. Stitched with deep gold thread in Old English style font was the name, *Mensa*.

"You really want me to sew my own patch on? That's like the ultimate pressure."

"Not like this will be a secret from you. Getting to sew it on yourself gives it that much more meaning."

"And I think he's right!" Aunt Nadia hollered from the back office.

Mensa lowered his voice. "You need to use weaker batteries in her hearing aids."

I laughed. "She doesn't wear them."

"What don't I wear?" she called out.

"Don't worry about it," I hollered over my shoulder.

"I wanted to be able to surprise you... and this is better than giving you the cut in front of a big audience at the clubhouse."

"Why don't I hear the sewing machine running?" Nadia asked, and she was standing right behind Mensa. "Move it, Whitney Janelle. I'll get this done for you... consider it an early wedding gift."

My brows drew together. "I thought you wanted me to up my game."

She waved her hand at me. "You'll get to up your game starting tomorrow because mark my words, this is the *last* cut I'm sewing for anybody. I'm just thrilled I get to do one for someone I love."

I felt tears well in my eyes. "Aunt Nadia! You can't sneak attack me with the sweet stuff. I love you."

"Love you, too, but get outta here so I can concentrate. And no necking in the back."

Mensa came back to the shop at five-thirty-one. *Right* after Aunt Nadia had left. "Did she get it done?"

I grinned. "Yes."

His eyes gleamed with pride and desire. "Then you're leaving your car here, putting on that cut, and riding back to the house on the back of my bike."

I cocked my head. "It's only fifteen minutes from here to the house, honey."

He came closer. "I didn't say we were headed straight to the house, Blume... there might be a detour along the way."

Once I grabbed my purse, I shrugged into my cut. The scent of brand new leather was almost overwhelming... or maybe it was the feeling of wearing something that carried so much meaning to my man.

He hummed his approval, deep and gravelly. Then he held me tight to his body, kissed me long and hard, bending me over his arm. He broke the kiss, but didn't pull his face back very far. "Never thought you could get more gorgeous, but I was wrong."

"You wanna know something, handsome?"

His lips tipped up. "What?"

"I'm wrong."

He shook his head and straightened. "What are you talking about?"

I grinned, went up on my toes, and pecked his lips. "Every time I think I can't love you more, you prove me wrong. I hope you keep doing it for the rest of our lives. Let's ride, because I can't wait to get on your bike wearing your patch."

***

Thank you for reading. If you want more of Mensa and Whitney, scan the QR code below to sign up for my newsletter and get their bonus epilogue!

SCAN ME

The Riot MC Biloxi series will continue.

ACKNOWLEDGEMENTS

Massive thanks to you, the reader. I'm honored that you choose to spend your time with my words and characters. I appreciate it more than you'll ever know!

Thank you to Jerri Willliams for your book, *FBI Myths and Misconceptions: A Manual for Armchair Detectives* as well as your podcast, FBI Case File Review. I very much appreciate your taking the time to answer my FBI questions. Every episode of the podcast further proves that fact is always stranger than fiction. Any errors are my own.

Thank you to my family for putting up with me and giving me the time to write.

Many thanks to my reader group. I appreciate all the input I get from you ladies, and I hope you find the group to be as entertaining and useful as I do.

Kudos to Enticing Journey, Wildfire Marketing, the influencers, and bloggers who take the time to share my books and read them! Your help is very much appreciated!

Thank you to Golden Czermak at Furious Fotog. You capture some of the best images with every shoot. Thanks to Zach Fox for giving the camera such fabulous side-eye! That look in that pose represents this character so well.

Thank you to Barbara J. Bailey for wrangling my words into shape!

Much appreciation to the Jacksonville Public Library for providing writers with such great facilities to research and work on their projects.

253

FIND MORE KAREN RENEE

Please visit your favorite book retailer to discover other books by Karen Renee:

The Riot MC Series
Unforeseen Riot
Inciting a Riot
Into the Riot
Calming the Riot
Foolish Riot
Respectable Riot
Starting the Riot
A Friendsgiving Riot – a short story found in Romancing the Holidays
Rough Riot
Fighting a Riot

The Riot MC Box Set Series
The Riot MC Box Set #1 (Books 0.5, 1, 2, & 3)
The Riot MC Box Set #2 (Books 4, 5, & 6)

The Beta Series
Beta Test

The O-Town Series
Relentless Habit
Wild Forces
Abrupt Changes
Holiday Fixation (An O-Town short story) – found in Romancing the Holidays, Vol. Two
O-Town Series Complete Box Set

Riot MC Biloxi Chapter Series
Harm's Way
Brute's Strength
Roman's War
Cynic's Stance
Gamble's Risk
Block's Road
Tiny Problem
Finn's Fury
Mensa's Match

Riot MC Next Generation Series
Break Out
Break Away

ABOUT KAREN RENEE

KAREN RENEE IS THE award-winning author of the Riot MC, Riot MC Biloxi, Beta, and O-Town series of books. She once crunched Nielsen ratings data but these days she brings her imagination to life by writing books. She has wanted to be a writer since she was very young, but it's taken the time for her to amass enough courage and overall life experience to bring that dream to life. Some of those life experiences came from the wonderful world of advertising, banking, and local television media research. She is a proud wife and mother, and a Jacksonville native. When she's not out and about with her family, you can find her at her local library, the grocery store, in her car jamming out to some tunes, or hibernating while she writes and/or reads books.

www.ingramcontent.com/pod-product-compliance
Lightning Source LLC
Chambersburg PA
CBHW060708190726
48289CB00002B/596